P9-EJZ-717

"Are you a cowboy?"

Julia asked, but she fell asleep before he could answer.

Ryder straightened from her bedside, his eyes fastened on her sleeping face. She was a thing of beauty the likes of which he'd never seen, and he was starved for the company of another human being. But whoever she was, she had no business being here, and she damn sure couldn't stay once she recuperated.

Ryder pulled the remaining canvas shoe from her foot and turned it over curiously before putting it down. Everything about her was strange, from the way she dressed to her manner of speech. Yet he could tell right off that she was a lady, from the tip of her red-blond hair to her dainty toes.

He blew out the candle in the lantern and moved to the old rocker in front of the fireplace, his Sharps rifle in his arms. It was going to be a long, long night.

Dear Reader,

The year is coming to a close, so here at Silhouette Intimate Moments we decided to go out with a bang. Once again, we've got a banner lineup of books for you.

Take this month's American Hero, Micah Parish, in *Cherokee Thunder.* You met him in the first book of author Rachel Lee's Conard County series, *Exile's End,* and now he's back with a story of his own. Without meaning to, he finds himself protecting woman-on-the-run Faith Williams and her unborn child, and suddenly this man who shunned emotion is head over heels in love. He's an American Hero you won't want to miss.

Reader favorite Ann Williams puts her own spin on an innovative plot in *Shades of Wyoming.* I don't want to give anything away, so all I'll say is beware of believing that things are what they seem. In *Castle of Dreams,* author Maura Seger takes a predicament right out of the headlines—the difficulties a returning hostage faces in readjusting to the world—and makes it the catalyst for a compelling romance. Award-winner Dee Holmes checks in with another of her deeply moving tales in *Without Price,* while March Madness find Rebecca Daniels writes a suspenseful tale of a couple thrown together and definitely in danger in *Fog City.* Finally, welcome new author Alicia Scott—a college student—whose *Walking After Midnight* takes gritty reality and turns it into irresistible romance.

And 1993 won't bring any letup in the excitement. Look for more of your favorite authors, as well as a Tenth Anniversary lineup in May that you definitely won't want to miss. As always, I hope you enjoy each and every one of our Silhouette Intimate Moments novels.

Yours,

Leslie Wainger
Senior Editor and Editorial Coordinator

SHADES

OF

WYOMING

Ann
Williams

INTIMATE MOMENTS

Published by Silhouette Books New York
America's Publisher of Contemporary Romance

If you purchased this book without a cover you should be aware that this book is stolen property. It was reported as "unsold and destroyed" to the publisher, and neither the author nor the publisher has received any payment for this "stripped book."

SILHOUETTE BOOKS
300 East 42nd St., New York, N.Y. 10017

SHADES OF WYOMING

Copyright © 1992 by Peggy A. Myers

All rights reserved. Except for use in any review, the reproduction or utilization of this work in whole or in part in any form by any electronic, mechanical or other means, now known or hereafter invented, including xerography, photocopying and recording, or in any information storage or retrieval system, is forbidden without the permission of the publisher, Silhouette Books, 300 E. 42nd St., New York, N.Y. 10017

ISBN: 0-373-07468-9

First Silhouette Books printing December 1992

All the characters in this book have no existence outside the imagination of the author and have no relation whatsoever to anyone bearing the same name or names. They are not even distantly inspired by any individual known or unknown to the author, and all incidents are pure invention.

®: Trademark used under license and registered in the United States Patent and Trademark Office and in other countries.

Printed in the U.S.A.

Books by Ann Williams

Silhouette Intimate Moments

Devil in Disguise #302
Loving Lies #335
Haunted by the Past #358
What Lindsey Knew #384
Angel on My Shoulder #408
Without Warning #436
Shades of Wyoming #468

ANN WILLIAMS

gave up her career as a nurse, then as the owner and proprietor of a bookstore, in order to pursue her writing full-time. She was born and married in Indiana, and after a number of years in Texas, she now lives in Arizona with her husband of over twenty years and their four children.

Reading, writing, crocheting, classical music and a good romantic movie are among her diverse loves. Her dream is to one day move to a cabin in the Carolina mountains with her husband and "write to my heart's content."

For my sister, Mable Wardell,
and her "cowboy," Leo.
Thank you for showing us the Wyoming
few people get to see.

Chapter 1

She was lost!

Julia brought the red Porsche to a grinding halt and stared at the vast stretch of emptiness around her. There wasn't a house, tree or telephone pole within sight. She hadn't passed another vehicle since...she couldn't remember when.

She'd been driving for hours, ever since leaving the motel that morning in Thermopolis, Wyoming. After a while everything had begun to look the same, the paved road had given way to hard-packed dirt and she'd gone from one deeply rutted road to another without taking note of where they led.

She supposed she'd been a fool to neglect getting a map and marking her route, but the truth of the matter was that she simply hadn't cared enough to do it. For three days, ever since leaving Los Angeles, she'd been on the road, headed...nowhere.

Looking at the countryside around her, noting how it looked the same in all directions, a sweeping panorama of undulating hills, covered with silver sagebrush and back-dropped by snowcapped mountains, she realized she'd found just that—nowhere, U.S.A.

She sighed, heavily. It was hot, she was tired, thirsty, and in need of a bathroom. Her eyes dropped toward the dash and she realized she was in need of fuel, as well.

Taking off her sunglasses, she glanced up at the sky. When had the dark clouds rolled in? The sky had been a deep azure blue when she'd started out that morning. Sometime in the past few hours, during her preoccupation with unhappy reflections of the past, the sky had changed. Now it was gunmetal gray.

A rumble of thunder sounded in the distance and she glanced toward the darkest of the clouds. A shaft of white lightning darted between earth and sky, a beautiful, awesome sight that made her catch her breath and shiver. She wasn't in the habit of being alone with—or at the mercy of—Mother Nature.

She turned off the air conditioner to conserve fuel and lowered the windows, considering heading back the way she'd come, then thought better of it. Somehow that smacked of going back, and she'd promised herself she'd never do that—never return to Los Angeles and the life she'd left behind.

Only pain and emptiness awaited her there.

Folding the sunglasses, she placed them on the seat beside her, took her foot off the brake pedal, and let the car glide slowly forward, picking up speed. Perhaps there wasn't a place on the whole planet where she could find happiness.

Certainly, Julia couldn't do as her mother wanted and return to the East to live. She'd tried that once and it hadn't worked. She didn't fit into her mother's "old world," society background.

But then, neither had she really fit into the ultramodern crowd she'd gotten mixed up with in California. Oh, she'd pretended to, rather than give up and go back East to live with her mother. She'd pretended for five years, to be exact.

It was only because she'd met Mariette and they'd become close friends that she'd stuck it out in California for as long as she had. She'd even managed, thanks to her friend's urging, to make a name for herself among the elite crowd by having a showing of her paintings in a prestigious art gallery.

Her no-nonsense style of capturing people and their emotions on canvas had caught on in a big way. She could have made a lot of money with her paintings if she'd wanted, but she didn't need to sell them to live.

It was her friendship with Mariette that had convinced her to give California a fair try. She settled in and allowed herself to get caught up in the "live for today and to hell with tomorrow" life-style, so fashionable in some circles.

But tomorrow came. And it came with a vengeance.

It came for her on a dark, stormy night six months ago. Julia had returned after being gone all night and found Mariette lying crumpled on the bathroom floor, so still...so white...so cold...like a beautiful statue made of marble that had never known life....

A few days ago, Julia had stood in that same bathroom looking into the floor-to-ceiling mirror. Dressed in a nightgown she'd worn for a week, hair in a wild tangle around her head, eyes dull and lifeless, she'd contemplated a bottle of sleeping pills in one hand.

Was that the answer? Suicide?

How had life become so worthless? It had been days since she'd left her apartment or spoken to another human being. She couldn't remember the date, or when she'd last eaten a meal.

She felt used up, wrung out, as though all the life had been drained from her and all her hopes and dreams for the future a lie. There was no bright tomorrow, no happy everafter, for anyone. All that awaited the human race was death; a legacy of emptiness after a life filled with pain.

She was tired of the fight....

When had it happened? When had the joy gone out of life?

She hadn't come into the world feeling that way. She'd been born the only child of wealthy parents in a long line of ancestors who had made a name for themselves by helping to shape history. Some were even listed in the history books.

Her mother could trace her family back to the American Revolution. But Julia had been a disappointment to her

mother from the start. She'd been more interested in drawing pictures than in dancing lessons or modeling classes, and
had no interest at all in academic studies.

After her paternal grandmother died and left her an an-
nuity, Julia had left her widowed mother to her women's
meetings and fund-raisers and moved as far away as possible, clear to the other side of the world. There she had a
brief, disastrous marriage and lost a baby.

Beaten down by life, needing the comfort of family, Julia had gone home to Boston to stay with her mother. She'd
even tried to conform to her mother's style of living, but
once she'd recovered from what her mother called her *Eu-
ropean phase,* Julia had known it was never going to work.
She and her mother were too different to live under the same
roof, or even in the same part of the country.

And that was how Julia had ended up in California. Still
serious, or perhaps serious again was the right phrase, about
her painting, she'd worked hard to the exclusion of all else
and garnered a showing. The showing had introduced her to
southern California society, and she was a hit.

It took awhile for Julia to realize that Mariette and her
crowd were into things she'd managed so far to steer clear
of—drugs and alcohol. Julia soon learned her friend had a
problem, an increasingly bad dependency on cocaine.

At first Julia had tried to help the other woman, but
eventually she'd gotten sucked into the morass surrounding
Mariette, and from there her life had gone quickly downhill. It had taken Mariette's death to shock her back into the
real world, but nothing had changed since her days after she
returned from the Continent. She was still out of step with
everyone else.

That was when she began to wonder if the problem lay not
with everyone else, but within herself. She didn't like herself very much and especially not what she'd become. So she
went into hiding and after a time reached the conclusion that
the only way out was the one Mariette had ultimately chosen. A clean break—death.

She was on the point of doing something to that end when
her eyes had fallen on a photograph of her dead roommate
taken during happier times. At that instant something in-

side her had snapped and she'd thrown the bottle of pills at her reflection so hard it cracked the mirror.

She'd had to get out of there. Changing quickly into street clothes, she'd grabbed her purse and car keys and run from the house, knowing she was running for her life. Either she got out of the city now, leaving it and its unhappy associations behind, to search for a new meaning to life, or she knew she'd end up like her friend—dead on the bathroom floor, without anyone ever knowing how desperate her situation had become until it was too late.

That was three days ago. Now she was coasting down a hill somewhere in the middle of Wyoming, without a clue to her present location.

A bellow from overhead drew her eyes skyward. The storm was drawing closer, bringing with it a cool breeze. It kicked up dust and fanned the tops of the silver-green shrubbery lining both sides of the road. The short curls escaping the colorful silk scarf holding Julia's long, curly red hair back from her face blew in the wind as the pungent scent of sagebrush filled her nostrils.

In a few minutes it was going to rain cats and dogs—or maybe out here it rained snakes and toads, she thought with a wry trace of amusement. In any case, the storm was closing in and so was night.

She supposed she ought to be frightened. To be caught alone at night in an unfamiliar part of L.A., with a close-to-empty fuel tank, could be dangerous. It stood to reason that getting caught in this wild, desolate country in Wyoming under similar circumstances would pose an equal threat.

It was her own fault. She'd left the motel that morning in the same careless manner she'd left California, telling no one she was going, taking nothing but her purse, some clothes and a sketch pad and drawing pencils.

Julia glanced down at the pristine face of the sketch pad on the seat beside her. She hadn't touched it since she'd laid it there. Most of the day had been spent in a kind of fog, going over the events that had led up to her precipitate departure from California.

Even though she'd taken the time to purchase the tools of her trade, the lack of inspiration that had plagued her since her friend's death continued to prevent her from using them. Her creativity was buried deep beneath an overpowering feeling of inertia.

A strong gust of wind shook the car, bringing with it the promised rain. Julia automatically switched on the windshield wipers as a flurry of large, cold drops pelted her through the open window. She took her foot off the gas, letting the car slow as she raised the window and turned on the headlights.

Night in this country came swiftly, she noted as the diffused light from a watery sun dropped behind the tops of the distant mountains. Mountains that never seemed to get any closer, but remained always just out of reach.

The low-fuel light on the dash blinked on, warning her she would soon be running out of gas. Julia scanned the horizon worriedly.

Was that a light? She blinked and it was gone. Slowing the car as it crested the next hill, she squinted and stared hard into the distance. It was difficult to see through the rain-streaked window with any accuracy, but she thought she saw the light again, for a brief instant, and then it was gone.

For a while she lost sight of the light completely and forgot about it as she drove through the increasing downpour, fighting the deepening ruts it was creating in the dirt road. Eventually, the rain slowed and stopped, but the storm continued its show of lights in the heavens. And when she saw the light again, she still wasn't certain whether it was real, or merely part of the storm's dazzling display.

All at once the car's engine sputtered, coughed a few times, bucked beneath her hands, and died. With sinking spirits, Julia guided the car to the bottom of the hill and onto the soft, uneven shoulder. There it coasted to a stop.

That was that, she thought with a sigh of regret. Now she was well and truly on her own.

She'd read somewhere that it was safer to stay with your vehicle than start off on foot. In most cases that was probably true. But the locked doors were little comfort to her in her present predicament.

She was without food or water in a land where people were at a minimum, and her need for a rest room was in-

creasing with each passing moment. Waiting for someone to
come to her rescue under these circumstances seemed rather
idiotic.

Julia pulled the keys from the ignition, grabbed her
handbag, stuffed the sketch pad inside, and stepped out of
the car. Staring into the growing darkness around her, she
realized she didn't have a flashlight.

She'd really prepared herself for this trip, she thought
with a snort of self-disgust. How was she going to find her
way in the dark?

Providence, however, appeared to be looking out for her.
With her first steps away from the car, the clouds rolled
away from the moon and allowed it to spill its white light
onto the ground, lighting her path.

It wasn't like having a searchlight to guide her path by any
stretch of the imagination, but it was better than the previous pitch black. Julia stood a moment to take stock of her
present location in relationship to where she'd last seen the
light.

Picking a spot to her right, in the phantom light's general direction, she began to angle toward it. She was about
to leave the road behind, but at this moment that didn't
seem such a bad idea. The road was awash with water and
sandy mud.

A wide stream of swiftly flowing water had created a gully
at the edge of the road and Julia did her best to find a spot
narrow enough to cross. After a couple of yards, she gave
up and stepped directly into it.

Her white canvas shoes sank deep in mud. It clutched at
her feet and ankles, making it close to impossible to retain
her footing. She struggled on for a few steps when her right
foot twisted beneath her. She floundered, arms flapping
wildly, and fell, losing her purse in the fray.

She was literally up to her elbows in muddy water. Feeling around on the ground beneath it, she managed to get a
solid purchase and used both hands to push herself to her
feet. Soaked to the skin, she stepped carefully through the
last of the water and stood at last on firm ground. Peering
around in dismay, she wondered where her purse had
landed.

Stumbling against a pyramid of sand, located a few feet from the edge of the rushing water, Julia kicked at it, almost losing her footing again, and wondered what it might be. And then she recalled a documentary she'd seen not long ago about large red ants, fire ants, whose bite could be more painful than a bee sting.

Did fire ants live in Wyoming?

All at once she could feel thousands of tiny feet crawling all over her body. Brushing at her arms and slapping at her skirt, she did a kind of dance away from the mound of sand and stumbled over something lying beside it.

Her purse! Bending over, she grabbed it, shaking it in case it too were under attack from the miniature red devils. Her skin brushed against the spiny skeleton of a dead bush and she took a sudden sidestep and tripped over a stand of sagebrush.

There weren't any ants, she realized as she went down for the third time, scattering the contents of her bag among the tangle of brush in her path. The feel of their tiny bodies moving against her skin had only been her imagination.

Now, thanks to her idiocy, everything but her sketch pad, wedged tightly in her purse, lay somewhere at her feet. She shook her head in irritation and felt around on the ground at her feet. With a feeling of triumph she came up with two drawing pencils, a comb and her wallet. Her car keys, makeup and the bottle of sleeping pills she'd brought along at the last minute were lost somewhere among the thick clumps of green bush and dry brush. She continued to search on hands and knees for a few minutes, but still came up empty-handed.

The clouds had returned and what little light there had been instantly disappeared. Suddenly the wind picked up, howling around the hills and across the valley, blowing her hair into her eyes and almost ripping the colorful scarf from her hair. She gave up and climbed despondently to her feet.

Clasping the purse with both hands, she decided that finding her car keys would have to wait until she returned in daylight. She hadn't moved far from the car, she'd simply have to remember that her keys would be somewhere this side of it.

She stood for a moment and looked in all four directions to get her bearings before walking any farther. When she finally moved, she came up against an incline and found herself struggling to climb a hill. It wasn't a difficult climb at first, but soon it became steeper and more rocky. Shouldering her bag, Julia used her hands to pull herself up the craggy face of rock.

The hill was in reality a ridge, and it took more than half an hour for her to get to the top. Along the way, she managed to lose her watch, one of her shoes and her wallet.

At the top she stopped to rest. The aerobic class she'd taken three days a week, until six months ago, hadn't prepared her for mountain climbing. Stretching out, she laid her hot cheek against the cool rock and breathed in uneven gasps. After a time, she raised her head and uttered a half-strangled cry.

The light! There it was! It hadn't been a part of the lightning, or a figment of her imagination, after all. It was real!

She struggled to her feet, anxious for the sight of another human being. With the first step forward she lost her balance as her foot came down on emptiness, and arms flailing, she flew out into space.

A startled scream followed her as she fell, landed and rolled to the bottom of the hill. Fortunately, this side of the ridge was less rocky than the other and covered with sandy soil. It cushioned what otherwise might have been a fatal plunge.

Julia came suddenly to rest against a rigid cushion of pungent sagebrush. The breath was knocked from her, and for a time all she could do was lie with eyes closed and gasp for air. She was afraid to move in case anything was broken or there was another drop-off close by.

Finally, breathing normally once more, she opened her eyes and slowly focused on the sky overhead. One by one, she tried her limbs, and then her spine, as she cautiously sat up. Everything, thank God, appeared to be in working order.

Everything, she amended a moment later, clawing her way to her feet, except her right knee. It hurt like the dickens! But, glory be, somehow she'd managed to keep hold of her purse. Clutching it to her as though it were a talisman, Julia raised her chin firmly and marched on, broken but not bowed.

She had no idea how long she walked, or rather limped, after that. It could have been a few minutes, or it might have been hours. Eventually, the light got closer, and she could make out the shadowy outline of a building set back a little to the right of it.

The building, she discovered on closer inspection, appeared to be a very primitive-looking log cabin. Her hopes for a hot bath, maybe even a meal and a bed for the night, dissipated into thin air.

The wavering glow of the light drew her attention from the disappointing sight of the cabin. Well, at least that was a sign of humanity. Someone was here. That surely meant a bathroom of sorts, possibly a telephone, and best of all, transportation!

Determinedly she made her way toward the light, then, with a frown, came to a stop. It didn't make sense to her, but the light appeared to be coming from within the side of a mountain. Moving a painful step closer, she realized it looked like an old mine shaft. Wood shored up the sides of the mountain and spanned the top, providing a doorlike entrance at the bottom of a slightly sloping path leading to it.

Should she yell and make her presence known before entering, or should she even enter it at all? Mine shafts could be dangerous, especially old ones. Besides, the idea of entering an old mine in the middle of the night without any idea of what she'd find inside was more than a little frightening.

However, on the other hand, she couldn't simply stand here, waiting for whoever was inside to come out. Hobbling closer, using one hand for support, Julia called weakly, "H-hello—is anybody there?"

She listened intently, but no sound came from the black, yawning maw before her. The long day and the mishaps she'd encountered since leaving the car were taking their toll. She knew she had just enough strength left to go a little farther before falling facedown and lying there for at least eight hours straight.

Julia started forward, the steep incline causing her to increase the amount of weight put on her injured knee. She hesitated, the pain so sharp it took her breath away.

Supporting herself against the mountain's rugged surface, she threw a brief, hopeful glance back toward the cabin, just in case it showed heretofore undetected signs of life. But it remained shrouded in silence, dark and just a little bit sinister-looking silhouetted against the night sky.

Julia wearily faced the mine. The pain had finally subsided, so she took another cautious step and felt her feet skid on loose sand and rock. She didn't fancy sliding down the path by the seat of her pants, so she gritted her teeth and put an equal amount of weight on both legs. The injured one buckled, pitching her forward against a wood support at the mine's entrance.

Swallowing a gasp of pain, she caught herself, took a shaky breath and called in a loud voice, "Hello! Is anybody there? I saw your light! Please," she muttered as she stepped through the entrance, "someone be here."

At that instant she felt a stinging blow—saw a burst of white light—and then . . . nothing. . . .

"Oh-o-o. . ." Julia moaned. Her eyes opened slowly, only to have them snap shut again almost immediately in defense against the sudden onrush of nausea.

Lifting an unsteady hand toward her forehead, her fingers encountered something soft and wet. They drew back in horror.

Blood? Her fingers tested the substance cautiously against themselves. No, blood would be sticky. Pushing a finger beneath the wet object, Julia found a lump the size of a goose egg in the process of growing on her forehead.

"What . . ."

"You planning on fainting again?"

Julia's voice cut off in the middle of a moan and her eyes snapped open. She raised her head and focused on the owner of the deep, rumbling voice coming from somewhere above her.

"Wh-who are y-you?"

"I was fixin' to ask you the same thing," the man replied, pushing back the curled brim of his wide-billed western hat with the first two fingers of one hand. Resting back on his haunches, he stared at her quizzically.

Julia's breath became motionless as her glance was captured and held by a pair of deep, lustrous brown eyes, rimmed with thick black lashes and set below black, arched brows. The black brows and lashes were a startling, but very attractive, contrast to the thick blond mustache growing above a wide, sensuous mouth.

"I—I—oh-o-o. . ." Her head dropped back and her eyes closed, as everything began to swim out of focus. She wasn't certain if the dizziness was caused by the knot on her head, or the unexpected attraction to the man kneeling at her side.

"You gonna be sick?"

"No." She gulped. "D-dizzy. . ."

After a few moments the dizziness passed. Julia opened her eyes to find the man bending over her, a speculative look on his solemn face.

"What happened—did you hit me?" she asked all in the same breath, a sudden frown of accusation marring her pale features. As far as she could reason there was no other explanation for the lump on her forehead.

"No, ma'am," he responded instantly, lifting his hands up and withdrawing from her. He made an abrupt nodding motion with his head, indicating the low central beam supporting the roof, and said, "You didn't duck."

Julia followed the man's movement with questioning eyes and realized almost immediately the accident had been her own fault. She should have paid closer attention when entering such an unfamiliar structure.

"Oh—sorry," she apologized softly.

"If you feel like moving, I think you'd rest some easier in the cabin."

Aware of the hard ground beneath her and an increasing variety of aches and pains, Julia agreed with him wholeheartedly. The only problem she could see with the plan was the fact she didn't think she could stand, much less walk.

But she needn't have worried; her gallant rescuer had everything well in hand. Removing the wet cloth from her forehead, he stooped and lifted her easily into strong, muscular arms. Julia wanted to make a token protest, but wisely kept her mouth shut.

As they neared the spot where she'd so recently been felled, he ducked to maneuver his tall frame through the low entrance and his face drew close to hers. Julia smelled tobacco on his breath, and for a brief instant his rough cheek brushed against her skin.

She jerked back instinctively, feeling her heart miss a beat. And though he made no comment, she felt a momentary tightening of the muscles in the arms bearing her weight.

Once they had stepped into the crisp night air, he straightened slowly, keeping his eyes focused straight ahead, and carried her silently, without seeming effort, toward the dark cabin.

Julia's skin tingled where his beard had rubbed against it, and she had to restrain herself forcefully from lifting a hand to touch the spot on her cheek. She'd never liked what was popularly termed "designer beards" on men, considering them nothing less than crude.

They reached the cabin after what seemed an inordinately long period of time. Her knight errant pushed against the door with a booted foot before Julia could make the effort to reach out and open it. The door swung back, its rusty hinges creaking in protest, and they entered the dimly lit room.

It was impossible to see much of the room's interior. The only light came from a fireplace centered along one wall, where only a few glowing coals gleamed redly.

Julia blinked, screwed up her eyes in an effort to penetrate the darkness, and winced as the bruise on her forehead throbbed in protest. Her host seemed to know exactly where he was going without benefit of light. In a moment, Julia felt softness beneath her as he lowered her to a bed.

"Just lay there a spell and rest while I go get the lantern."

"Wait!" Julia raised herself on one elbow to call hurriedly after him. "I—" She hesitated, reluctant to discuss such a personal matter with this stranger, but it wouldn't wait any longer. "I need to go to the ladies' room."

"This is the only room there is."

"No," Julia said with a frown. "I mean, I have to go to the ladies' room—you know—the rest room."

"You can rest here—"

"No, no—the toilet!" What was wrong with him? Didn't he understand plain English? "I have to go to the toilet."

"It's outside."

Somehow, she'd known *that,* or something similar, would be his answer.

Making his way back to the bed, he lifted her and strode toward the door. In darkness, they moved outside and around to the back of the cabin, past a rough corral where an animal stirred in the deeper shadows, then they traveled down a narrow path toward a small building dimly outlined in pale moonlight.

"I'll go fetch the light while you take care of your business," he told her matter-of-factly, standing her on her feet and turning away. He halted after only a few steps and turned back. "You can manage—can't you—without any help?"

"Yes," Julia answered swiftly, "yes, I can manage perfectly well on my own." He was turning away as she added slowly, "There aren't any...snakes—or anything—in here...are there?"

"I doubt it," he answered, pausing to look back over his shoulder. When she didn't move, he added somewhat reluctantly, "Maybe I ought to take a look first, just in case."

Julia released her pent-up breath in an inaudible sigh, only to catch it again when he stalked off in the opposite direction.

"Where are you going?" she called, hobbling a step after him.

"I'm going to get the lantern, so I can look inside. Isn't that what you want?"

"Oh—yes." She cast a quick glance toward the rough wooden structure. "I'll just wait right here, shall I..." she added, letting her voice trail off as she looked after him and saw his tall figure swallowed up by the night.

"Please hurry," she murmured softly, hobbling toward the outhouse.

The sudden loud scrape of something sharp against rock, somewhere nearby, caused her to draw back in alarm against the rough wall. She hardly noticed the feel of splinters penetrating her cotton blouse as she squinted into the darkness, looking for what had made the sound.

"Is s-someone there?" she asked weakly.

A small avalanche of dirt and rock greeted her words. She gasped and cringed back in fear.

"Something bothering you?"

Julia's head whipped toward the voice, her hands flying up in a protective manner as she flattened herself against the building at her back.

"Oh, it's you," she breathed, heart racing with fear.

"Were you expecting somebody else?" he asked carefully, lifting the lantern to peer into her face.

Was that a note of suspicion she detected in his voice? "N-no, of course not. I heard something—" she motioned toward the hillside "—over there."

"You want me to take a look?"

"No! I just want to...do what I came to do...and go back to the cabin and lie down."

He nodded, noting the pale color of her cheeks and the bruised look around her eyes. She looked plumb tuckered out and about ready to drop in her tracks. The goose egg on her forehead had turned a deep blue, and he'd be surprised in the morning if she wasn't sporting at least one shiner from it.

Lifting the wooden latch, he opened the sagging door of the outhouse and stepped inside. A moment later, he backed out again.

"Nothing in there to harm you." He nodded toward the open door and Julia hobbled toward him, squeezing past his chest to step inside.

"Please—" She stopped him as he was about to turn away. "May I keep the lantern with me?"

He handed it to her and their fingers brushed in the exchange. Julia quickly drew back, feeling the light touch all the way to her toes. Her precipitous movement almost dislodged the candle set in the glass bell making up the lantern and he grappled with it to keep it from happening.

"Th-thank you," she whispered, feeling a fool for her skittish behavior. Keeping her eyes lowered, she added in a soft voice, "If you want to go along the path a little way, I'll call when I'm ready."

It might have been better if she'd gone inside in darkness, she thought an instant later. She wasn't at all impressed with the primitive facilities. Nor was she certain, upon first reflection, what use there was for a pile of old newspapers.

A short time later, newly educated about the use of newspaper, Julia opened the door to find her host standing right outside. Her face flamed as she extended the lantern toward him.

"You keep it," he told her, lifting her off her feet. He pulled her against him decisively, almost as though he expected—and dared her—to object.

Julia stiffened and tried to hold her body rigid to keep from making contact with his chest, but her reserve of strength had reached its limit. The night air verged on being cold, and the warmth of his chest tempted her to make use of it.

Inevitably, she relaxed against him, wondering idly about the sweet, somewhat pungent odor she detected on his clothes. Her eyes began to drift shut. A pounding sensation, directly behind both her eyes, had begun to make itself known, and everything began to take on a dreamlike quality.

Julia was unaware of falling asleep, nor was she aware of burrowing her face beneath the man's chin. She had no idea her warm breath, moving rhythmically across the skin of his neck, was making him uncomfortable, or that he was becoming more aware of her as a woman than he wanted to be.

With the sweet scent of her hair filling his nostrils, its softness creating a need in him he was hard-put to repress, her reluctant host paused and gently removed the lantern from her lax fingers. It would be easy enough to hold it and still carry her, because she was as light as a feather.

His mind filled with questions about her. Where had she come from? He'd been as surprised to find her lying on the floor of the mine shaft as he would have been if he'd stumbled upon a dead man.

She looked like she'd been through hell. Crossing this country on foot, he well knew, could be hell. And it looked like that's exactly what she'd done.

Inside the cabin, he set the lantern on a table and lowered his rare burden to the nearby bed. He was removing his arm from beneath her when her eyes blinked open. Looking him straight in the eye, she smiled.

His breath became buried in a score of feelings he hardly recognized. Whatever her reasons for being here, she was the prettiest woman he'd ever seen, goose egg, mud and all.

"My name is Julia. What's yours?"

"Ryder," he answered deeply. "Ryder McCall."

"Ryder," she murmured softly as though testing the sound of it on her tongue. "Are you a cowboy?" she asked, snuggling down against the pillows.

"Well, ma'am." He stood back and pushed at the brim of his hat with two fingers before answering. "I punched a few cows in my time. So I s'pose, among other things, you could call me a cowboy."

Julia nodded, letting her eyes drift shut. She opened them abruptly and focused on his face. "I'm glad I found you...I've been looking...for someone...for a long, long time...."

Ryder straightened slowly, his eyes fastened on her sleeping face. She was a thing of beauty the likes of which he'd never seen, and he was starved for the company of another human being, but she had no business being here and she damned sure couldn't stay.

Ryder pulled the remaining canvas shoe from her foot and turned it over in his hands curiously before setting it on the floor beside the bed. Everything about her was strange, from the way she dressed, to her manner of speech. Yet he could tell right off she was a lady, from the tip of her red hair to the ends of her dainty pink toes.

He barricaded the door for the night and built up a fire in the fireplace to stave off the night chill. Then he blew out the candle in the lantern and moved the old rocker to a spot in front of the fireplace, conscious all the while of the young woman sleeping in his bed.

Taking his Sharps rifle down from the wall, he lowered his long frame to the rocker, hearing it creak in protest as he settled comfortably on the seat. He laid the rifle across his lap and settled back with his head resting against the high back of the chair, his eyes on the bed. It was going to be a mighty long night.

Chapter 2

Julia stretched, yawned and opened bleary eyes. Pushing the tangled red hair from her face, she winced and touched the bump on her forehead with a careful finger. Her glance slowly focused on the rough beamed ceiling overhead and she blinked in confusion.

Where was she?

Raising herself on one elbow, she looked around the room's dim interior, sniffing the air like an animal scenting danger. Her nose wrinkled. What was that strange scent? It reminded her of something....

And then she remembered. Sitting bolt upright, drawing the scratchy wool blanket to her chin, she looked for the stranger—the cowboy—from last night. But the room, or cabin rather, was empty, except for herself.

A fire in the stone fireplace blazed brightly, casting flickering shadows on the walls of the room. Julia surveyed what she could see of its contents. It didn't take long—there wasn't much to see.

The walls were made of rough logs without paint or adornment. In a far corner to one side of the fireplace sat a corner cupboard with sagging doors. A few feet from it stood a rough, square table and two straight-backed chairs.

On the edge of the table sat a wooden bucket, and beside it, a metal drinking cup. To one side of the fireplace was a small three-legged table.

Julia's eyes slid to the uneven wood floor and the shaggy hide of an animal spread before the fire; its long black fur appeared matted with dust and age. A rocking chair was placed nearby. On the walls and ceiling near the cupboard hung a few large black pots in different sizes and an assortment of long-handled cooking utensils the likes of which Julia had never seen outside a museum.

The single window in the room was situated in the wall beside the closed door, and wooden shutters were latched across it. Julia could see a thin stream of light filtering through the cracks where the rough boards didn't quite meet.

Her eyes fell on a saddle resting on the floor below the window with a bedroll lying across the seat. Well, that answered any questions she might have had about where her host had spent the night.

Julia's gaze moved to the foot of the bed and lingered on an old wooden chest with chipped black paint and leather straps across it. Beyond that, in the corner, stood an oblong metal tub, and beside that, a small, wooden cradle.

Was her host married? Where was his wife—the child?

What did it matter? She was only here overnight and the night appeared to be gone. Though she had no idea of the time, since she'd lost her watch during her trek up the hillside, she knew it was time to find the cowboy. Her car was sitting on a lonely back road in the middle of nowhere, and she had no doubt a Porsche, even in Wyoming, would net a car thief a hefty sum of money.

Throwing back the covers, she scooted toward the edge of the bed and lowered her feet to the floor. Just before her feet actually touched the floor she experienced a momentary regret at leaving the bed's soft haven of warmth. The cabin might be primitive, but whatever the cowboy used for a mattress was pure heaven, and she had slept like a baby.

Julia shifted her weight to her feet and felt the right one buckle beneath her. A shaft of burning pain shot from her knee all the way to her spine. She dropped quickly back onto the bed, feeling slightly sick.

The leg she'd injured the night before was too sore to bear weight. It was painful just moving the knee joint. Great! Now what? How was she going to get anywhere if she couldn't stand and walk? How could she drive if she couldn't use the gas pedal?

Pulling up the hem of her mud-stained, ankle-length cotton skirt, she gave a shudder at the sight of her misshapened knee. God, she hoped it wasn't permanently damaged. What was she going to do all by herself in the back of beyond with an injured limb?

Wait, she wasn't exactly by herself. This crude cabin did come with an owner, a cowboy of sorts. She stood up and hopped on one foot, supporting herself with a hand on the mattress, to the end of the bed, around the trunk, using it for support, and along the wall to the door. After a momentary struggle, she managed to open the heavy wooden door and leaned against it to catch her breath.

Her eyes scanned what she could see of the immediate area. Almost directly in front of her were two Y-shaped sticks of wood crossed with another piece of wood supporting a round iron pot. To the left of that stood a rough wooden bench with a large wooden tub sitting on it. The remains of a wagon—the pioneers would have called it a prairie schooner—were on the ground a few yards from the cabin. Resting against it was an old plow with leading straps, the kind oxen, mules or horses used to pull.

Failing to catch sight of the cowboy, Julia moved through the doorway and outside. The roof of the cabin extended outward, creating an overhang that served as a porch with a dirt floor. She paused there to scan a larger area, looking for her host.

When she still failed to see any sign of him, she opened her mouth to give a shout, hoping to attract his attention, wherever he might be. A slight sound to the right of her found its way to her ears. Julia turned—and stood transfixed.

Him! The cowboy—she couldn't remember his name—was bent over what she recognized from western movies as a horse trough. He was busy sluicing his head, neck and face with water—and he was naked from the waist up. Black suspenders, attached to brown trousers, hung down around his thighs.

Julia's captivated eyes traveled from light brown hair streaked with blond, down long, sinewy legs, to scarred brown boots sticking out from the ends of his trousers. Her gaze made the return trip in a leisurely fashion, taking in the manner in which the trousers molded themselves to the man's powerful thighs, narrow hips and flat stomach.

She watched as he cupped both hands into the water and splashed it against a powerful chest sprinkled lightly with curly brown hair. Shaking the way a dog shakes water from its fur, he made a slight gasping sound as the cold water struck his bare chest, and then splashed himself again.

Julia felt her mouth turn dry as he sucked in his breath the instant the cold water found its way down skin tanned the color of old copper, causing the muscles across his chest to bunch and his flat stomach to become even flatter. Her eyes followed the trickle of water as it became lost in the dark hair arrowing toward the low waistband of his trousers.

In sudden need of a douse of cold water herself, Julia held her breath as the object of her voyeurism picked up a towel. He dried his hair, wiped his face and rubbed vigorously at his chest. Her lips parted for speech, but before her mind could formulate any words, he pushed the trousers well below his navel and used the towel to remove the moisture from belly and hips.

Julia glanced quickly away, turning her eyes toward the mountains, feeling suddenly guilty for gawking at him unaware. But after little more than a few seconds, she couldn't seem to help it, her gaze wandered back—and found a pair of rich brown eyes, filled with some undefined emotion, locked on her face.

Her host quickly reached for a blue chambray shirt hanging on a nail beside him. Ducking his head, he grabbed the shirt and turned away, sliding it quickly over head and shoulders and tucking it into his pants. Pulling the suspenders up over both shoulders at the same time, he ran a hand through his wet, curling hair, before turning to face her with a light stain of red on both cheeks.

Julia was amazed at his obvious discomfort. How many men did she know who would show embarrassment at being caught in a similar situation? Most of them would use it as a prelude to a come-on. But not this one...how strange...

"Morning, ma'am." He picked up his hat from the corner of the water trough, pushed the rawhide strings tied together at the back, and placed it on his head. "You feeling some better this morning?"

"Yes," she answered quickly, trying to hide her embarrassment at being caught watching him. "Except for my knee," she blurted.

Lifting her skirt, she stared down at the swollen knee in growing irritation. He made no comment, and Julia glanced up at him curiously. She was amazed to see a sudden deepening of the flush across his tanned cheekbones.

Ryder dragged his eyes from the sight of her bare leg and glanced toward the mountains in the distance. Without taking his eyes off them, he reached toward the brown leather belt hanging on the nail where his shirt had hung.

Julia's eyes widened as she watched him strap the gun belt and holster around his narrow waist. He positioned the holster containing a .45 Colt low on his right hip, glanced up and suggested in a flat voice, "Maybe you should stay off your feet awhile. Let's go inside and get you settled, then I'll fix us some vittles."

Vittles? Julia looked at him strangely, wondering what language he was speaking, while at the same time realizing she'd embarrassed him by lifting her skirt to show him her bare leg. Where was he from, Mars?

Despite her curiosity, she now felt embarrassed herself. Slightly flustered, she turned away, thinking maybe she should have stayed inside and waited for him to come to her. With that thought in mind, she moved quickly toward the door.

"Here, let me help you."

Before she could move or make a protest, Julia felt herself swept up into strong arms and instinctively threw her

own arms around his neck for support. She was instantly
shocked at the impact his gentle grip made on her senses.
Tilting her head back, she peered at his face so close that
even in the shadow created by the curled brim of his hat, she
could see tiny creases at the corners of both eyes. Up close
like this, there was a vulnerability obvious in their dark
depths impossible to detect at a distance.

Ryder felt her eyes rest on his face and felt compelled to
meet their green glance. Julia swallowed tightly, and for a
long moment neither moved.

In the ensuing silence, a fly whizzed past their heads, a
bird trilled in a nearby tree, a soft breeze stirred the scent of
pine in the air, and Julia felt as though something momentous was about to happen.

Ryder's glance flickered before traveling slowly over her
face, searching her eyes. Julia felt a tingling sensation in the
pit of her stomach and bit down on her lower lip. At the base
of her throat a pulse began to beat and swell. Ryder's eyes
fastened on it and couldn't seem to look away.

The muscles in his arms grew tense and began to tremble. An answering tremble began somewhere deep inside
Julia.

Ryder's glance drifted up toward Julia's lips. Her arms
tightened instinctively around his neck as his head dipped
slowly in her direction.

There wasn't one single thought of denial in her mind as
her eyes drifted slowly shut and she lifted her head. An instant later her eyes popped open again in surprise.

The man wasn't preparing to kiss her as she'd thought—
he was ducking to enter the cabin. A deep sense of shame
flooded her, spreading a flush of heat over her entire body.

She peered through the cabin's gloom and once again
noticed the wooden cradle.

"Has your wife gone to town?" she asked as he lowered
her to one of the two chairs at the table and propped her
foot on the seat of the other one.

Though he looked a bit startled, he straightened and
turned away without making an answer. Crossing the room
to the window, he opened the shutters wide and took a deep

breath. Julia's eyes noted the breadth of his chest and recalled a vivid picture of that same chest stripped bare.

From the window, Ryder strode to the fireplace and removed an old-fashioned coffee boiler made of granite, hanging over the fire on a black iron trammel attached to a chimney bar. He poured liquid from it into a tin cup and took the cup to the cupboard.

"I—is there something wrong with your wife?" Julia asked hesitantly, wondering why he didn't seem to want to talk about his family.

"I'm not married," he answered curtly, lifting the lid off a brown stoneware jar. "You like your tea sweet?"

"Yes, thank you," she replied in surprise, her eyes going toward the empty cradle.

He wasn't married. Now why should that thought set her stomach aquiver? She would only be here long enough for breakfast, and then, in a few hours, if she was lucky, she'd be in her car on the way out of the state.

A huge black fly buzzed into the room through the open door and landed on the table close to Julia's right hand. Her eyes widened at the size of it, and she fluttered her fingers at it in repulsion, trying to make it go away.

Its hairy body twisted and turned as it seemed to eye her with interest. After a time it must have gotten bored looking at her, because her antics to try and shoo it away certainly weren't working, yet it streaked off the table and whizzed around the room.

Ryder didn't seem to notice when it buzzed around his head, but swatted at it when it landed on his sleeve.

"I thought the insects were bad in Texas," Julia couldn't help commenting with a grimace of distaste.

"Insects?" the man asked, pausing to lift a black brow in her direction before adding a scoop of thick yellow honey to the cup in his hand.

"The fly." She nodded toward the creature as it dive-bombed the lid on the honey jar before swooping toward the open door.

"Oh, they're not bad yet. Just wait till it gets hot. After a fresh kill in the summertime, they're thick as ticks on a dog's belly. That's when you can't keep 'em out of anything."

"Kill?" Julia asked in alarm, picking up on that word alone.

"Mostly buffalo—I've seen 'em so thick on a buffalo hide the critter looked like it was movin' even after it was dead. First time I saw it for myself, I got right up on the buffalo, ready to shoot, 'cause I thought it still had some life left in it—till I saw there wasn't nothin' beneath the hide, nothing but swarms a' black flies."

Julia shuddered at the picture he painted. She felt her gorge rise, and a moment later, when he placed the cup on the table before her, she glanced down to see something floating on the surface and swallowed thickly. He must have seen what she was thinking in her face, because he bent over and peered into the cup.

"Only dregs from the tea," he murmured, slanting her a look.

Something in his manner made her scrutinize him closely and she realized he was enjoying her obvious discomfort. She decided right then and there she'd drink the tea and damn with him.

Taking the cup in both hands, she held it below her nose and sniffed at the rising steam. Over its rim, she watched as Ryder poured himself a cup, noticing he took his straight, without honey.

"I caught some fine trout in the river early this morning, while you were sleeping. I'll make breakfast as soon as I've had my tea."

"Oh," Julia protested quickly, "I really can't stay." There was something eerie about this place, as though the rest of the world had moved forward in time, while this cabin and its occupant had remained fixed in one period. Despite the fact she found him very attractive in a raw, earthy way, she felt constrained to go, and as soon as possible.

"I do appreciate your hospitality," she was quick to add, "both last night and this morning, but I really must be on my way. I'd appreciate it if you could help me to the nearest town."

"Later," he said curtly, brushing aside her polite chatter. He sat down on the three-legged stool and rested his shoulders up against the wall. Stretching out his long legs and crossing his booted feet at the ankles, he sipped his tea.

"You're not from around these parts," he added, noting her glare of rebuke. She was a feisty one. It figured—with that bright red hair.

Uneasy beneath the intensity of his stare, Julia wanted to protest, but after a moment's consideration decided it might be more prudent to remain silent. She was, after all, at his mercy. Besides, it wasn't as though he'd done anything to make her feel anxious, he'd been a perfect gentleman—well, not *perfect,* but a gentleman nonetheless.

And it wasn't as though she was headed somewhere in particular, or someone was awaiting her arrival. A few hours' delay would make no great difference. Besides, once she got past the crude outer exterior, the man intrigued her in a strange sort of way. After the terrible emotional inertia she'd suffered in the past six months, feeling an interest in something again felt good.

Julia raised the cup toward her lips and sniffed its contents with interest. It had the same pungent aroma she'd noticed upon first awakening.

"What kind of tea is this?" she asked curiously.

"Sagebrush. I make it myself."

She lifted it to her lips and took a cautious sip. Wrinkling her nose at the unusual flavor, she stared at her host from beneath half-lowered lids. She couldn't help being curious about him. Who was he, and what was he doing living here alone, making like Daniel Boone and Davy Crockett?

The hot tea trickled down her throat, making her stomach growl, reminding her she hadn't eaten since the evening meal she'd had alone in her motel room the day before yesterday. Her host had mentioned fish for breakfast, and at first thought the idea hadn't appealed, but the more tea she drank, the more she was willing to give it a try.

"I'm sorry—I don't remember whether I introduced myself last night. I'm Julia Southern." She waited a couple of beats, and when he didn't offer his own, she prodded, "And you are?"

"McCall, Ryder McCall."

Julia took another sip of the aromatic tea. The flavor must grow on you, she decided. It was actually beginning to taste good.

"Do you live here alone, Mr. McCall?"

Did he hesitate a fraction before replying?

"Yes."

She didn't bother asking if he had a telephone. From what she'd already seen that morning, it was obvious that was too much to hope for.

"I didn't see a conveyance of any kind outside, so I suppose that means you won't be able to take me to town yourself. I wonder—"

"Conveyance?" he asked, curling his upper lip beneath the blond mustache.

"Yes—have I said something to offend you?"

"No," he answered shortly.

"Then I don't understand. You will be able to help me get to town, won't you?"

"No."

"No?" She felt a momentary surprise at the curtness of his reply.

"No, I don't go to town."

"Well..." She felt nonplussed by his attitude. He was being deliberately obstructive. "What about a neighbor, could I get help—"

"I don't have any neighbors."

"No neighbors! But everyone has neighbors—"

"Nope, not everyone," he contradicted her, getting to his feet. "I don't."

"I see. Well, then, I suppose it must be lonely, living here all by yourself—especially in winter. I understand the winters here can be rather harsh." She didn't know what else to say. She wasn't certain what the man was up to; she couldn't classify his attitude. He wasn't threatening—not exactly—but he wasn't friendly, either. She got the feeling he was still deliberating over what his attitude toward her should be, and the jury wasn't in yet.

"I like it," he answered steadily.

"I beg your pardon?"

"I said, I like living alone."

Julia studied his stern face, then shrugged. "What do you do when you need to go to town?"

"I don't."

"You don't?"

"No." He moved abruptly away from the table toward the fireplace.

Apparently, their conversation was at an end. From what little conversation they'd had she'd learned he didn't like people, so be it. She was no threat to his isolation, all she wanted was a way into town.

Despite his obvious antagonism, she didn't want to make him angry. She glanced at her swollen knee. The way things stood, she was in need of help, and his was the only help in sight.

"Is there anything I can do to assist you?" she asked, watching him work in silence.

"No...thank you," he added belatedly, without a glance in her direction, letting her know he could be polite when the need arose.

It seemed he was a man of few words, and that suited her just fine. But as the seconds multiplied into minutes, she began to feel piqued by the fact he could so easily ignore her. It didn't matter, because, whether he liked it or not, after breakfast, even if she had to crawl, she was heading for the nearest town.

A little later, as she glanced around the cabin's crude furnishings, even after telling herself she couldn't care less, she couldn't help wondering what had made him give up the comfort of modern society to live in this way. She didn't think she could do it—despite the way her life had turned out.

"E-excuse me," she murmured to his stiff back. "I'm sorry to have to ask—but would you happen to have a comb I could use? Mine was in my purse and I lost it last night."

Ryder turned with a long-handled fork in his hand and looked at her without replying. After a moment he moved around the bed to an antique cherry wardrobe standing in the corner that Julia had somehow missed seeing during her previous assessment of the room. Its fineness seemed out of place compared to the crudeness of the rest of the cabin's furnishings.

From the top of the wardrobe Ryder removed two objects, crossed the room and handed them to her. Julia stared down at the ivory comb and matching brush. Her eyes widened. "Oh, how lovely," she murmured, turning the brush over and seeing the gold inlay of a grape-leaf design on the back. "Where did you get them?"

"In the trunk." Turning back to the fireplace, he deftly flipped the fish sizzling in an iron skillet over the fire.

Julia removed the silk scarf at the back of her head and began to draw the brush through the knots and tangles in her red hair. The cabin was filled with the aroma of cooking fish, and nothing she could remember had ever smelled so appetizing. She could hardly wait to taste it.

However, when he placed a plate on the table before her and handed her a two-pronged fork, she stared down at it without moving.

Ryder pulled the three-legged stool up to the table and sat down across from her. Picking up his fork he tucked into his food with relish. After a few moments he realized she wasn't eating.

"You don't like fish?"

"I like fish," she answered slowly, shifting her attention from the plate containing trout, a hard biscuit of some kind and a spoonful of canned peaches, to his face.

He gave her a keen look. "Then what's wrong?"

"I—" she hesitated. "Could I please have a damp cloth to wash my face and hands?"

Ryder straightened, laid his fork across his plate and pushed the stool back from the table in an abrupt movement. He crossed the room, lifted a cloth from the corner of the cupboard and strode outside. A moment later, he returned and handed the cloth to her without a word.

Julia scrubbed her face and hands with it while he stood towering over her. When she was finished, skin tingling from the coarseness of the material, she placed it in his waiting hand and watched as he turned and pitched it across the room. It landed on the exact spot where it had been when he'd picked it up.

Taking his seat, he lifted his fork, then hesitated before resuming his meal. He met her eyes with a questioning glance.

Julia smiled tentatively, willing to forgive and forget. "Thank you," she murmured, dropping her eyes to her plate and lifting her own fork.

"You're welcome," he replied, forking fish into his mouth.

"I know it's none of my business," she began a few minutes later. Her eyes were fastened on the chipped edge of the plate sitting on the edge of the table before her. "I know I'm only a stranger passing through, but I can't help being curious. Is this your permanent home? I mean, are you living here because you *want* to?"

Ryder swallowed grimly. A muscle tightened in his lean jaw. The dark eyes flashed a firm warning. "You're right," he agreed succinctly, "it's not your business."

The silence between them stretched for what seemed an eternity. He couldn't help wondering what she was doing here, but an unwritten code of the West forbade him to ask.

All at once, as though he couldn't help himself, Ryder asked, "What's wrong with the way I live?"

Julia glanced at him and looked away. It really was none of her business. She wouldn't have welcomed a stranger's intrusion into her own style of living.

"Nothing." She shook her head. Running a finger around the rim of her cup, she added, "I'm sorry I said anything. Please, accept my apology. How, or where, you live is none of my concern." Her voice trailed off and she picked up her fork.

He studied her for a moment longer before resuming his own meal. "How did you find your way here in the dark?" he asked around a mouthful of fish.

"Just luck, I guess," she answered with a slight curve to her lips he didn't miss. "I spotted your light about the time the storm hit."

Ryder stopped eating. "What storm?" he asked softly, narrowing his eyes on her face.

Julia stopped eating at the tone of his voice and glanced up at him curiously. "The storm I got lost in last night—the reason I'm covered from head to toe in mud.'' Her voice took on an edge as the expression in his eyes grew speculative.

"The sky was clear and the stars were out when I carried you inside last night," he said deliberately.

"Then it must have passed over by then," she felt compelled to insist, without realizing why.

What did it matter whether it had stormed or not? It could have stormed on one side of the mountain and not the other. What mattered was that she was here, needing his help to get away.

"Where are you from? Did you travel a long way in this…storm?" His eyes searched her face and seemed to be reaching past her eyes into her mind.

"California—" she replied slowly, watching him push his empty plate aside, "I came from California."

Ryder stood and crossed the room to the cupboard in a slow, hip-rolling gait Julia found oddly sensual. When he returned he carried items she didn't recognize.

"That so?" he said, resuming the conversation. A moment later he was placing a small square of dark paper in a wooden tube. He added tobacco from a pull-string pouch down a small funnel into the paper and poked it into place with a small rod.

"I figured you to be from back East," he added, removing the cigarette, licking the open edge of paper and pressing it down flat with his thumbs.

"No," she denied without thinking, following his precise movements with a kind of fascination. As she realized what he'd said, she amended, stammering, "That is—I am originally, I was born in Boston. How did you know—I don't have any accent left."

Ryder smiled as he placed the finished cigarette in his mouth. "It's a little trick I picked up when I was a kid. We traveled a lot."

"Was your father a salesman?"

Ryder shoved the stool back almost violently and climbed to his feet. Julia jumped at the sudden clatter and followed him with wide, startled eyes as he moved to the fireplace and bent to light the cigarette. Taking a long pull on it, he straightened and stood a moment longer with his back to her before turning to face her.

"You travel from California all alone?" he asked as he moved the cigarette from one side of his mouth to the other.

"Yes." Clearly, his own beginnings were to remain a secret. She wondered why.

"It's a long way for someone like you to come alone."

Julia shrugged, irritated at the way he expected her to answer his questions, while refusing to answer any of hers.

"Where you headed?"

"I...don't know." She was on the point of admitting she had no particular destination in mind and then thought better of it. It would be imprudent to tell a stranger no one knew where she was, or where she was headed.

"Bad things happen sometimes to people traveling alone." A silken thread of warning ran through his voice. Julia shivered and gave him a sharp look. Was he threatening her?

"Are *you* one of those 'bad things'?" she challenged, suddenly tired of this cat-and-mouse game they'd both been playing.

An inexplicable look of withdrawal came over his face. He spun and threw the half-smoked cigarette into the flames with undue force.

Now what had she said? "Where—exactly—are we?" she asked stiffly.

"Where—exactly—" he mimicked her "—would you like to be?"

Anywhere but here, she was thinking as she replied, "I don't know, someplace where I can get help. Is there a town nearby?"

"Two days' ride from here," he answered.

"Ride?"

"That's right, on horseback."

"You have a horse?" she asked quickly. "Then you could take me—"

"I told you, I don't go to town," he cut her off sharply.

"Why not?"

"Town's got nothing I want."

"But—" she protested.

"I got some things to take care of outside. You just rest and I'll be back in a while." Hoisting his saddle, he strode out the door.

"But, you don't understand—" she called in growing frustration at his disappearing back.

What was wrong with the man? One minute he acted as though he could hardly bear her company, and the next, he was refusing to help her leave.

Chapter 3

Julia's eyes darted around the cabin. The minutes stretched into an hour. She began to wonder where he'd gone and if she *should* be afraid of him. He lived in a museum, yet he didn't appear to be aware of that fact. And his story about the buffalo had either been contrived to upset her, *or a figment of his imagination.*

The interior of the cabin started to become oppressive. Why would someone live like this... unless there was something terribly wrong with his thinking—or he was hiding from something.

A sudden chill danced across her skin. Rubbing her arms, she recalled his mentioning danger for a woman traveling alone. She was well aware people sometimes disappeared on cross-country trips. Travelers and hitchhikers frequently were victims of fatal crimes....

Had his seemingly innocuous remark been in actual fact a warning of his own evil intent? Had she stumbled into the hideout of a madman?

The skin across her scalp prickled and pulled tight, her stomach knotted painfully in sudden fear. Her eyes darted to the empty plate and cup sitting on the table.

She tried to tell herself everything was all right, that the man was only an eccentric and that's why he lived here, like this, all alone, but she couldn't seem to convince herself of that fact.

She began to shake. What if he'd poisoned the food? The drink?

The flavor of the tea had been strong—almost medicinal. Was that tight feeling in the pit of her stomach even now the beginning of a slow, painful death from poisoning?

The door to the cabin flew back, and startled, Julia let out a soft cry. In sudden panic, eyes darting around the room, she wondered how she'd get away from him with her right leg in its present condition.

What if he attacked her? The back of one hand brushed against something cold, drawing her glance. The fork!

By the time the tall, menacing figure filled the doorway, she was clutching the fork in one hand. As he advanced slowly toward her, Julia raised the fork and drew her arm back, prepared to use it if necessary as a weapon.

Ryder stopped on the far side of the table and stood looking from her strained expression to the upraised fork in her hand. "Was the food that bad?" he asked, a hint of humor curling a corner of the sensual mouth.

How could he look so ordinary and sane, standing there with a hint of a grin on his handsome face, when he was planning to murder her and dispose of her body?

"Here, I hope this will do."

Julia stared from the thing in his hand to the sudden glint of shyness in his dark eyes. It took a moment for her to realize the significance of what he held. A crutch. He'd fashioned her a makeshift crutch from a tree branch.

Julia blinked rapidly and turned her face away, trying to get a grip on her emotions. She wasn't certain which feeling was the strongest, that of relief at the realization he wasn't about to bludgeon her to death in a fit of maniacal fury, or foolishness for even thinking that was his plan.

"Thank you," she finally managed through unsteady lips, "that was . . . thoughtful—"

"No, ma'am," he cut her off, the shyness leaving his face as his glance came to rest on the upraised fork. "I just figured it would be a might easier on my back if I didn't have to haul you around—or worry about you falling and hurting your other le—" He swallowed the rest of the word and substituted, "yourself any more."

It wasn't polite to mention body parts in conversation with a lady. He'd have to keep reminding himself of things like that, because he hadn't had that many conversations with a lady and his manners were a might rusty. Taking off his hat, Ryder ran a careless hand through the pale strands of hair lying across his forehead and swept them back against the top of his head.

Julia was struck anew by the unusual contrast between the light brown hair, black brows and lashes. He was a remarkably handsome man, and the virile cowboy image suited him perfectly.

Being an artist, she was used to analyzing people and their character-types. Sometimes, she even played a little game in her mind in which she thought of people she knew and tried to match them with characters in movies. She knew she couldn't have picked an image any more suited to this man than the one he'd already chosen for himself, a kind of Gary Cooper with a dash of Indiana Jones.

"You ready to turn loose of that yet?" He indicated the fork and reached for it. Julia gave it up without a struggle. "What that le—" he caught himself "—what you need is a good soak in the river."

Julia looked startled, a hint of returning fear darkening her eyes.

"To take out the soreness," he explained, nodding without looking at her leg, "but first you got to learn to get around on this," he added, holding the crutch out to her.

Julia was very conscious of his nearness a moment later as he placed a tentative arm around her shoulders, keeping as much distance between them as possible, and helped her get to her feet. There was nothing in the least for her to object to in his handling of her as he helped her walk back and forth across the rough planked floor. He was very careful to keep his hands from touching anything but her shoulders, and his hip didn't so much as come within brushing distance of hers.

A short time later, satisfied she'd be able to use the crutch without causing herself further injury, Ryder suggested they move outside. It wasn't as easy manipulating the crutch over uneven ground. By the time they'd moved around the cabin to the corral, Julia was out of breath. Stopping to lean on the crutch and catch her breath, she admired the small vegetable garden growing near the cabin.

"It looks like you have a green thumb," she commented with envy. She couldn't manage to keep a houseplant alive, even when the florist assured her it took almost no maintenance.

"Only thing I do is plant it, nature takes care of the rest." He shrugged, rejecting the intended compliment. "I'll pick some fresh vegetables for supper. You like chicken stew?"

"Sounds great," she murmured softly, curious about his reaction to a simple compliment. She didn't bother to mention the little matter of her impending departure. What was the use? Apparently he took no note of things he didn't want to see or hear.

However, despite his help, or lack of it, she fully intended being reunited with her car long before supper. It would be difficult, but with the crutch he'd so thoughtfully provided, she could manage on her own. How far could the nearest neighbor be?

An image of empty, undulating hills tried to push itself to the surface of her mind, reminding her of the country she'd driven through yesterday, but she, too, was adept at rejecting things she didn't want to acknowledge.

"Come with me, there's someone I want you to meet."

Someone? Julia followed him curiously to the back of the cabin. He'd told her he lived alone.

The roof at the back of the cabin extended outward, forming a shelter with three sides. A corral had been built across the front and was attached to the walls of the cabin. It housed a magnificent black stallion.

This, Julia realized, admiring the animal's beauty and strength, must be the animal she'd heard the night before, when she'd visited the outhouse. Its presence also explained the sweet, pungent odor she'd noticed on Ryder's clothing as he'd carried her to the cabin.

She noted the horse was saddled and wondered if her host had changed his mind about taking her to town. On the tail end of that thought came another less pleasant one. Did he expect her to ride the beast?

If so, he was in for a surprise. She knew nothing about horses, and after observing the size of this one, decided she liked it that way. In the cabin, when he'd mentioned riding horseback, she'd imagined a much smaller version. If he intended using this great beast to take her to town, he'd better have a wagon stashed somewhere out of sight.

Ryder drew a reluctant Julia a few steps forward, but didn't press her when she refused to go any closer, and introduced her to Midnight. She duly admired the horse's shiny coat, thinking Midnight was an appropriate name for the animal, because he was indeed as black as the night sky.

Sensing her nervousness—how could he not, when she eyed the stallion with slightly widened eyes and cringed every time he snorted or made a move in her direction— Ryder reached behind him and pulled a thick clump of coarse buffalo grass, then instructed softly, "Hold this out and let him take it from your hand."

Julia looked from the horse's powerful jaws to the flimsy shoots of grass and shook her head. "I—I'd rather not."

She drew back as the animal pushed his large head through the bars of the corral toward the grass in Ryder's hand, and gave a nervous jerk when he whinnied in protest, because he couldn't reach it.

Ryder hid a slight grin at her skittish behavior, thinking she was the greenest tenderfoot he'd ever seen, then he remembered the way she'd lifted a fork against him in her own defense and sobered instantly. Grabbing hold of her hand, he turned it over and pushed the grass onto her palm.

Julia balked at the move, but with the crutch in one hand, it was hard to refuse. She bit her lip as he forced her rigid palm closer to the corral and held it beneath the stallion's muzzle.

Midnight sniffed at her hand, shied back at the unfamiliar scent and danced nervously around the corral. Ryder explained that the stallion wasn't used to her scent, yet, then couldn't help adding impatiently that he sensed her fear, too, and softly urged her to calm down and stand still.

Julia closed her eyes and turned her head aside, hoping that when he was finished proving whatever it was he was trying to prove, she'd still have a hand left at the end of her wrist. Without warning, she felt the horse's breath blow warm and moist against her skin and twisted her head slowly to see him nibbling the grass down toward her fingers.

She would have dropped the rest of the grass once she felt the sandpaper touch of the animal's tongue, but Ryder tightened his grip, lifting her hand toward the horse's muzzle. Julia's fingers closed in protest, and she tried to wrench her hand away, but Ryder only used his other hand to calmly pry her fingers apart so the remainder of the grass lay within easy reach.

Midnight's long tongue snaked out and curled around the remaining stalks, inadvertently sweeping across the sensitive skin on Julia's palm. Her hand jerked, but Ryder wasn't through with her yet. Raising her empty palm, he pressed it against the horse's forehead, intending it as a caress, but Julia's fingers curled into a tight, hard fist as she resisted his efforts. Speaking softly, in soothing tones, gentling her as well as the horse, Ryder slipped his fingers beneath hers and loosened them, spreading them out flat against the horse's soft coat.

But by now Julia was barely aware of the horse. It was the warmth and strength of the hand covering hers, the solid wall of chest, the strong, muscled shoulder pressing against her, the soft crooning whisper of Ryder's voice in her ear that held her undivided attention.

Midnight's nervous dancing had stopped. He snorted and blew loudly, lifted his magnificent head up and down as though he was agreeing to something, then stood quietly beneath Julia's hand.

"There, now you're friends," Ryder murmured in satisfaction.

Confused by the feelings he was creating within her, Julia couldn't help wondering silently, *And you and I, are we friends now, too?*

Ryder dropped her hand abruptly and unbarred the gate. Leading the stallion from the corral, he mounted him with fluid grace. Trotting up beside her, he motioned to her.

"Give me your hand."

"Where are we going?" she asked in apprehension. It looked a long way from the ground to the stallion's back.

"To the river. A soak in the cool water will do your injury a power of good. Leave your crutch here, you won't need it."

"I don't think I want to—"

Ryder's arms slipped beneath her from behind, causing her to drop the crutch in surprise as he lifted her to the saddle in front of him. Julia grasped the saddle horn as though it were a lifeline, noting that it was indeed a very long way to the ground.

She didn't know which kept her most on edge during the short ride—trying to keep her body stiff so she wouldn't rest back against the man's chest, or trying to breathe as shallowly as possible, so his arm wouldn't lay across her chest.

"Is it far to the river?" Julia whispered on an expelled breath, hoping he hadn't noticed how her nipples had grown tight when his arm had brushed against her just now.

"Over that hill." Julia glanced in dismay to where he pointed. They were headed toward the mountains—the mountains that never seemed to get any closer.

As though reading her thoughts, he added, "Don't fret yourself, it's not as far as it looks."

Half an hour later, Julia sat on the bank of the river beneath a canopy of cottonwood trees. The trip hadn't been at all unpleasant. It was beautiful country. They'd ridden from a valley of green cottonwoods, willows and mountain ash to the banks of the river, where the rocks were worn smooth by water, wind and time.

She'd even gotten used to riding in the crook of the man's arm and felt just a little sad to have the ride end.

"How do we do this?" she asked, feeling a flush of embarrassment stain her cheeks. As grateful as she was to him for the consideration he'd shown her so far, she had no intention of sharing a bath with him, even in a tub the size of a river.

"Shall we take turns?" she added when he made no immediate answer.

"You bathe, I'll keep watch. There's just one thing. You ever swim in a river before?"

"No," Julia responded slowly, "but I have in the ocean. Isn't it about the same?"

"I don't know," Ryder answered with a shrug. "I've never been in the ocean. Anyway, the middle of the river has a mighty strong current. Stay away from it," he admonished sharply. "It's dangerous. You do that and you'll be just fine."

He handed her a piece of brown soap and dropped a bundle he'd untied from the saddle's cantle onto the ground. "There's a change of clean clothes in there. I'll be keeping watch from up there." He pointed to the brow of a hill a little way downriver. "If you need me, just cup your hand around your mouth and give a holler—don't worry, I'll hear."

Taking hold of Midnight's reins, he turned away. Julia stood watching as he and the horse climbed the hill. When they'd gained the top safely, she turned in the opposite direction and hopped along the bank a short distance.

Finding shelter behind a huge rock surrounded by trees, she began to disrobe. Every now and then she peeked out from behind the rock to check on Ryder's position.

The last time she looked, he'd made himself comfortable by sitting cross-legged on the ground, his back to the river, with his rifle lying across his knees. Midnight stood nearby, munching on thick clumps of the short buffalo grass.

Just exactly who, or what, Ryder was keeping watch for escaped her, but she wasn't going to ask any more questions. It did little good in any case, since he didn't answer most of them.

She knew nothing about him, whether he was sane or just a hermit who liked living alone. If he was a hermit, hiding from people, so be it, it was nothing to her. And if he was crazy, well, that had nothing to do with her, either. The world was filled with crazy people who didn't bother anyone. She'd even met a few.

She would simply take her bath, change clothes—though she couldn't imagine what he'd brought for her to change into—then ask him, beg if necessary, to take her to his nearest neighbor, if he continued to refuse to take her to town.

Standing in her underwear, two scraps of dainty white lace, she picked up the curious piece of soap he'd given her. It smelled awful, but as long as it did the job she could stand it, just this once.

Julia made her way awkwardly toward the river's edge. It wasn't easy without the crutch. She thought about sitting down and scooting, but didn't want to ruin the expensive, delicate underwear. They were the only pair she had with her, everything else was in her suitcase in the car.

Once she'd reached the water's edge, she hesitated. The idea of undressing in the open, even though the place was secluded, made her uncomfortable. She cast a quick look behind, toward Ryder's solid back. If she didn't want to ruin her underthings, they had to come off.

It proved more difficult than she'd imagined. She should have stayed near the rock, where she'd have had something to lean against for support while she removed them.

Dropping the soap to the ground, she reached behind her with one hand, balancing on one foot, and managed to unfasten the lace bra and work it down her arms. Hanging it from a tree branch drooping near the water's edge, she began to work the panties down over her hips, glancing around nervously to make certain there were no uninvited observers.

Everything went fine until she tried to slip the foot of her uninjured leg from the panties. The small branch of the tree she was using for support broke suddenly with a sharp snap. Arms flailing, Julia lost her balance and fought to regain it, but it was a losing battle. She staggered back, slipped in the mud, and fell into the icy water.

A moment later, spluttering, shivering from the cold, she rose to the surface. Using one hand, while paddling to stay afloat with the other, she pushed the hair from her eyes and tried to figure out where she was.

The water felt like melted ice. Her skin tingled and her teeth chattered with cold. All at once, she spotted the lace panties drifting toward the center of the river. Without a moment's thought for her host's warning, she struck out toward them, intent on retrieving her only pair of panties.

Julia's hand touched the softness of fine lace at the same instant she realized she was in trouble. The river was deep at its middle and the current swift, but worst of all was the treacherous undertow. It was pulling her beneath the water's surface.

"Help!" Choking on a mouthful of water, coughing and spluttering, she called again, "H-help!"

What was it Ryder had said? Cup your hand round your mouth. She couldn't even get her hand up to her mouth— unless she wanted to slide beneath the water's surface.

The water was carrying her along at a fast pace, and Julia had no idea how far she'd come from the point at which she'd entered the water. Raising her head, she managed to get a fleeting glimpse of the bank and what lay before her. She wished she hadn't. The river narrowed and twisted up ahead, boiling with white foam. That meant rocks—and danger.

Julia gathered her strength and propelled herself as high as she could in the water and screamed, "H-e-l-p m-e!"

Exhausted by the constant battle to keep from being sucked beneath the water, she took a deep breath and slid beneath the water's surface, rising a moment later, gasping for breath.

She was going to die!

A week ago, she'd wanted to die. Now, with death imminently at hand, she knew that was no longer true. With every fiber of her being, *she wanted to live!*

Taking a deep breath, throwing her head back until her eyes were filled with nothing but blue sky, she bellowed, "R-y-d-e-r, h-e-l-p m-e!"

Ryder was just thinking of calling to the woman to see if she was about finished with her bath when he heard the sound of his name bellowed in fear. Gaining his feet quickly, he whirled to face the water.

He didn't waste time looking for her on the riverbank, or near the water's edge. He knew she must be somewhere near the middle of the river. He scanned the water quickly and spotted her almost immediately. She was headed for the shoals where the water twisted before entering a narrow canyon with steep rock walls and large, deadly spires protruding from the water's surface.

If she reached the canyon alive, she still wouldn't last long, because the canyon led to a waterfall. And no one could survive the five-hundred-foot drop to the waiting rocks below.

Sliding his rifle into the buckskin sling over the saddle horn, Ryder mounted Midnight and galloped along the edge of the cliff. There was only one chance to save her. A rock arch curved over the water a short distance from where the river narrowed before entering the canyon. It was a long shot, but if he could make it in time, before she passed that point, he just might be able to save her.

As he dismounted, his hand was already reaching for the grass rope coiled and fastened to his saddle. He scanned the water quickly as he removed his hat, gun belt, boots, socks and shirt. It took only a few seconds to spot the woman's bright head bobbing in the water.

He wished there was some way he could let her know he was on his way so she'd be ready for him when he got close enough to reach her. But he knew the sound the water made moving through the canyon, added to that of the falls up ahead, would cover any attempt he made to call out to her.

Dressed in suspenders and trousers, Ryder tied one end of the rope around the wide trunk of an old cottonwood growing near the tall bank, and the other end he knotted snugly around his waist. Stepping out onto the rock arch, he prepared to dive, waiting until he was certain to hit the water a little way in front of Julia. He knew he'd have only one shot at it, so it had better be good.

Taking care to keep his feet and legs from becoming tangled in the rope, he sprang up on the balls of his feet and lunged forward. The dive was neat and clean. His body arched through the air like an arrow plunging toward the water's surface. The rope followed him down. It was his lifeline—his and the woman's.

Julia didn't see the spectacular dive, but she did see him hit the water a few yards ahead of her. At first she was only thankful to see him, and then she realized he was in the same danger as she was herself. She didn't know about the waterfall, but the thought of vanishing between the towering cliffs up ahead terrified her almost to the point of hysteria.

She lost sight of Ryder as she slid beneath the water, but caught sight of him again as her head broke the surface. He'd moved downriver toward the worst of the rocks. She was exhausted from fighting the pull of the water trying to suck her beneath its murky surface, and her breath burned in her lungs, but her fear at the moment was for Ryder. Was she about to witness his body being battered against the rocks before experiencing the same fate?

Striving to keep afloat, she lost sight of him again as she was whirled in the water like a bobbing, spinning top. When next she spotted him, it appeared as though he'd moved closer.

Was that possible? Was he a strong-enough swimmer to fight against the deadly current and win? The thought made Julia's heart leap in her breast.

Yes! He was closer! He was closer, and she was heading directly toward him. All at once she realized he was trying to tell her something, shouting words she couldn't make out before they were swallowed up in the ever-increasing roar of the river, and waving one hand.

Without warning Julia smacked up against something solid in the water and felt a burning trail of fire along her right side. Rocks! He'd been trying to warn her she was drifting toward the rocks.

Julia threw herself to the other side and skimmed past the next rock without making contact. Ryder appeared to be moving closer now at a much faster rate. He was no more than an arm's length away.

Suddenly Julia realized something was wrong. He wasn't in the same spot—he wasn't directly ahead of her any longer. She'd changed course when she'd thrown herself away from the rocks. He wasn't going to reach her! She threw herself toward him.

Ryder treaded water and lunged in her direction, his hand reaching toward her. Julia stretched, straining with everything in her to keep her head above water and make contact with his hand. Their fingertips touched, lost contact. She bobbed beneath the water, struggling in panic to get to the surface, terrified she'd move past him without realizing it.

Her head broke the water's surface, and in a blind panic she expected to find him gone. She was wrong. Somehow, he'd managed to move toward her again. Their fingers touched, his slid between hers, clutching at them. And then his other hand was wrapping itself around her delicate wrist.

Ryder drew her toward him slowly while fighting the pull of the water's current against the rope. When she was close enough, he enfolded her against him, holding her slippery body in his arms. With her pressed safely against his heaving chest, he pulled the two of them up the rope toward the riverbank.

It seemed to take forever, but finally they both lay against the wet sand, breathing heavily, gulping in mouthfuls of air, thankful to be alive.

At first Julia wasn't aware of her nakedness. She felt the coarse sand against her cheek, tasted the sweet air filling her lungs, felt the warm kiss of the sun on her body and thanked God for life—and Ryder McCall.

Opening her eyes without moving her head, she saw him through a gap in the strands of red hair all but covering her face. Only a scant few inches separated them.

"Tha-nk you," she panted. "I seem ... to be in ... your debt ... once again."

Ryder blinked and looked up at her, water beading his dark lashes, sticking them together in tiny clumps. It ran in rivulets from his dark blond hair, coursed down the planes of his face to his chest, and dripped from the sides of his thick mustache. Except for the rapid tempo of his breathing, he lay without moving, his eyes locked on hers.

All at once something flickered and sprang to life below the surface of their dark depths. Easing himself away from the riverbank, his glance shifted from her face downward. Slowly and seductively, his eyes traveled over the rounded swell of a firm breast peeking from beneath one curved arm. The deep hollow of a narrow waist and gentle rise of a softly rounded hip beckoned to him to continue his examination, despite the voice inside telling him it was wrong.

By the time his eyes had reached the long, tapering thigh and graceful calf, Ryder was filled with a need so great, he thought he might burst with it. His dark eyes smoldered with fires barely under control as they flew back to her face.

In that one searing glance, Julia was made fully aware of her nakedness and all its implications. The pupils of her green eyes dilated in fear. Surely he wouldn't save her from the river, risking his own life in the act, and then do something so vile as—no, she wouldn't even think the word.

He was moving toward her. Julia felt her heart stop dead and then begin to race in alarm. She drew back in fear, but all he did was lift a swathe of wet hair from one cheek and smooth it back behind a small ear. His fingers lingered against her skin, slid around the sensitive outer curve of her ear, down the side of her neck, to the silky smoothness of her shoulder.

Julia shivered and felt her nipples grow painfully hard.

"You're about the prettiest thing I've ever seen." His hoarse whisper broke the strained silence. A second later, his warm breath feathered her skin as he leaned forward and placed a soft kiss against the raw scrape along her right side.

Julia's eyes drifted shut at the touch of his lips. So gentle was the caress she hardly felt it. But when his mustache brushed her skin, she quivered and shrank away.

Ryder drew back, his dark eyes filled with a seething passion. He needed her more at that moment than he'd ever needed anyone in his life.

Julia lay still, staring at him with wide frightened eyes, afraid to move in case the flimsy restraint he held on the dark passion she saw blazing in his eyes broke free and swamped them both. She was shocked at herself to discover that though she found him and the way he lived very disturbing, at the same time, he excited her. She sensed a wild, untamed streak in him that called to something in her.

There was a toughness about him missing in the men she knew—yet at times he was almost courtly in his manner toward her. She'd never in her life met a man like him.

But there was none of that courtliness in his expression as he looked at her now. The skin on his face looked as though it had been stretched too tight across the bones of his cheeks, the fine nostrils flared, and the sensuous lips were held rigidly taut against the palpable tension in the air between them.

Julia was well aware she owed this man her life, in fact, she owed him much more. Not only had he saved her at the risk of his own life, he'd made her realize just how precious was the gift of life. She'd always be grateful to him for that.

Grateful, yes, a voice inside her reasoned, but gratitude didn't stretch to cover what she saw building behind his eyes.

Ryder saw the varied emotions passing over her face and seemed almost to read her thoughts. For a moment he resisted the obvious answer to a question he hadn't yet spoken aloud.

Julia noted that resistance and grew tense, prepared to do battle if necessary to retain her dignity.

All at once Ryder's eyes closed; his head dropped forward and the tension suddenly drained from his body. He turned away. Getting to his feet, standing with his back to her, he loosened the rope around his waist with unsteady fingers.

"I'll get your things," he murmured in a voice devoid of emotion. "Don't go near the river while I'm gone. I think you've soaked in it long enough for one day."

Julia sat up, crossed her arms over her bare breasts, and bent forward, letting her long hair shield her face. She let her breath out in a long, relieved sigh. Just for a moment, she'd thought she was in real trouble. There had been such a hot, determined look on his face, she'd been afraid he wouldn't take no for an answer.

God, would this odyssey her life had become, never end? All she wanted was her clothes and a way to get to her car. Maybe her mother had been right when she'd told her she wasn't capable of taking care of herself. She certainly hadn't done a very good job of it up to now.

* * *

Ryder threw a brief glance over his shoulder, noting Julia's air of wretchedness. Who was this woman who had so nearly caused him to cross the bounds of civilized behavior and become the animal society had labeled him?

She brought out a side of him he didn't want to know. The both of them would have been better off if she had never showed up at the cabin.

Maybe he should point her in the right direction and let her go. Maybe she was nothing more than she said, a traveler in need of help—*but what if she wasn't?*

Chapter 4

Julia's body moved stiffly against the gentle sway of the horse's slow, steady gait. On the ride to the river *she* had been trying to keep from making intimate contact with her companion's body, but on the ride back she had Ryder's full cooperation in the endeavor.

She felt like an idiot. She'd done exactly what he'd told her not to do and nearly paid for it with her life, nearly taking his in the bargain.

No doubt he thought her a complete fool. She certainly felt like one. But she'd made so many wrong decisions in the past few years she supposed another one was par for the course in her case.

Since they'd left the river he'd maintained a stiff silence, broken only by the sounds the horse made as Midnight picked his way through the rocky hills toward the valley below. She felt certain he would be only too glad to see the back of her.

With that thought in mind, she was determined one way or another to leave for the nearest town as soon as they returned to the cabin and she was once more in possession of the crutch he'd fashioned her.

Her mind kept flashing back to that last scene between them on the riverbank, but she wouldn't let herself think about it. What she'd seen, or what she imagined she'd seen, in the man's dark eyes was better left forgotten. Just thinking about it made her feel unsettled.

If she were going to think about it at all, it was to tell herself the man had only been reacting, as most men would, to the naked body of a halfway attractive woman.

Back off, a voice inside warned sternly, *don't get mixed up with this one. This one is dangerous.*

She listened to the voice of reason and knew instinctively it was right. Besides, after California, her emotions were still too raw to even contemplate risking them on a man like the one holding himself so stiffly behind her.

Even at that, she had a feeling that wherever life took her in the years ahead, as long as she lived, she would never forget Ryder McCall.

Hoping to ease the tension between them for the rest of their brief trip, Julia searched around in her mind for a safe topic of conversation. Off to her right, through the thick grass, she glimpsed two wooden crosses.

"Are those graves?" she asked in surprise.

Ryder glanced in the direction she indicated and nodded as she turned to him for an answer.

"Can we ride closer?"

Ryder gave a slight pull on the left rein and Midnight veered in the direction of the graves situated on a slight rise about a thousand yards from the back of the cabin. The horse halted dutifully, sunlight reflecting off his silky coat, as the man pulled back on the reins. And when Ryder let them hang loose in his hands, Midnight lowered his head and began to nibble leisurely at the clump of grass near his feet.

Julia stared at the two mounds of earth with rocks piled around their outer edge. Her glance shifted to the wooden cross on the closest grave. The letters on it looked as though they'd been burned, rather than carved, into it.

Julia read aloud, "Sarah Purdy, 1856—1875." She made a swift calculation and whispered sadly, "She was only nineteen. That's too young to die."

Her thoughts were on Mariette as she glanced toward the second cross. It read very simply, "Baby John, 1875."

Julia's throat closed up. Her own child had been only a few months old when she'd lost her, and she'd barely been twenty at the time.

"Life's hard for a woman," she murmured softly, thinking about how much she had in common with the one lying here. "I guess it doesn't matter what century you're born into—it's all the same." She didn't notice the slight puckering of Ryder's brows as he stared at her.

"Life's hard on us all." He shrugged. "That's the way it is, the way God intended, I guess. I always figured it meant he wanted us to know nothing worth having came easy."

Julia lifted green eyes rimmed with sadness toward his face, but his glance was focused on the cabin in the distance, an odd determined expression written there. His words had surprised her. She'd already decided, on the strength of what she'd seen so far, that he lived as he did because he couldn't cope with today's society and had escaped it by making an uncomplicated life for himself on the prairie.

Some people might consider the lengths to which he'd taken it as a little crazy, but who was *she* to judge *him?*

Wasn't she on the run?

But now, her eyes narrowed on his face. She was confused. His words hadn't sounded like those of a man who'd retreated completely into the past because he thought it was easier than facing reality.

He intrigued her. She wished they'd met under different circumstances. At any other time, their coming together might have been a stroke of pure luck for the both of them. They might have helped each other before things got out of hand, but now it was too late.

She was being forced to weigh her life and reestablish her values. And she had a feeling Ryder was doing the very same thing.

They were both searching desperately for something to believe in, some reason to hang on in a world gone crazy, a world in which neither quite fit. But she suspected they would only confuse each other more if they spent too much time in each other's company. Her search would have to take her elsewhere, and Ryder would have to seek his own salvation without any help from her.

Julia was lost in her own unhappy contemplations when Ryder's glance moved suddenly to her face. Their eyes met, and something rippled beneath the calm surface of his dark eyes. Julia felt her heart skip a beat. This would never do.

Tearing her glance from his, she sought refuge from the rekindling of the dark fires building in his eyes. "It looks as though they're a recent addition." She gestured a little desperately toward the crude wooden markers.

"They've been there since I got here." The deep timbre of his voice vibrated along her nerve endings. "I guess they must be part of the family that lived in the cabin before me. Thanks to them, I've had a roof over my head and food in my belly."

"Oh, surely not." Julia's finely drawn brow arched like a question mark above her left eye. Forgetting the sexual aspects of their proximity, she turned to ask in a dubious voice, "I mean, in all that time, wouldn't things have . . . spoiled?"

Ryder shook his head. "This mountain air favors a man and his possessions—and it hasn't been all that long a time."

Well, time was relative, she supposed. A hundred years to an archaeologist might seem a short span indeed. But to her, a century was . . . unimaginable.

"Have you seen all you want to see?" Ryder asked a bit testily. His hands tightened on the reins, causing Midnight to dance about nervously as though he sensed his master's disquiet.

Ryder didn't much like being reminded of his own mortality; there was still a lot of life left for him to live. That's why he'd stayed here for so long, when it would have been safer for him to move on.

"Yes," Julia answered him softly, "I'm ready to go." And she was, ready to get back to her car and head in a new direction, before she found herself probing too deeply into this man's reasons for being here.

Clicking his tongue, Ryder coaxed Midnight to move. Julia's glance rested on the two lonely graves for as long as she could see them. She couldn't help wondering about the young woman and child buried there.

Outside the cabin, Ryder told her to stay put while he dismounted and disappeared around the side of the building. A moment later he returned, carrying her crutch. Propping it against the corner of the cabin, he reached for her. Hard fingers curved around her body, his thumbs grazing the underside of her breasts.

Julia couldn't withhold a sudden sharp intake of breath. He frowned and muttered, "Sorry," adjusting his hold.

He'd forgotten, until her gasp reminded him, about the raw scratch running along her right side. It wouldn't do for him to remember it too clearly, not if he wanted to forget how she'd looked lying on the bank of the river a little while ago, without a stitch on.

Julia's eyes focused on his chin and stayed there as she felt him accept her weight. She didn't know what to do with her hands. They finally found a resting place on his shoulders, and her eyes moved as though with a will of their own toward his grim mouth.

He looked as embarrassed as she felt. Speech was beyond her, but she gave a slight nod of thanks as he released her. The instant her toes touched the ground, he stepped back. Julia regained her balance and made herself busy settling the crutch beneath her arm while her color died down.

"You need to rest after your scare," her host muttered, turning away.

"No!" His back stiffened at the quick protest. "I really think it's time I was getting on my way," she added when he turned to face her. "Before I know it, it will be dark again, and I don't want to... overstay my welcome," she finished lamely.

"You aren't. I'd tell you if you were."

"But you don't understand," she protested on the point of explaining about her car. Perhaps, despite his retreat from society, he'd understand the possibly disastrous ramifications of an expensive car left unattended for too long, even in this part of the country.

"Rest now," he insisted, trying to sound soothing, despite feeling anger at being put in the middle of a situation he neither liked nor wanted. "We'll talk later, and if you don't want things stiffening up on you, you'd better rest while I rustle us up something for supper."

Julia swallowed her protests and allowed him to persuade her. She really was tired after her ordeal at the river, and a little rest before leaving was probably the only sensible thing under the circumstances.

But she'd stay only a little longer, she assured herself quickly. If she couldn't persuade him to take her to a neighbor for help before dark, she'd walk.

"All right, you win. I do feel a bit tired." She smiled a bit wanly and pushed the hair back from pale cheeks that had caught the sun. The few steps to the door seemed like a mile.

"Bar the door while I'm gone and don't open it till I return," he said tersely, turning away. "I'll have to see about gettin' you a hat, before you turn the color of a ripe strawberry."

Julia stood beside the door, staring at his stiff back. A dull ache in her knee moved up her thigh to her hip and the scratch on her side began to burn abominably. She really did need that rest. But she'd caught his muttered words and couldn't help again wondering why, if he didn't want her there, he kept making excuses for her to stay?

Was it because he really didn't want her to leave? Was he tired of this life he'd chosen cut off from other people? Or maybe he felt himself slipping away from reality and was clutching at an unexpected straw—her sudden appearance in his life—to help him hang on to it.

She couldn't afford to get mixed up with someone like him. She had problems of her own. She couldn't take the chance on becoming involved with an emotional cripple. Her own emotional well-being was too fragile, right now.

A tiny voice inside that wouldn't be silenced compared the man's needs with that of her dead friend, Mariette. Mariette had been slipping away from reality, too, through the use of drugs. If Julia hadn't been involved in her own attempt to escape from reality in alcohol...perhaps the other woman would still be alive.

"I really don't see the need to bar the door," she protested aloud, more because she was irritated with her own thoughts than because she really gave a damn whether the door was opened or closed.

"Bar it!" he ordered, pivoting on his heel to face her grimly.

"But you'll be—"

"Gone for a while," he finished for her. "Do as I say and bar the door."

"All right," she answered faintly, the trembling in her limbs increasing. She was just too tired to argue. If he wanted the door barred against some *imaginary* intruder, who *might* show up unexpectedly in this idyll he'd created, then she'd bar the damned door!

"Oh," she added as an afterthought, whispering with a hint of satisfaction in her voice through the narrow opening as she closed the door, "don't bother with a hat, I won't be here long enough for you to trouble yourself about my needing one."

Ryder's eyes glared at her through the door's narrow margin. He looked as though he wanted to say something more, but his lips remained clamped firmly shut.

Why didn't he just go so she could lie down?

"I'll be back before dark."

Julia nodded without really listening to the words, but his tone stayed with her. Was he making a promise, or a threat?

Without another word Ryder stomped away, and Julia dropped the heavy wooden bar into place with a sigh of relief. She was glad he was gone. At the moment all she wanted was an hour or so of uninterrupted sleep.

Turning to face the interior of the cabin, she stood for a moment, letting her eyes adjust to the darkness after the bright sunlight outside. The room lay in shadow. She lifted the loose bodice of the dress away from her sticky body and blew out her breath, fanning the damp hair curled against her forehead. What this place needed was central air-conditioning.

She had no idea where her host had gotten the dress he'd brought to the river for her to change into, but it certainly was hot. Looking over her shoulder toward the door, her eyes slid to the window. He'd probably never know...

A few minutes later she stood with closed eyes and lifted her face toward the cool breeze blowing through the open shutters. Satisfied, she turned to survey the room in the shaft of light now streaming through the small square.

She had every intention of taking a short rest in order to be ready for the ordeal ahead of her, should she be forced to leave this place on foot. She'd already made up her mind that if he wouldn't take her back to civilization, then she'd get directions from him and make it there under her own steam. After all, she'd found her way to him, hadn't she?

But after a few minutes of lying on the bed, staring at the ceiling, Julia found she couldn't sleep. She wondered where Ryder had gone and when he'd return.

Her eyes kept popping open every time she closed them, and so finally she gazed around the cabin, her thoughts on Mariette, Ryder, her own past mistakes, and finally, the young woman whose grave rested out back. Had that woman laid here sometimes, like this, awaiting the birth of her baby, wondering when her husband would return?

No, of course she hadn't. At least not right here, on this same bed. The 1870s were well over a hundred years in the past. This bed and mattress, the bed coverings, couldn't possibly be that old, despite the fact Ryder had indicated things lasted longer in these mountains. Maybe his belief that the cabin's contents were that old was a part of this fantasy world in which he lived.

Her conscience smote her at the thought. If that were the case, he really needed someone's help to bring him back into the real world. Who was there to help him, but her?

Julia's eyes moved to the trunk at the foot of the bed and lingered. Did it belong to him? Was there something inside that might help her to understand him better and his own special needs?

Curiosity got the better of her, and Julia found herself sitting in the rocking chair shortly thereafter, lifting the trunk's cracked and peeling lid. She hesitated all at once. She had no right to snoop into the man's personal belongings.

But, then, it might not be his. Besides, a part of her was very curious about the man . . . and he'd never know . . .

The trunk contained a wedding dress, some hand-stitched baby clothes, a large family Bible, an unfinished quilt and a diary, none of which belonged to Ryder McCall.

Julia admired the fine stitches on the baby clothes with a poignant tear in her eye, marveled at how well-preserved the wedding dress appeared to be, and carefully returned everything to the trunk. All except the diary.

She opened it to the first page and read, *Presented to Sarah May Douglas, May 15, 1868, for her twelfth birthday.* It was signed, *Samuel and Dorothea Douglas, her parents.*

The diary spanned five years. The early handwriting was childish, but very neat. The first entry was a list of all the birthday presents Sarah had received that day. Julia continued to read.

A long while later, Julia climbed on the bed, her knee aching abominably, and read the last entry with compassion stirring in her heart. The young woman was desperately frightened, her baby was due in a few days' time and she was all alone. Her young husband had left on a cattle-buying trip three months back, and being big with child and sick with the heat of summer, she'd stayed behind. He'd assured her he would only be gone a few weeks, but he'd been gone so long . . . she feared something must have happened to him. . . .

Closing the book, Julia held it in both hands, staring down at the deep, rose-colored, satin binding. How was it that the satin hadn't lost its deep, rich color, she wondered curiously.

Opening the book again, she ran light fingertips over the smooth pages. They were crisp and white, not dry and brittle, or yellowed with age.

After a minute, she closed the book thoughtfully and placed it beneath the pillow beside her. Her eyes felt heavy with the strain of making out the young woman's handwriting in the dim light.

Lifting her head and spreading her hair out on the pillow, she sighed deeply and closed her eyes. It must be about time for Ryder's return. She'd just take a short, fifteen-minute-or-so nap, and be ready for him when he arrived.

Her last fleeting thought was that she hadn't found anything belonging to Ryder in the trunk. She'd hoped she
would. She had decided there must be some dark mystery
behind his being here and wished she could solve it before
she had to leave . . . time was so short. . . .

A fiddle played in tune with a mouth harp, and a deep
voice called, "Swing your partner, 'round we go."
Julia laughed up at the tall cowboy holding her in a loose
clasp, his dark eyes barely visible beneath the wide brim of
a tall white Stetson. They were both breathless from the
dancing—and the excitement of being this close to each
other in a room full of people.
She had been wanting him to kiss her all evening. With
longing, her glance rested on the sensitive lips below a thick
blond mustache. They parted suddenly and moved as he
began speaking. She strained, listening, but couldn't make
out the words above the sound of the music and the talking, laughing crowd.
All at once, the lips became a firm line and the arms
dropped as he backed away from her. As his figure withdrew, it began to fade, becoming shadowy and indistinct—
as though seen through a cloud of smoke.
Julia strained toward him, but her feet felt like lead
weights, and she couldn't move them. "What?" she
shouted. "What did you say? I can't hear you."
Again his mouth moved, and she heard a word or two.
"Louder!" she shouted. "Speak louder!"
His figure was fading fast in the smoke-filled room. But,
suddenly, the words he'd spoken made sense.
"Open the door! Julia, open the door!"
Julia's eyes snapped open. She stared at the ceiling overhead in bewilderment. What had happened to the roof of
her house? Where was the cream-colored ceiling and pale,
peach-tinted walls of her bedroom?
"Julia! Damn it—open this door!"
That voice sounded vaguely familiar and extremely agi-
tated. Who . . . and then it all came back to her. Julia knew
who dared to yell at her in that harsh-sounding voice.
Ryder!

Sitting up, she scooted toward the edge of the bed. Something hit the floor with a soft thud. Glancing down, she saw the diary and felt a rush of sudden panic.

She bent over and scooped it up, holding it pressed against her chest with both hands, heart pounding, eyes riveted on the door. She didn't want him to know she'd read it! For some reason, it seemed imperative that he not find out she'd gone through the things in the trunk.

Sliding toward the foot of the bed, she grabbed her crutch, and lumbered to her feet. As quickly as possible, she replaced the book where she'd found it, well, as near to where she'd found it as she could remember, and called, "I'm coming."

"I'm coming," she called again in answer to a heavy blow struck against the wooden door, rattling the cabin's walls. "I'm coming."

She struggled to lift the heavy bar and dropped it to the floor, but before she could straighten, the door was shoved inward and Ryder's tall, dark silhouette filled the empty space. Over his shoulder, Julia noted that dusk had fallen.

Without warning, hard hands grasped her shoulders and held her. Julia looked up into his face, or what she could see of it that wasn't shielded by the brim of his hat. She couldn't make out his expression, but she could see the glitter, like tiny flames, in his dark eyes.

"Are you all right?" he asked in gruff tones.

"F-fine," she answered dazedly, staring hard at his eyes. Why was he so upset?

"Why didn't you answer when I called?" he asked curtly, his fingers biting into her flesh.

"I... fell asleep. I'm sorry," she found herself apologizing.

She could feel the tension in the arms holding her and her heart began to race in response. Abruptly his arms relaxed and dropped completely away from her—*just as they had in the dream she'd been having a little while ago.*

Now he'd fade away, she was thinking, recalling the dream and how bereft she'd felt as he'd done just that. In silent protest, as though in a trance, Julia moved toward him. She felt very tired all at once, too tired to think about anything, except how nice it would be to feel the strength of this man's broad chest beneath her cheek.

Ryder's breath caught deep in his chest. He stood unmoving, arms dangling at his sides, neither repelling nor encouraging her, yet accepting her weight. He realized he liked having her this close, but at the same time he didn't trust the sensation—any more than he trusted her.

Julia wasn't aware of his ambiguous feelings. A sense of peace, almost of homecoming, stole over her. It didn't make any sense, this feeling of rightness she felt at being in this man's arms, but at the moment she didn't care. She didn't even mind the sharp poke in her ribs from the wide buckle on the gun belt he wore.

"I thought something had happened to you," Ryder muttered against his will. "You didn't answer when I called . . . I thought you'd been . . . hurt."

"No, I'm fine." She swayed back so she could look up into his face and gave him a small, reassuring smile, before once more nestling her face against his shirt. "I just fell asleep," she murmured against him, her warm breath penetrating the cotton fibers of the shirt.

"It feels nice—" she hesitated, then continued in a difficult voice "—knowing someone was concerned about me."

Julia felt him stiffen. Had she said something wrong? In a moment he had put her away from him and crossed the room to stand before the fireplace.

"The fire's low," he muttered brusquely. "I'll get some wood."

He made a wide berth around her as he passed from the cabin to the growing darkness outside. Julia stood without moving as the door closed behind him. Had she *imagined* the concern, the momentary softening in him?

Had she *imagined* the air of anger about his taut figure just now?

Ryder stood leaning against the center pole supporting the cabin's porch. What was the matter with him? Why did he feel responsible for her? He didn't want to; she was a grown woman and she'd made it here all the way from California—nevertheless, he did.

All the time he'd been hunting, he'd worried about leaving her at the cabin alone. He'd spent more time worrying about that, than in checking his traps. As a result, he'd inadvertently set loose a prairie chicken twice the size of the one he'd brought home.

Ryder slapped the pole with an angry fist. He didn't want her here, damn it, sleeping in his bed, filling his mind with thoughts he had no business thinking. He tried to excuse his concern by telling himself he was only practicing western hospitality, giving her a place to stay until she was on her feet again. But that just didn't wash.

She was a beautiful woman, and he hadn't been this close to a beautiful woman in years. All she had to do was look at him, those green eyes sparkling, and he . . .

Ryder pushed the brim of his hat to the back of his head and wiped at the sweat on his brow with the back of one hand. His hand slid to his chest, covering the spot where her cheek had rested.

All at once his hand fell away, and Ryder snorted in self-disgust. What was he doing, acting like a mooncalf over a woman? So what if she was one of the first women he'd seen in over a year? It was that kind of foolishness that got a man hanged.

If he was smart, he'd take her to the nearest trail leading away from the cabin and forget all about her—*no, not yet.* Not until he'd figured out why she was really here. Her story just didn't set right with him.

Ryder straightened away from the pole and turned toward the firewood stacked along the end of the house. It was getting late and there was still supper to cook. If it were only himself, he'd have been satisfied to make a meal of hardtack and dried venison, but there was the woman to consider. . . .

Julia offered her help tentatively, a bit surprised when he readily accepted it and set her to slicing tomatoes and scraping corn off the cob for the stew he'd promised her. They worked in companionable silence. She learned what it was like to prepare a meal with none of the modern amenities—not even running water.

It was interesting, even the part where she helped Ryder pick the feathers off what he called a prairie chicken, then watched as he singed the pinfeathers in the open fire. The cabin had a peculiar smell for a little while after that, but later, sitting before a meal of chicken dumpling stew, sliced tomatoes and biscuits, she had no complaints.

She was touched when Ryder came in from outside and laid a damp cloth at her elbow before they began the meal. His own face looked pink, as though he'd scrubbed it at the water trough before entering the cabin.

They were both hungry, having eaten nothing since the fish he'd prepared for their breakfast that morning, and both ate without making conversation. Julia ate everything on her plate with relish. Spearing the last dumpling with her fork and popping it into her mouth, she glanced up to find her host eyeing her with approval.

Laying the fork across her plate, she sat back with a full tummy, strangely content for a woman who had no clear idea of where she was, or where she was headed.

What would her mother say if she could see her now? Julia almost laughed out loud at the thought. There was no question about it, she'd be outraged by the primitive living conditions, and make immediate arrangements to have Julia visit a psychiatrist as quickly as possible.

It was totally dark outside, but inside, candles and the fire's muted glow softened the roughness of their surroundings. The room had a very cozy feel and Julia felt thoroughly relaxed.

A voice at the back of her thoughts reminded her she'd done nothing the whole day about getting back to civilization except talk about it. Her expensive automobile might even now be in the hands of ruthless car thieves.

She shrugged mentally, it was too late to worry about that now. If the Porsche was gone, she couldn't do a thing about it.

A few hours ago, she'd been driving with no clear destination in mind, searching for a place to hide until she had come to terms with the latest disaster in her life. Where was she going now? In which direction did she head, when she left here?

A muscle jumped in the calf of her injured leg and pain shot outward from the knee. Julia stifled a sudden moan and adjusted her position.

She knew she would only be fooling herself if she told herself she could walk out of here tomorrow. There was no way her knee would be well enough tomorrow, or even the next day, for that kind of trip.

Her glance rested on Ryder's profile. And maybe that was all right with her. A few days filled with rest, sunshine and food might be just what she needed.

Julia relaxed and watched as Ryder went through what was becoming the familiar ritual of making a cigarette. She was completely unaware of the moment casual interest became total fascination.

Her gaze settled on the blond hair growing on one muscular forearm; the flickering light from the candles turned each hair into a single strand of pure gold.

"Would you like one?"

Julia's eyes fluttered and darted to his face. "I—I beg your pardon?"

Ryder held out the cigarette he'd just fashioned. "I know ladies don't usually smoke—at least not in public." He thought wryly of his mother and her friends. "But there's no one here 'cept the two of us, and I promise not to tell."

Julia stared into his dark, unfathomable gaze without answering.

"Well, yes or no?"

Julia raised one clearly defined eyebrow. She refused to pander to the game he played with the past. "That kind of male chauvinism vanished an eon ago. Besides, I don't smoke." She used to, but that seemed like another lifetime ago. One of the many things she didn't want to remember from her past.

Ryder blinked and shook his head. There she went again, using those highfalutin words he didn't understand. Putting the cigarette between his own lips, he leaned toward the candle. Did she do it deliberately, to try to keep him off balance? Their glances met across the flame, and he saw her give a slight shiver.

"Anything wrong?" he asked curiously, giving her a narrow, glinting glance.

"No, nothing. I was just thinking about gathering up the dishes."

"Leave them."

Julia paid no attention. She was stacking things together when he spoke again, startling her.

"Leave them," he ground out harshly. "I'll take them to the river, later, and do them myself. Sit down by the fire and relax." He stood, waiting for her to accompany him.

Julia did as she was told, taking a seat in the rocking chair facing the fire, lying her crutch on the floor at her side. When the meal was finished, Ryder had allowed the flames to die down, and now there was little left of the fire but glowing coals.

Ryder had brought his saddle in and placed it in the corner of the room beneath the window. Now he moved it closer to the fire, and instead of sitting on a chair, he lowered his long frame to the floor and sat, one knee bent, smoking his cigarette and staring into the dying embers.

Julia began to feel a little uncomfortable. The silence was getting on her nerves. She had no idea how to start a conversation with this man—none of her earlier attempts had met with much success. Obviously, he wasn't interested in world affairs, or the state of the nation's economy....

Come to think of it, neither was she. But that didn't settle the question of what to talk about to a man who walked with one foot in the present and one in the past.

"Supper was very good." She shattered the silence abruptly.

Without relinquishing his contemplation of the fire, Ryder nodded.

"Where did you learn to cook?"

"Here and there," he replied noncommittally.

"I took cooking classes once, but I only learned to follow a few basic recipes."

Ryder looked her over critically, scanning the gentle contours of her face. It was a face untouched by harsh winter winds or the heat of a dry blazing sun. His glance shifted to the soft white hands. These were not the face and hands of a woman who'd ever walked behind a plow, or scrubbed the dirt from clothes on a riverbank.

"Don't suppose you had to," he replied after a moment, returning his gaze to the fire.

Stung by his remark, conscious as always of her family's affluent background and resenting the prejudices it sometimes evoked in other people's minds, she opened her mouth to blast him with words of anger, then closed it again without uttering a single word.

He was right. She hadn't wanted to learn to cook, just because her mother insisted on it. They employed an unreasonably expensive chef, hired specifically to cook delicacies for her mother and her mother's friends.

"And did you—*have* to learn to cook, I mean?" she couldn't help asking.

He shrugged, sat forward to flip ash into the fire and settled back against the saddle, stretching his long legs out before him, crossing his booted feet. "Only if I didn't want to eat my food raw," he replied slowly.

Julia grinned, and Ryder, glancing in her direction, felt something painful clutch at his chest. She was beautiful even with the purple bruise on her forehead. He guessed she wasn't vain, either; she hadn't once asked him for a mirror.

Julia noted his stare and lifted a hand to her hair self-consciously. What was he thinking? Was he looking at the sore place on her forehead, the tangled rat's nest of her hair...or was he remembering how she'd looked at the river....

"Excuse me." Face flushed a deep pink, she half rose from the chair. "Can you tell me where the comb you lent me earlier might be?"

Ryder was on his feet instantly, flipping his cigarette into the fire, glad of something to do so he wouldn't be so conscious of her nearness.

"Sit still. I'll get it."

Julia dropped back into her chair. A moment later he returned with the comb. "Here." He handed it to her and went to open the door and stand with his hands behind his back, looking outside.

Julia studied his profile, wondering why his figure looked so strained. Did her presence make him uncomfortable?

She lifted the comb and began the awful task of trying to remove the tangles from long, permed hair without benefit of a decent shampoo and conditioner. A sharp twinge in her right side forced a low murmur of discomfort from between stiff lips. She'd forgotten about the scrape on her side. It hadn't bothered her much until now.

"What is it?" Ryder heard her smothered gasp and faced her.

"Nothing." She gave him a fleeting smile and lifted the comb, unable to withhold a slight grimace.

"Nothing? How does nothing make you look like that?" he asked half angrily.

Julia lowered her hand and shrugged. Maybe she was being silly. She just hadn't wanted to remind him of her foolishness at the river.

"It's the scrape from the rocks this morning . . . it's kind of sore. . . ."

Ryder released his breath slowly, unaware he'd been holding it. How could he have forgotten about that?

"It's all right," she reassured him. "I heal quickly."

He appeared to accept that and turned back to the open door, listening to the sound of katydids in the silence that followed. Julia plied the comb to her hair. After a couple of quickly swallowed yelps and a few smothered damns, Ryder couldn't stand it any longer. Stomping to her chair, he took the comb from her fingers and told her to stand up.

Julia obeyed with some difficulty, wondering what he had in mind. A moment later, she knew. Pulling the saddle around so she could perch on it, he knelt behind her and slowly began to remove the tangles from her matted hair.

A pall of silence descended over them. For a while it was a waiting, hold-your-breath kind of silence, but after a time Julia found herself relaxing. She forgot the identity of the person working behind her. Wrapped in a warm cocoon of contentment, the outside world and all its problems only a vague memory, her eyes fluttered and grew heavy.

Into that golden void, the deep timbre of Ryder's voice made itself heard. He began to tell her about his hunting trip that afternoon and how he'd spotted a herd of wild mustangs in the distance.

By the time the tangles were gone from her hair, Ryder had launched into a story about a pair of young antelope he'd seen at play. Julia listened without really hearing his words. Their cadence, the rhythm of his hands smoothing the comb through her hair, lifting the strands, separating them and smoothing them with his fingers, had begun to make her drowsy.

He was in the middle of another tale about a couple of prairie dogs when he noticed Julia's head had begun tilting farther and farther back, until it rested against his chest. She gave a gentle snore, and he realized he'd talked her to sleep.

Laying the comb on the floor, he turned the sleeping woman into the circle of his arms. Taking care not to awaken her, he gained his feet, lifted her and carried her to the bed. As he laid her down she rolled over onto her back.

Without bothering to do more than loosen the long hair beneath her head, he stood back and headed outside. When he returned a short time later, he carried a few silver-green leaves in one hand. Placing the leaves in a cup, he poured into it a small amount of hot water from the pot hanging over the fire. A pungent odor wafted from the cup to his nostrils.

When the leaves were thoroughly moistened, he removed a soft cloth from the corner cupboard and, taking the cup, he moved toward the bed. Careful, so as not to awaken her, Ryder turned the sleeping woman over onto her left side and propped her there with one of the feather pillows.

His eyes traveled over her slight figure. She was so finely made, his throat ached just to look at her. A pulse began to beat at his temple. Women like this one were not the kind men like himself normally had any truck with.

A heat began to grow inside him. Sweat moistened his upper lip and beaded his forehead. His breathing quickened. What if she awakened and found him bending over her? She'd probably think—he'd best get to what he was about.

Pulling the blanket to her hips, he reached beneath it with an unsteady hand and quickly slid the full skirt up her lithe limbs, careful not to touch her. With the raw wound exposed, it became obvious why lifting her arm earlier had been painful. The skin around its uneven edges looked puffy and slightly blue.

Ryder determinedly kept his glance from straying to follow the line of her rib cage up to where the smooth skin filled out and hinted at the curve of a full breast. Swallowing thickly, feeling the heat rise steadily in his lower body, he concentrated on relieving the soreness caused by Julia's injury.

With gentle fingers, he removed the softened sage leaves and carefully placed them over the wound. All at once, Julia stirred restlessly on the bed. Ryder hesitated. She lifted and turned her head to look groggily over her shoulder with unseeing eyes. Muttering something unintelligible, she laid back, letting her head drop down onto the pillow.

Ryder continued to hold his breath, waiting to see if she'd stir again, but the woman beneath him emitted a gentle snore and settled back to sleep. He waited a few seconds more and then went back to work. When the wound had been completely covered with sage leaves, he poured a small amount of warm liquid from the cup onto the cloth in order to keep the leaves moistened and then folded it over Julia's side. He placed a dry cloth over that.

Finished, he stood back and looked at his handiwork. He wasn't a medico, but he'd learned a few things about doctoring the years he'd lived with the Shoshone. And he'd learned a few more during the years he'd driven cattle north from Texas.

In the morning the wound would hardly trouble her. But he wasn't certain if the same could be said about the fact that he'd been the one to apply the poultice while she slept.

Normally another woman would have treated her, but that wasn't possible. He excused himself for treating her by telling himself he didn't need or want a sick woman on his hands. It was bad enough having a healthy woman to contend with right now; he didn't need the added worry of one sick with a fever because of a neglected wound.

Standing back away from the bed, he gathered up the remains of his handiwork and turned away. He'd had all day and evening to learn who she really was—if she wasn't who she claimed—and what she was after, yet he'd learned nothing. Like a besotted fool he'd combed her hair— *combed her hair*—and told her stories as though she were a child.

With a curse, he decided that maybe he deserved to be duped out of what he'd found by a little bit of a woman.

Chapter 5

Ryder was filled with self-disgust at the thought of how in a few hours' time he'd let this woman get beneath his skin and insinuate her way into his life. Not only had he risked his own life to save hers, but now he was playing nursemaid to her, as well. And the worse part of the whole thing was that now he didn't know if he planned on keeping her with him because he hadn't yet made up his mind about whether she was what she pretended to be, or because he simply couldn't abide the thought of letting her go.

He blew out the candle on the table, then threw a brief glance over his shoulder at the slight mound she made beneath the covers and felt a deep gnawing at his insides. He had to get outside and cool off before he did something neither one of them would ever forgive him. Once outside, he stood beneath the clear night sky, eyes raised toward the twinkling stars, and took several deep gulps of the bracingly cool night air.

The sky and stars reminded him of a dress his mother had worn when he was a child, made of black taffeta and sewn all over with clear glass beads. He remembered that as the light caught the beads, each one appeared to erupt with a burst of white fire, making them look like shimmering stars.

He'd liked seeing her in that dress. Until she'd become ill, she'd been a very beautiful woman with milky-white skin, clear blue eyes and hair the color of moonbeams.

Strange, he hadn't thought about her in a long time. He turned back toward the cabin, moved softly inside and took the makings of a cigarette from the cupboard. Outside, he leaned against the pole and rolled one. With the cool breeze from the mountains blowing over him, he considered what he knew about the woman inside.

She'd lied to him, he knew that. She said she'd come from California, yet it had been clear to him she knew nothing about riding a horse. So how did she get here from California? Did she walk all the way?

If she'd come by wagon, she'd still have had to deal with horses, or mules, or oxen. Where were they? Where was the wagon and why hadn't she mentioned it?

Another thing that didn't quite add up—anybody traveling in this harsh country of sun and wind and rain ought to look like it. Where was the dry, parched look to her skin, caused by hours spent beneath the blazing sun.

The only sign she had of being in the sun was the faint pink on her cheeks caused by their trip to the river, and if the short time they'd spent there had done that to her, what would days spent on a dusty trail, beneath a merciless sun, have done to her skin?

The condition of her hands belied her claims, too. They were soft and white, totally without the telltale calluses from hours of handling the reins on a wagon.

Her clothes were another matter. He'd never seen the likes of those dainty lace underthings she'd been wearing, not even among the women his mother had worked with in saloons in one mining town after another all across the West. He knew things and people were different back East; he'd met enough Yankees in his life to know that for a fact, but not even the ones he'd met had talked and acted like Julia Southern.

She laid claim to having crossed miles of Indian country. Alone? Without a gun? He didn't think that was very likely, not in these times, not with the Cheyenne and Sioux tribes on the move, killing everything white that crossed their paths. And what about the Apache?

He'd noticed Indian signs when he'd been running his traps earlier that day and that made him uneasy. The cabin was located on the edge of Shoshone lands. That didn't bother him, he'd lived with the Shoshone until he was almost twenty after his mother's death.

Washakie, the chief of the Shoshone, had been like a father to him, and he knew the old chief would have welcomed him back any time. But this time Ryder preferred to keep the tribe out of his troubles.

He didn't doubt the old chief was well aware of his presence near their lands. When he'd first moved into the cabin, he'd seen Indian signs in and around it more than once when he'd returned from a hunting trip. But no one had bothered him, and after a few months the signs had disappeared altogether.

Lately, the Indian signs had returned to the mountains and valleys where he hunted. But it wasn't the thought of the Shoshone that bothered him. Some of the signs left had been Cheyenne, but mostly Sioux. Neither tribe was particularly fond of whites.

Ten years ago, in December of 1866, about the time Ryder was getting ready to leave the Shoshone camp, Chief Red Cloud of the Oglala Sioux had slaughtered seventy-nine soldiers and two civilians just outside Fort Phil Kearny, located to the west of here. A couple of years later, Red Cloud had signed a treaty and was now, apparently, happily settled on a reservation.

But Crazy Horse wasn't. He was another strong Sioux leader and he hated the whites. In 1874, General George Armstrong Custer enraged him by invading the sacred Paha Sapa, the Black Hills, on a reconnaissance mission. Paha Sapa was a holy place belonging to the Indians, deeded to them by the Treaty of 1868.

Nothing the whites had done in the past had so enraged the Indians; it didn't matter that the treaty gave the army the right to enter Indian lands at any time, they didn't want the whites there. But it didn't matter what the Indians wanted;

when gold was discovered by Custer's expedition, the whites flocked to the Black Hills.

Crazy Horse had become incensed and began wreaking his vengeance on the white man at every opportunity. He still was, as far as Ryder knew, but this cabin was a long way from the Black Hills.

Ryder's eyes slid toward the mine shaft. He held the cigarette clamped between thumb and first finger and took a long drag on it, letting the smoke drift out leisurely through his nostrils.

He'd been out of touch with news of the Crazy Horse raids for the past year. The last he'd heard, Crazy Horse's camp was located somewhere near the Cheyenne River. There was a real hullabaloo going on among the nations over the government's offer to purchase the Black Hills and the Powder River lands from their chiefs.

Tempers were short among both Indian and white man; maybe it was time he cut his losses and made tracks out of here and in another direction. *But not until he'd settled the question of the woman.* It was his guess she hadn't traveled across country alone. So where was her companion—companions?

Ryder dropped the cigarette butt and ground it into the dirt with more force than was necessary. Shoving his hands deep into the pockets of his trousers, he strode around the side of the cabin to Midnight's corral.

He'd been keeping a close eye on the stallion since the Indian signs in the area had increased. Horse stealing was one of the young bucks' favorite pastimes. He was afraid one of these nights Midnight would end up in the hands of a brave who couldn't resist the temptation.

The black stallion heard his master's approach and whinnied a greeting as he moved from beneath the shelter and into sight. Moonlight danced on his sable coat as he trotted toward his master and friend.

Ryder lifted a carrot he'd pulled from the garden and held it beneath the animal's nose. Midnight sniffed at it, took it between his large teeth and crunched it noisily. When it was gone, he nuzzled Ryder's chest playfully, looking for another.

"What do *you* think, boy—" Ryder spoke in quiet tones, running a gentle hand down the stallion's forehead "—is the lady a liar?"

Ryder had found talking things over with the stallion sometimes gave him the opportunity to mull things over more clearly in his own mind. There were times, however, when he spoke to the animal simply to hear the sound of his own voice. Sometimes a man had to hear his voice just to remind himself he had one.

As far as Julia Southern was concerned, either she was telling the truth, she was after something, and he had a fair idea of what that "something" might be. If she'd been a man, he'd have known what to do about the situation. A gun could be a great persuader, and he'd have used it to persuade his guest to talk.

But a woman? No matter what the cost to himself, he knew he'd never be able to justify using a gun against a woman.

Midnight stomped his front hooves and cribbed the top of the corral, wanting another carrot.

"Stop that," Ryder admonished sharply, catching hold of his lower jaw, feeling the tongue slide like sandpaper across his palm. "You'll get splinters in your gums." The horse seemed content once he had the man's attention and nuzzled puppylike against his chest.

Ryder stroked the broad, flat nose thoughtfully. "She's not like any woman I've ever known—not that I've known all that many *ladies*." He laughed self mockingly, adding, "And she's definitely a lady, ain't she, boy?"

Giving the horse a final stroke, he turned away. He'd told Julia he'd do the washing up from supper, but it could wait until morning. He was tired and wanted to have a last look around before turning in for the night himself.

There hadn't been much sleep for him the last two nights. In fact, he hadn't slept much at night for over a year, but always before, he'd managed to get a few hours' sleep during the day.

Now there was the woman, and just possibly a visit from her friends, to consider. One thing was sure, he'd be sleeping with one eye open and his rifle close at hand from now on.

Ryder's silent figure blended with the night. He slid from bush to bush hiding in shadows among rocks and trees as he painstakingly examined the area for signs of uninvited guests.

There had been another reason, a reason he preferred to forget, for his lack of sleep of late. Try as he might, he couldn't get the picture of the woman sleeping in his bed out of his mind.

She was the most beautiful woman he'd ever seen. She was so...feminine—not helpless, but untutored about how to live in the West. He supposed that had something to do with the way women from back East were reared. It was that quality, that innocence that made him want to take care of her, and that made him mad.

One thing she didn't lack was spunk, because, whatever her reasons for being here, *she was here,* and that took plenty of spunk. It was the same kind of spirit that drove the women who moved West with their husbands. He'd seen them working alongside their menfolk in the fields, shooting and skinning buffalo, nursing a baby while they herded stock, helping to make a life for themselves and their families in a land that *took* life more readily than it sustained it.

Ryder admired those women, white and red alike—just as he couldn't help admire Julia, and he'd continue to admire her, if grudgingly, even if her reason for seeking him out had nothing at all to do with being lost and everything to do with personal gain.

He didn't have much to do with people. He'd always been a loner, because that's the way he liked it. Even the time he'd spent living among the Shoshone had earned him the name Walks Alone. He might have stayed with them longer if the sister of a friend hadn't begun to eye him with longing.

He'd felt the noose of responsibility growing tight around his neck and left their camp as quickly as possible so as not to offend the friend by turning down the young woman. He couldn't stand the thought of being tied to one place. He was a man who lived for his freedom.

It was for that reason he'd broken out of prison. He knew a prison break would add years to his sentence if they caught up with him. But it was a sentence he didn't deserve, because he was innocent of the charge of horse stealing brought against him.

He'd won Midnight fair and square in a poker game. The horse's owner, Chase Bartlett, hadn't wanted to honor the deal. The witnesses to the game had been cattle drovers like himself, hired to drive the man's cattle to market.

The drive had ended, and everyone was planning to head out the next morning in different directions. That last evening, until late into the night, was spent gambling.

The next morning, when Ryder had awakened, everyone was gone, and so was the black stallion he'd won in the poker game. Ryder followed Bartlett to his ranch, a day's ride away, on the horse he'd ridden on the cattle drive. At the ranch, he'd tried reasoning with Bartlett, but the man had refused to acknowledge his debt. He'd had his ranch foreman throw Ryder off the property.

That night Ryder returned and took Midnight, leaving the other horse in the corral. A posse had followed close on his heels and caught up with him the next day. He'd been arrested for horse stealing and no amount of protest on his part had done any good.

The men who could have given testimony on his behalf were long gone, scattered to the four winds. That's how he'd ended up in Laramie Territorial Prison. The judge's final remark to him before sentencing was about how lucky he was that Mr. Bartlett was a forgiving man, otherwise, he'd be having his neck stretched on the hanging tree at the edge of town.

Ryder had managed to regain the freedom taken from him by Chase Bartlett's lies. Now, in one way or another, Julia Southern threatened that freedom and he'd promised himself he would never go back to prison. He'd rather be dead than closed up by four walls, behind bars, again.

The simplest way to solve his problem would be to take the woman out and lose her. He knew the countryside like the back of his hand. He could get her so lost she'd never be able to find her way back to civilization—

Ryder stopped the thought right there, because he knew he wouldn't do it, no matter what trouble she brought him. He couldn't abandon her in Indian country.

If he were honest with himself, he'd admit there was another reason he wouldn't do something like that. He liked the company. If she hadn't showed up, he'd have been just fine alone. But she had, and she'd made him realize how much he missed the companionship of another human being.

Loneliness could do strange things to a man. He was beginning to worry that it had begun to addle his brain. In fact, that evening when he'd returned from hunting and she hadn't immediately answered his knock, was a prime example of just how addled he'd become. He'd been completely unsettled by the thought that she had up and left without his knowing it.

Was he willing to chance a bullet in the back, a knife stuck between his ribs—or a hangman's rope—to keep her here?

One thing was certain, he'd have to work harder to keep his guard up against her from now on. He might be nothing more than a trail bum on the run from the law, but he was smart enough to know she wasn't the kind of woman you took to bed and forgot all about the next morning. He'd keep his eye on her, but from a distance. He hadn't gained his freedom just to lose it again, and especially not to a woman.

Julia, unaware of her host's suspicions, slept deeply. A pair of dark eyes followed her into her dreams. Something about those eyes haunted her. She was drawn to them, yet at the same time she feared them without quite knowing why.

The next morning she awakened abruptly, a cold, soggy mess beneath her in the bed.

"What in the—"

Dragging up her skirt, she kept one eye on the empty place where Ryder's saddle had rested last night, and the other on the wet cloth and brown mess falling away from her side. It looked like—she didn't know what it looked like. Picking up a pinch of it between finger and thumb, she

raised it gingerly to her nose and sniffed. She recognized that
odor. Where had she—

"It's sage." Ryder stood in the cabin doorway, blocking
the early morning light, shirtsleeves rolled to his elbows,
holding the dishes and pans he'd washed from their dinner
the night before.

Julia hastily lowered her skirt and grabbed at the blankets, aware that after a brief, fleeting glance he'd transferred his gaze to the floor. She felt unaccountably
embarrassed at his having seen her bare skin. She didn't stop
to analyze how strange that should be, she who had worn
bikinis on crowded beaches all her life.

"I made up a poultice last night and put it on the
scratch." Ryder spoke matter-of-factly as he entered the
cabin and strode to the table where he emptied his arms. "I
should have awakened you," he added after a moment when
she didn't answer. Feeling awkward, he stood stiffly by the
table, not liking it at all, wishing she'd say something.

"You were sleeping," he explained, "I didn't want to
wake you . . . I did it to keep you from getting a fever."

"Thank you," she managed at last.

Surprised, Ryder glanced in her direction and saw she was
smiling at him shyly. A glimmer of an answering smile crinkled the corners of his eyes before he realized what he was
doing.

He sobered abruptly, gave her a short, curt nod, pulled
the brim of his hat low over his eyes, and without another
word stalked from the cabin.

Julia watched him disappear with a slight frown furrow-
ing her brows. She had a feeling she was beginning to get to
him, and she suspected she knew why. The man resorted to
anger, or did a disappearing act, every time it looked like
something personal was about to spring up between them.

If she'd been awake last night, no doubt he'd either have
given her the poultice and told her to apply it herself, or he'd
have maintained an air of angry silence through the whole
procedure. That realization might have upset her last night,
but now it didn't, because it meant she was getting beneath
his skin, and for some reason she felt compelled to do just
that.

Later that morning, when she'd finished straightening the cabin, or as much of it as she could on a crutch, Julia sat in the rocker to catch her breath. As the rocker moved back and forth, her eyes idly roamed the cabin. Ryder had mumbled something about wood and disappeared again a little while ago, leaving her alone.

She'd been tempted to go after him and force him to talk to her, just to annoy him, but didn't. She didn't want to anger him, she wanted to get to know him. That's why she was still here, instead of where she ought to be—making sure her car was still in one piece.

Some time during the night, she'd decided she couldn't just walk out and leave him. The guilt she felt over Mariette's death—Julia wasn't there when the other woman had needed her—had convinced her to stay, for a little while at least, and see if she could help Ryder.

Her eyes settled on her hands. With her thoughts on Ryder, she was only mildly appalled to discover that her usually faultlessly manicured nails were raggedly broken and encrusted with dirt.

Were these the hands of an artist? she asked herself mockingly. Smiling, she thought about the answer her "friends" in California would have given to that question.

Her gaze traveled from her hands to her clothes and the smile died. The shapeless dress Ryder had given her to wear at the river was wrinkled and stained with dirt. With a grimace of distaste, she decided that what she needed was a bath and a change of clothes—but clothes for her were becoming a problem.

She really ought to insist Ryder either take her to her car, or that he go for her, to get the few clothes she'd bought before leaving Thermopolis. But something stopped her.

She realized she was growing to like being here. The man made no demands on her at all. And though he maintained a certain distance between them, he treated her with consideration and respect. As a matter of fact, sometimes she had the absurd notion that he thought the very fact of his being male offended her sensibilities. There were times when his Victorian attitude made her smile, but it made her feel...special, too. She liked to think their...friendship...was making a little progress.

Earlier that morning, she'd gone with him to the river to do laundry. Ryder had looked at her with a deep frown when she'd asked him how they were going to get the filth out of the clothes without a washer.

"You are the washer," he'd told her succinctly with a shake of his blond head. "And this is how you do it."

He'd proceeded to wet down the clothes and rub them with the brown soap, which seemed to be a universal brand good for both personal hygiene and household cleanliness. Next he'd beaten the clothes with a rock, making suds, then he rinsed them in the river. They were currently spread over bushes at the back of the cabin, drying in the sunshine.

She'd noticed him eyeing her underwear, the ones she'd nearly drowned for trying to save, as they were spreading the clothes out to dry, and she'd have given a lot to know what was running through his mind at the time. He'd looked up and caught her watching him, and a deep tide of red had run up his neck and stained the tips of his ears. That's when he'd tilted the hat low over his face, mumbled something about wood and disappeared from sight.

Twisting around in the chair, she felt a slight twinge in her side and remembered the poultice Ryder had applied the night before. Surprisingly enough, it had worked. The man was amazing. Where did he get such knowledge?

That was another reason to be counted in favor of her staying here awhile longer. She wanted to learn from him. He was a man obviously at peace with himself and his surroundings—except for the slight paranoia he'd shown at the river when he'd insisted on "keeping watch" while she bathed with a rifle across his lap. The more she thought about it, though, the more she was convinced it must have been wild animals, bears, perhaps, that made him feel the rifle a necessary precaution.

Julia pushed herself from the chair to her feet. Her eyes had fallen on the trunk. A change of clothes was uppermost in her mind when she decided to look a bit deeper into its contents.

She hadn't gone through all the things in the trunk the day before when she'd found the diary. Maybe somewhere at the bottom she'd find something she could wear. Ryder had suggested during dinner last night that she look in the trunk and use whatever she needed from its contents.

Laying her crutch on the foot of the bed, Julia pulled the rocking chair forward and lifted the lid. Slowly, she removed everything she'd gone through the first time, laying the items on the floor. Underneath it all, she discovered two loose smocks similar in design to the one she now wore. There was also a set of tortoise-shell combs wrapped in paper and a long nightgown of fine lawn patterned with tiny yellow-and-green flowers and leaves.

The clothes gave off a musty scent, reminding her how long they must have lain in the trunk. They were surprisingly well preserved and free of moths. Holding the gown between her hands, she stared down at it, thinking of the young woman to whom it had belonged. A deep sadness welled up inside her. Perhaps she shouldn't wear the clothes, after all.

"Whew! It's hot out there," Ryder muttered, wiping the sweat from the inside band of his hat with a large colored bandanna. "I'm going fishing—" His words died as he caught sight of Julia's unhappy face. Moving closer he asked, "What's wrong?"

She looked up. "Nothing. I was just having second thoughts about . . . borrowing these clothes."

"Why?" He frowned, looking from the gown to her unhappy face. "Their owner doesn't need them anymore."

She hesitated before explaining. "I lost a friend—someone very close to me—not long ago. I packed her things and sent them to her family. Handling these things has reminded me of that time."

"We all die sooner or later." He'd accepted that fact a long time ago.

"I know," she answered sadly, her green eyes searching his face. "But, my friend—she shouldn't have died. Not the way she did—not so young." Again she hesitated before asking, "Do you think they know?"

"They?"

"Yes, those who have died, do you think there's something ... something more ... after death?"

"More?" he asked, the frown intensifying.

"Yes." Julia nodded.

He shrugged. "Indians believe that when this body dies you simply change form and continue life."

"Do you belive that?" she asked curiously.

"I don't know." He shrugged again, uncomfortable with the conversation. "They seem convinced of it. I s'pose one of these days I'll find out for myself—when it's my turn to go."

Julia shivered. "Are you ... afraid?"

Ryder straightened his shoulders and crammed his hat down on his head, turning away. "I'm not afraid of anything."

"I wish I wasn't."

The poignant tone of her voice stopped him. He turned back. "I'm going fishing," he said on the spur of the moment, then added, surprising her, but surprising himself even more, "Come with me."

"Fishing?" she asked. He sounded as though he actually wanted her company. If that were true, then it would be the first time since she'd stumbled across him and the cabin.

Because, though he'd shown no inclination to help her on her way, he showed no great desire for her company, either. Most of the time he found something to do to keep him away from her.

"You coming—or not?"

Julia nodded. "Let me put these clothes out to air. Later," she added quickly before he could exit the cabin, "when we come back—after the evening meal—would it be too much trouble to have a bath in the tub?"

"No trouble," he murmured tightly, refusing to let the image of her pale, naked body enter his mind. "No trouble at all."

A little while later, sitting on the bank of the river, munching on a ripe, juicy tomato plucked straight from the garden, Julia watched as Ryder threw his line into the water. What was he thinking with his eyes all screwed up in that manner?

"Do you have a family?" she asked abruptly.

Ryder stiffened an instant before his head swung in her direction. "Didn't your mama ever teach you it isn't polite to ask questions of a personal nature?"

She could tell by his expression he was debating about whether or not to answer the question. "I don't mean to pry," she murmured softly. "I just..." She shrugged and looked away.

"I don't have any family," he relented abruptly. "None that I know about. My ma's dead. I don't know about my pa—I never met him."

"You never met him?"

"My mother was a prostitute," he declared flatly. "Any one of her paying customers could have fathered me."

Julia was shocked into silence. She hadn't meant to open old wounds. Ryder met her eyes, and she was surprised to find nothing in his expression but signs of a faint curiosity directed toward her.

"Have I shocked you?" he asked with a hint of derision.

"N-no—well—yes," she amended. "But not by what you said, but by your attitude. You seem so...well—" She hesitated. "I guess *adjusted* is the word I'm looking for—you seem so well-adjusted to the idea."

Ryder shrugged. Before he could make any further comment a sudden tug on his line drew his attention. Lifting the line out of the water, he smiled at the size of the trout dangling from its end.

"What about your family?" he asked as he removed the fish and baited the hook. "Your parents still living?"

Julia's attention was focused on the hook he was baiting. It was a grayish-white and obviously not made of any metal she'd ever seen. "That's an unusual hook. I don't believe I've ever seen one quite like it. What's it made of?"

Ryder raised a brow in her direction, but only answered, "Bone."

"Bone?"

"Yes, I made it myself from the wing bone of a hawk."

Again he amazed her with his knowledge and ability. The bone hook seemed quite effective in catching fish. Subconsciously, she wondered why he went to such lengths to preserve an aura of the past, even in such a minor thing as a fishing hook, when it would have been much easier to bring along metal ones.

"My father is dead," she said, answering his question about her family, knowing instinctively that at this point in their relationship, it would do no good to bring up questions about his reasons for "hiding" from the present. "He died when I was a teenager."

"Teenager?" Ryder looked back over his shoulder with a frown.

"Yes, I was thirteen when he died. I was traveling when he had a sudden heart attack. It was fatal."

Ryder forgot his puzzlement over the unfamiliar term she'd used and watched the gathering sadness on her face. "You were close to your father."

"Yes. Father and I always got along well. We understood each other."

"And your mother?"

"Mother pushed me all the time. She was never satisfied with what I did. She wanted me to be the best—always the best—at everything."

Wiping tomato juice from her fingers onto the grass at her side, Julia lifted her crutch and got to her feet. Talking about her father brought back the pain surrounding his death.

She hobbled to the bank and stood for a time looking out over the clear blue water. What she didn't tell Ryder was that her mother had held the funeral before Julia could get back from Europe. Her mother had told her she'd done it for Julia's own good. Now Julia wouldn't have to remember him in a casket, but as she'd last seen him at the airport waving her off.

But Julia hadn't felt better knowing she'd never see him again. She wanted one last time to see his dear face, to tell him she loved him and say goodbye.

Julia knew her mother had resented the close tie between father and daughter. And she knew that was the real reason for her having gone on with the funeral without waiting for Julia's return.

She wandered back to where Ryder stood with his fishing line dangling in the water.

"Did you miss not having a father?" she asked him abruptly.

"You don't miss what you never had."

"I miss my father every day of my life," she couldn't help whispering passionately. "All he ever wanted was for me to be happy."

"And were you?"

"Until he died."

Ryder eyed her troubled profile. "What took you to California?"

"Escape," she admitted softly. "I was trying to escape my mother's domination." Turning toward him suddenly, she raised a haughty brow and asked, "Are you surprised I can admit that?"

The haughtiness faded abruptly and a lost look stole over her delicate features. "You aren't the only one who's learned to adjust ... to some things at least," she added after a moment's hesitation.

"What about the others—the things you haven't adjusted to?"

Julia folded an arm across her chest and locked her fingers on the crutch beneath the other arm. "I don't want to discuss them," she answered shortly.

"What brought you here?" he asked carefully, probing her face with curious eyes.

"Here?" she asked with a raised brow.

"To this territory."

"I was looking for something."

Ryder's insides grew tight with tension. "What?" he managed to ask in a normal voice.

"Treasure," she answered ambiguously, meaning the treasure of knowing peace. She couldn't come right out and admit what a mess she'd made of her life. She didn't want him to know the depths of despair to which she'd plummeted before finding the courage to climb out of the abyss into the sunlight.

She was searching for treasure, all right, but it wasn't the kind you exchanged for money. It was a new life, a new identity, one she could be proud of.

"What kind of treasure?" he asked tautly, eyeing her with slitted eyes.

"It doesn't matter," she answered with drooping shoulders. "I'll probably never find it." Then she added on a sudden note of determination, "But maybe I'll keep looking, anyway." She shrugged. "Who knows, maybe someday I'll find it when I least expect it."

Was she warning him she knew about the bounty on his head? Was she telling him in a roundabout way that he hadn't fooled her and she didn't give up all that easily?

"I think I'll take a walk along the water's edge." Even though she was standing in bright sunlight Julia shivered. Something about the changing expression in Ryder's eyes just now chilled her to the bone.

Ryder watched her go. She'd looked almost . . . scared for a moment. Scared of what? Who? Him? Or someone else? He'd thought he was safe—until now.

Julia sat on the edge of the bed contemplating the saddle resting near the fireplace. She felt bad about taking the only bed in the cabin. The cabin door opened abruptly and Ryder walked in. His head was bare for once and he carried his boots in one hand.

The blond hair curled wetly against the side of his head, lying in tight ringlets across his forehead and beside his ears. He'd put on a clean pair of trousers without the suspenders she was used to seeing him wear. The sleeves of the brown shirt he wore were full at the shoulders and gathered at the cuffs.

He looked younger and defenseless somehow without his boots. Julia's eyes rested on his hair, and her whole body tingled at the thought of how soft those blond curls must feel. Just for a moment she wished she were bold enough to find out for herself.

Glancing away, hoping he couldn't read her thoughts, she broke into nervous speech. "I wish you'd let me sleep in the chair. I'd be perfectly comfortable—"

"You'll sleep in the bed," he interrupted tersely, "and I don't want to hear any more about it." He nodded toward the saddle and bedroll. "I'll be just fine with that."

So, all right then, sleep on the floor and be damned to you, she thought, miffed at his tense attitude. Laying down, she turned over onto her side facing away from him and pulled the covers up to her chin. She was asleep in minutes.

The flames in the fireplace had burned low when she awakened abruptly a few hours later. She had no idea what had awakened her.

Raising herself on an elbow she looked around the shadowy room with sleep-narrowed eyes. Catching sight of the long-limbed body lying before the fire she smiled in relief and lay back against the pillows. Whatever had awakened her didn't matter as long as Ryder McCall lay only a couple of yards from her bed. Snuggling deeper beneath the quilt she drifted back to sleep.

Some time later she was awakened again, this time by the howl of an animal outside. She must have been dreaming, because there was a faint thread of the dream still unraveling in her head. She recalled a face, a face that smiled pleasantly one minute, then turned dark and threatening the next.

Julia rolled over and sought refuge in Ryder's comforting presence. Her heart jolted to a standstill as she again heard the lonely howl of the animal in the distance and realized at the same time that Ryder's blankets were empty.

With no clear thought of where she was headed, or of what she'd do when she got there, Julia threw back the blankets and slid her bare feet to the cool boards of the floor. She could only guess at the time, but felt as though she'd slept for hours. It must be somewhere near morning.

All at once the cabin door slid back and Ryder stepped inside, his rifle in his hand. Julia watched as he closed the door, barred it, and moved cautiously into the room.

He glanced toward the bed and halted abruptly, realizing she was sitting on the side of it watching him. His steps turned in her direction.

Julia looked up at him with wide eyes, aware of a sudden tension filling the space between them as he stood over her, the rifle still clutched in one hand.

She was the first to speak. "S-something woke me up—s-some kind of animal outside—"

"A coyote on the prowl." The timbre of his voice sounded deeper than usual.

"You were gone." She couldn't help the accusing ring the words seemed to acquire in the following silence.

"I know," he answered softly. "How long have you been awake?"

"I don't know." She pulled the quilt across her lap, aware all at once that she was wearing nothing beneath the thin nightgown. A nightgown that covered her from neck to ankles, but under the circumstances it seemed provocative, nonetheless. "N-not long. I was having a bad dream."

"Well, I'm back now, and you know it was only a dream. You can go back to sleep." He hesitated when she didn't move but sat staring at him with large eyes.

"Come on." Laying his rifle on the floor, he put a hand against her shoulder and at the same time raised her feet to the mattress. "Lay back and go to sleep."

Julia let him assist her and gave a sigh of contentment when the covers rested beneath her chin. "I'll sleep now," she murmured, "now that you're here."

As he was turning away, she caught at his sleeve and stopped him. "You aren't going out again?" she asked anxiously.

"No," he answered tightly, withdrawing from her touch. "I'm in for the night."

Julia was asleep almost as soon as her head touched the pillow.

Ryder stood for a long time staring down at her sleeping face with a grim set to his mouth. Just when he was beginning to think he had her all figured out, she confounded him again.

He was hardly aware of reaching out to smooth a strand of bright hair back from her lips. He could do such things while she slept, things he didn't dare even contemplate while she was awake.

She'd almost caught him tonight. How long would he be able to keep his secret from her, the secret he suspected she was there to try to ferret out?

Chapter 6

Julia left the cabin and stood for a moment in the bright sunlight, feeling its heat penetrate the thin material of the loose smock and warm her skin. Nights in the mountains were chilly, she discovered, but the days were sunny and hot.

Lifting her face to the sky, she let her eyes drift shut and gloried in the feeling of peace that slowly settled around her heart. She hadn't felt this carefree since the summer before her father's death, when he'd taken her and her mother for a holiday on the coast of Spain.

In the last few days it seemed as though she'd left all her troubles somewhere back on the road with her car. Maybe that was the real reason she hadn't approached Ryder with the idea of finding it, even to get her clothes.

She glanced down at the drab color of the dress she was wearing and then lower to the deerskin moccasins on her feet. Brown had never been her color, but the dress was comfortable enough and the moccasins were softer and easier on her feet than any shoes she'd ever worn.

Her glance lifted and moved around the empty yard, looking for her host. As usual, he seemed to have disappeared. She considered wandering around to the back of the cabin to see if he was working in the garden, but her eyes

drifted toward the entrance to the old mine shaft and curiosity stirred.

She'd been at the cabin for four days now, and Ryder
hadn't mentioned the mine once in all that time. Neither had
she, but that was because it had slipped her mind until now.

The place seemed to have little to do with Ryder's life, so
she hadn't given it a second's thought. But now, looking at
it, she felt intrigued. She'd never been anywhere near a real
mine until the night she'd stumbled into Ryder McCall's life.
And it was a light coming from the mine that had led her to
him.

What could he have been doing in there at night? She decided to take a look inside and find out.

Maneuvering the crutch down the slight incline toward the
entrance of the shaft wasn't as difficult as it appeared. She
used the rough surface of the hillside for a handhold, making the short descent easier.

At the entrance she paused and remembered to duck her
head, but once inside she halted again, met with an impen-
etrable darkness. If she was going to go exploring, she
needed a flashlight. That, however, didn't seem likely, she
realized with disappointment, given her host's lack of
modern amenities.

Suddenly, she remembered the lantern Ryder had used the
night of her arrival and wondered what he'd done with it.
Thinking it was probably back at the cabin, she turned to go
in search of it when her hair brushed against something
overhead. She heard a soft metallic creak, gave a slight jerk
of surprise, and looked up.

She wouldn't have to search for it, after all. The lantern
swung from a nail in one of the wooden timbers above her
head. The only problem now was lighting the candle inside
the glass bell. And since she didn't carry matches or a
lighter, that meant a trip to the cabin, where a fire always
burned in the fireplace.

A short while later, Julia again stood in the dark mine
shaft, lantern in hand. She hadn't seen Ryder on her trip to
the cabin, but this time she was glad. Somehow, the more
she thought about it, the fact he hadn't mentioned the mine

and never seemed to go near it whenever she was around, seemed a bit suspicious. Was he hiding something?

Just for a moment she allowed her thoughts to run wild and envisioned him as having committed some crime for which he had to elude the law. Might she find something, like a cache of money or stolen jewelry, hidden somewhere inside?

The idea seemed fantastic, nevertheless she couldn't totally wipe it from her mind. After all, before a few days ago, she'd never seen the man before in her life.

Holding the lantern aloft in one hand, she took stock of her surroundings. Above her, large wooden beams formed a kind of cradle that appeared to cup the ceiling. One large timber ran down the center of the shaft with smaller arms branching off it and extending outward toward the walls where they appeared to be fastened somehow to the rock.

Julia was surrounded by rock, rock ceiling, rock walls and a rock floor. Having taken that all in, she began to move down the narrow passage away from the entrance.

As she progressed slowly down the tunnel, she began to note a change in the air. It became cooler and felt slightly moist against her skin. Just for a moment, an intense feeling of dread swept over her. She shivered and stopped.

The inside of the shaft was like an underground burial crypt, and being inside it, alone, felt almost like being buried alive. The fetid smell of rock and earth filled her nostrils, and as anxiety spread she seriously considered turning back. But curiosity was a potent magnet; she pulled herself together after a few moments and allowed it to drag her forward.

She was no great judge of distance and had no idea how far she'd traveled when she came to a point where the tunnel branched into two separate passages. The new tunnel veered off to the left, while the one she'd been following continued on a straight course.

Swinging the lantern in first one direction and then the other, she shrugged and followed what appeared to be the main shaft. After a few yards, the ceiling began to slope downward and the wooden cradle overhead disappeared.

Julia began to feel claustrophobic as the walls and ceiling narrowed around her. All at once her crutch bumped against a shelf of rock at her feet and she lurched to a stop. Raising the lantern, she squinted into the darkness and saw what appeared to be a large cavern.

She stepped into the chamber and held the lantern high, looking around in amazement at the spacious room with its tall, cathedrallike ceiling. From outside the mine there was no indication that a cavern of this size was contained within the mountain.

After the initial shock had worn off, Julia began to take note of a variety of strange objects she couldn't begin to identify in the dim light. Moving closer to get a better look, she almost stumbled over a wheelbarrow made of wood with iron wheels and handles.

On the floor beside it lay a pick, a flat-bladed shovel with a bucketlike scoop, an anvil, a handheld drill and a sledgehammer. Beside that sat a wooden bucket filled with dirt and rock.

It looked as though *someone* had been mining—something. Bending down, she sifted some of the debris in the bucket through her fingers curiously.

"What are you doing in here?"

Julia jumped and nearly dropped the lantern. Whirling as agilely as possible with a crutch in one hand and the lantern in the other, she faced a very angry Ryder. He held a single candle close to his face, and his expression was enough to scare anyone.

"I—I was just l-looking around," she stammered. "I wasn't bothering anything—"

"You have no business in here." He strode toward her, furiously snatching the lantern from her startled fingers. "I don't like people snooping into my private affairs."

Blowing out the candle he held in his other hand, he glared at her as he shoved it in a pocket, then bent to look her directly in the eye. "This mine is none of your concern—do you understand? It's dangerous to go poking your nose into things you know nothing about."

"Y-yes...I'm sorry." She noted the stern lines of his face and backed away from the angry glitter in his dark eyes. "I w-was curious—that's all.'' She flinched at his sudden movement, as though she expected him to strike her.

Ryder swallowed the hot, uncontrollable part of his anger and straightened away from her. She looked terrified, and suddenly he decided to press his advantage while he had it. Drawing closer, he rasped, ''Who are you? Why are you here? What are you after?''

''I—you know who I am—I told you why I'm here, and I'm not after anything.'' She managed, despite her fear, to inject a note of indignation into the last.

''What if I don't believe you?'' He stepped closer, crowding her against the rough wall at her back. ''You ask a lot of questions—pry into things that don't concern you—for somebody who's just lost. Who sent you?'' he goaded, noting the wary look in her frightened eyes. ''Are you working alone? Or you got someone out there waitin' with a gun?''

''My God,'' she whispered in renewed fear, ''you are crazy!'' Brandishing the crutch in both hands, she pushed it between them, causing him to back off.

''Let me go,'' she pleaded suddenly, her eyes locked on his relentless expression. ''I won't tell anyone you're here. I won't tell them about the mine—I won't tell them anything—I promise!''

Ryder's fury grew with each word she uttered. So, she *was* on to him, and now that she'd been caught she wanted to make a deal. He wrenched the crutch from her nerveless fingers with one hand and whipped it behind her, using it to press her up against him.

Julia looked at him with terror, realized she was totally at his mercy, licked suddenly dry lips and whispered, ''What are you going to do to me?''

''I could break you in half,'' he answered coldly, tightening his arm until the buckle on his gun belt became a part of her belly. He felt the slight quiver as she caught her breath and leaned closer, until his face was only inches from hers. ''I could leave you right here, bound and gagged, and no one would ever find your carcass.''

''W-why?'' she asked with what little voice she could muster. The bar across her back made it almost impossible to breathe. "Why would you want to hurt me? I've done nothing to you."

He felt her body quaking with rigors of fear, and all at once he felt ashamed. What if she was telling the truth? What if her only offense was that of finding him when he didn't want to be found?

She was scared out of her wits with fear of him, and still she persisted in her story. Maybe she was what she claimed to be—and maybe he was a fool.

He let her go so abruptly she stumbled backward and would have fallen if he hadn't dropped the crutch and caught her shoulder to steady her. He held her upright while she regained her balance.

"Are you all right?" he asked in quieter tones, seeing the agitated rise and fall of her breasts, becoming all at once very much aware of her as a woman.

"Y-yes, fine." She sidestepped away from him, her hands going to the wall behind for support, and he let her go.

"Look, I didn't mean to scare you—" He broke off. Now why had he said that? He was angry with her and *had* meant to scare her, scare her into telling him what he wanted to know, and to prevent her from any further meddling.

Yet, at the same time, part of his anger had stemmed from fear—not for himself—but for her. Once again, she had him riled to the point he didn't know which side of the horse to mount.

"Come with me," he said abruptly, "I want to show you something." He led the way to the point where the two tunnels came together, forming a Y. He stepped around the corner into the opposite tunnel and paused, waiting for her to catch up.

They'd gone about a hundred yards into the second tunnel when Julia became aware of a drastic change in temperature. It suddenly got colder, and an unidentified sound filtered to her ears. She quickened her pace and moved closer to Ryder. He stopped abruptly, and she barely managed not to bump into his back.

"There—" He broke the silence abruptly, and his voice rang hollowly, bouncing from wall to wall. "Careful," he warned as she drew closer. He lifted the lantern and stepped aside so she could see where he pointed. "That's what you might have walked into if you had taken this tunnel instead of the other one."

Julia eased up beside him and looked past the light, down over the sheer face of a cliff and at what lay below. Her eyes grew wide with shock.

Before her lay a cavern twice as large as the one they'd just left, only this one was filled with black roiling water.

"It's an underground river," Ryder explained. "It comes down out of the mountains and swells each spring with the melting snow. If you'd stumbled into that, God only knows where you'd end up."

"I had no idea," Julia whispered, drawing closer to him, forgetting her fear of him. She'd almost chosen this tunnel. If she had . . . Shivering, she murmured, "Please, can we go?"

The stark reality of what might have happened kept her from asking the many questions running through her mind. Questions about who he thought she might be and why someone would be after him with a gun.

When they left the shaft, Julia found a spot in the sun and sat for the next few hours basking in its warmth, trying to dispel the memory of icy, black water. As the sun rose higher, Julia finally forsook it for shade.

Leaning her back against a rock, she watched Ryder work with Midnight. He seemed tireless as he exercised and groomed the beautiful animal.

Julia sensed the feeling of shared love between the two, man and beast, and found herself feeling envious of the horse. She couldn't help it; ridiculous as it sounded, she envied the close relationship between the two.

Ryder's anger with her a little while ago had terrified her, but later, there had been real concern for her in his voice when he'd shown her the underground river and apprised her of what might have happened if she'd unwittingly stumbled across it on her own. That had made it easier for her to forgive him for his anger and suspicion.

Her curiosity, however, had been aroused by the questions he'd asked. Were they an indication he was running away from a *who* and not a *what* as she'd previously suspected? She could understand that, too. Wasn't she bent on staying clear of her mother?

She knew she ought to be eager to get away, considering he'd as much as threatened her life. He had problems, there was no doubt about that, especially if he expected someone to come looking for him with a gun. She had problems of her own, and she didn't need the added worry...

But what if they could help each other? Was she a fool to think she could help him? Maybe he needed professional help... and maybe, like Mariette, he just needed someone with him to get him through the night.

As for her, how could he possibly help her? She shifted her position on the hard ground. What could this man know that would help *her?* Coming from the background he'd described, he'd have no conception of people like her mother, her ex-husband, Gabriel, or Mariette.

No, the idea was preposterous. Not only that, her knee was much better. She could almost walk without the crutch.

Just this morning, she'd hopped out of bed feeling so well she hadn't even thought about grabbing the wooden support. A moment later, a slight twinge of pain had reminded her she was standing upright without it. Just as she'd reached for it, Ryder had entered the cabin. He'd stood for a moment without moving, and feeling unaccountably guilty, she'd launched into speech.

"I'm sorry—" she clutched at the high neck of the gown "—I should have been up long before now. I just woke up."

Without comment he'd excused himself and backed out the door. But Julia had an uncomfortable feeling that her date of departure had been decided.

A soft breeze stirred the branches of the cottonwood behind her, bringing her thoughts back to the present. She looked up through the leaves and closed her eyes for a brief moment. She was beginning to think she didn't ever want to leave this place. Julia smoothed the skirt over her knees with an impatient hand and darted a glance toward Ryder.

No, it would be better if she left.

From the corner of her eye she caught sight of a bright speck of yellow and turned to see a butterfly flitting from flower to flower in a bed of lacy pink blossoms. Her gaze wandered out over the lush valley, rich with growing things, and drifted toward the rugged, snowcapped mountains in the distance. It was such a contrast and yet so very beautiful.

She heaved a sigh and relaxed tense shoulder muscles. Just being here was helping her. She didn't want to leave this place—not yet!

Her attention moved back toward the man, and she put the unhappy thought about leaving out of her mind. For the moment at least she could simply enjoy being here.

As she became absorbed in watching man and beast, she was struck by the similarities between the two. The same leashed power evident in the stallion's muscular haunches was revealed in the bulging thigh muscles of the man. The fighting spirit she saw in the stallion's black, fiery eyes, was the same expression she'd seen in Ryder's eyes a short while ago when he'd confronted her in the mine.

She heard the sound of Ryder's deep voice in the background of her thoughts, speaking low to the animal. Periodically, his words were met with a snort of response from the stallion.

The sound of the wind and the music of the birds, along with the even drone from an occasional insect, combined to create a soothing symphony that all but lulled her to sleep. How could she give this up? Why should she have to?

Added to this sense of peace was an ever-growing need to know more about the man, Ryder McCall. Who was he? Where had he come from?

She tried, but couldn't stem the flow of questions flooding her mind. The more she watched him, the more she wanted to know about him.

The inadequate amount of information he'd offered her the day before had only whetted her desire to know more. She tried to picture him growing up in some big-city ghetto. The kind of life he must have lived during his formative years was no doubt a part of the reason he'd sought sanctuary in these quiet mountains.

All she knew for certain was that his mother had been a prostitute and his father was unknown. A sad story, but unfortunately, not an uncommon one in this day and age, when life seemed to be lived by the split second rather than by the hour. She had firsthand knowledge about living life in the fast lane, but she didn't want to think about herself.

She wanted to know about the man inside Ryder McCall, the one he hid from the world. She wanted to touch his soul—and she knew without a doubt that she could only do that by painting him.

As she looked at him, standing so tall and straight in his cowboy garb, she realized he could have been posing for a western movie poster. If she were posing him, she'd have him remove the sweat-stained shirt, leaving the muscles across shoulders and chest bare, to be kissed by the sun.

Leaning suddenly forward, she realized she wanted to paint him. She had to! Her mind began to formulate a pose.

All at once the enthusiasm drained from her and was re- placed by a sense of frustration. She had a feeling the man would never agree to pose for her, and besides, she didn't have any painting supplies.

Suddenly, Julia's eyes narrowed and she straightened abruptly. She couldn't paint him—but she could sketch him!

A few minutes later, seated at the base of the tree with pencil and paper in hand, she eyed Ryder's broad back for a long moment before concentrating on the paper. Her fin- gers flew; she paused to use a finger to do a bit of shading, and began again.

As she worked, her thoughts became as furiously busy as her hands in an effort to plot her strategy. She'd do the sketch without asking, then offer it to him as a gift to show her appreciation for his hospitality.

If the sketch appealed to him, he just might agree to al- low her to paint him. And if he agreed to that, Julia would have an excuse, now that her knee was nearly healed, to stay here for a little while longer.

She hesitated for a moment to look deep within herself, assessing her motives. She'd found something here she hadn't been able to find in any other spot in the world. She'd found peace, and in that peace, a healing process had be- gun.

The wounds were deep and old, starting with the death of her father, including her disastrous marriage, the loss of her own child, and culminating with Mariette's death a few months ago. Leaving California had brought to a close a lifelong conflict stemming from choices she'd made in an attempt to "find herself."

She could admit now that she hadn't been as interested in finding herself as she'd been in running away, or proving to herself she was nothing like the woman from whom she ran—her mother.

This time with Ryder McCall had done that for her, or at least his allowing her to share the peace he'd found had helped to accelerate the healing process. And now she wanted to help him, too.

Despite her thoughts while in the mine cavern, she didn't believe him to be mentally unbalanced. That had never seriously been a consideration. But sometimes, when she looked behind the dark eyes, she saw something she thought she recognized: a faint expression of desperation.

Apparently, despite his extreme efforts, he had found only a measure of the peace he sought.

Even though he appeared to be well-adjusted about the fact of his birth, she was convinced there was something more in his past he couldn't handle. She wasn't a psychologist and didn't claim to be, but somehow, she felt certain her continued presence would do him good.

While reasoning that out in her mind, her pencil had been flying steadily over the drawing pad. She paused to compare her drawing with the real subject and was pleased with the results. After a moment's contemplation she once more fell to work, so deeply immersed in the forming shapes, she forgot everything else.

Ryder lifted Midnight's left foreleg and checked between the shoe and hoof. A rock or burr caught between the two could cripple a horse in a short span of time, and being without a horse in this country could cost a man his life.

He'd been aware almost from the first of being under scrutiny by Julia. She'd been restless all morning. At first he'd thought it was because he'd walked in on her as she was getting out of bed that morning and after that she felt too embarrassed to show herself, but later he'd realized that wasn't it.

After breakfast, while she'd done the washing up, he'd gone to work in the garden. That was where he'd been when he'd realized he hadn't seen her for a while. He'd gone to look for her, worried that she'd wondered off and might be in trouble.

The Indian threat was real, and he knew he was going to have to do something about it before long. But he hadn't mentioned it to her, because getting around on a crutch kept her from going any great distance from the cabin.

When he didn't immediately find her, he'd become suspicious. In growing desperation he'd searched the cabin for the second time and then the root cellar. He'd even wondered if she'd sneaked off for a rendezvous with a partner while his back was turned.

And then he'd thought about the mine. She hadn't mentioned it since the night she'd arrived, and that seemed mighty suspicious to him. It would have been normal for her to show some interest and ask him about it.

When he didn't find the lantern where he'd left it, he knew she must be inside, and he'd been mad enough to eat the Devil with his horns on. She'd hornswoggled him into believing her and played him for a greener.

It wasn't until he'd actually entered the mine shaft after lighting a candle that he'd thought about the underground river and remembered how she'd nearly drowned. He feared that it might already be too late to save her. No matter how many times he told himself he didn't trust her or that she wasn't his responsibility, he still felt responsible for her.

Then he'd found her poking around in the cave, and his anger had grown swifter than a dust storm on the prairie. If he hadn't suddenly become aware of her as a woman and backed off, he didn't know what might have happened. Maybe keeping her here hadn't been such a smart idea, after all.

After they'd left the mine he'd followed her around the back of the cabin and watched her take a seat in the sun alternately shivering and rubbing her arms. He suspected she was remembering the underground river and what might have happened to her there.

When he'd finished weeding the garden and moved to the corral to give Midnight a rubdown, she'd moved to a spot beneath the gnarled trunk of a cottonwood and sat watching him work. He thought she'd fallen asleep, but a few minutes ago she'd gotten up and disappeared around the side of the cabin.

He'd followed close on her heels, determined to keep track of her from now on. She'd entered the cabin and he'd waited outside, wondering what she was up to this time.

He'd barely made it back to the corral ahead of her, when she'd come walking into view with something clutched in her hands. It took a moment for him to realize she had paper and pencils and that she was writing something.

He kept an eye on her without appearing to, and slowly a feeling of unease crept over him. She would write for a few moments and then she'd pause to study him and then write some more. He was flummoxed until he began to savvy what she must be doing.

She was putting his likeness on paper. And the only reason he could think of for her to do that, was so someone could use it to identify him. *She was making a wanted poster!*

He couldn't let her do that. Her injury was almost healed, he'd seen that when she'd negotiated the uneven path in the mine without too much trouble. The time had come for him to get shed of her.

Julia was finally finished with her work. As Ryder's face had come to life on paper, she'd stared down into the eyes she'd drawn and wished she could see what was behind their haunted expression.

Now it was evening and the meal was finished. Ryder had gone through his ritual of making a cigarette and was in the process of lighting it when Julia showed him her sketch.

"Well, what do you think?" she asked when he sat staring at it without speaking.

"It's a very good likeness," he commented obliquely.

"Yes, it is. I think it's one of the best I've ever done."

"Why did you make it?"

"Why?"

"Yes, why did you sketch *me?*" His eyes were on her face, searching for hidden motives.

"You're a very good subject—both you and Midnight," she added, nodding to the picture of both man and beast. "I'd like to paint you—the both of you—but since I haven't any paints or brushes, I did the next best thing."

"Have you done a lot of these?"

"A fair number," she admitted.

"Back in . . . Boston, was it?"

"That's right. But, actually, I didn't do a lot of this sort of thing in Boston—not pencil sketches like this. I started doing this kind of thing after I moved to California."

"A wild place, California."

"Have you ever been there?" she asked carefully, unconsciously holding her breath as she waited for his answer.

"I was there . . . once. But I didn't stay long."

"Why was that?" she asked quickly.

"I didn't like the people. You get paid for doing drawings like this?" he asked, changing the subject.

Julia shrugged, trying to hide her disappointment. She had thought for a moment that she was about to learn something more about him, something that might answer the questions chasing themselves around inside her brain.

"Sometimes," she answered, "but mostly I do it for fun. This one is for you."

"You're giving it to me?" he asked carefully.

"Yes, I'd like you to have it."

"Why?"

"My way of saying thank you for the hospitality you've shown me. After all, we are strangers."

"Not anymore," he denied softly, a dark, dangerous gleam in his eyes.

Julia swallowed and managed a smile. "No," she agreed, "you're right, we aren't. I hope we're friends. The sketch is something to remember me by when I've gone."

"Oh, you're not going anyplace yet," he said quickly, then added by way of explanation, "Your . . . injury isn't healed. And truth to tell, I've liked having someone to talk to these past few days. It can get mighty lonely by yourself after a while.''

"Yes, I imagine it can," she agreed faintly.

"I like it that way, you understand," he was quick to add. "But it never hurts to break the monotony."

So, that's what she was to him, a break in the monotony. Julia couldn't help a slight twinge of irritation at the thought. She'd hoped he'd be pleased by the sketch, but he'd seemed more suspicious than pleased. Not that he didn't seem anxious enough to have her stay. For a moment her pulses had leapt at the realization, and she'd been almost willing to admit she not only found him intriguing, but very attractive, as well. Then he'd admitted it was because he was lonely and she'd been firmly put in her place.

The evening went downhill from there. Ryder thanked her for the drawing, excused himself and disappeared. Julia waited up for him for a while, wanting to discuss the idea of doing a painting of him, but she eventually turned in, convinced he didn't like the sketch any better than he liked her.

The fire had burned low and the cabin was filled with the sounds of night when he returned from his evening stroll— at least that's what she assumed he did every night before turning in. She didn't really know, because he never invited her along.

Julia lowered the blanket an inch and peered at him from between slitted eyes. Her breath caught at the back of her throat. He was watching her, and the look on his face had nothing to do with attraction.

Chapter 7

Early the next morning Ryder awakened Julia as the sun was peeking over the mountains.

He placed a pair of buckskin trousers identical to the pair he was wearing on the bed beside her, along with a matching pullover shirt. "Put these on, they're better for horseback riding than what you're wearin'."

"Horseback?" she repeated groggily, not yet fully awake. "What—"

"We're going on a trip into the mountains."

"Trip? But—why?"

"I want to hunt some larger game. The meat I been snaring is fine for a meal now and then, but it's time to stock up for winter."

"Winter? But, spring is barely past."

"I know, but summers are short here in the mountains."

"You can leave me here—I don't mind," she assured him quickly, more fully awake with each passing second.

"No. It isn't safe." He still didn't mention the Indians, because he and Julia would be traveling in Indian territory and he didn't want a nervous woman on his hands. "Besides, I have a ... surprise for you."

"Surprise?" Julia held the blanket up to her chin and scooted up in the bed. "For me? What kind of surprise?"

"If I tell you, it won't be a surprise, now will it?" he asked with a quirk of one black brow.

"No, I guess not, but—"

"Get dressed. Breakfast is waiting." He pointed to a plate of dried meat and hardtack.

Julia eyed the plate without enthusiasm, but before she could make another protest he was out the door and gone.

She joined him a short while later, feeling ridiculous in the buckskin. Midnight was saddled and, as the saying goes, looked loaded for bear. Not only were there two bedrolls tied behind the saddle, but a pair of brown leather saddlebags had been added, as well. The Sharps rifle was riding in a sling to the right of the saddlehorn, over which Ryder had placed his coiled lariat and the long straps of two canteens, one on each side.

As far as his own getup went, Ryder was a sight to behold, mounted on Midnight and dressed in soft, golden-yellow buckskin. The shirt laced up the front and was fringed at the shoulder seams. He'd traded his boots for a pair of moccasins that came halfway to his knees with a short fringe around the cuff and down the back.

The handle of a knife was barely visible protruding from the top of the right moccasin, and the Colt .45 was strapped to his right hip. This time, the rawhide strap on his hat was pulled tight beneath his chin, and the hat's curled brim shaded his expression.

Julia stood and waited for him to lift her onto the saddle. But before he did, he reached behind him and pulled out a beat-up looking hat and crammed it down on top of her head.

"Tie the string beneath your chin so it won't blow off. The sun gets hot after a while."

She did as she was told and felt almost giddy as his hard hands reached for her and lifted her onto the saddle before him. He held her securely in the circle of his arms as they rode away from the cabin.

Even though he'd continued to shun the familiar use of her name, Julia felt as though he had accepted her into his life, at least for the time being. As for herself, she was fighting the thrill of being this close to him. He looked like a western movie hero, and she felt a little bit as though she was in some epic western herself.

She knew from the last ride they'd taken that it was impossible to maintain any distance between them while riding in this fashion and didn't bother trying. All it had got her the last time was a stiff neck and sore spine.

They didn't talk much as they rode, and lunch consisted of more dried meat and a sip of water from one of the canteens. Julia was rather excited at the prospect of sighting horses in the wild and thought at one point she'd done just that. But before she could get Ryder's attention they were gone and she shrugged mentally, thinking what she thought were horses were probably only cattle, anyway.

The trip took the whole day, and it was close to sunset when they arrived at a spot surrounded by tall, craggy mountains. Steam rose from the ground and formed pools of water.

"It's a natural hot spring!" Julia exclaimed. She slid from the horse before Ryder could dismount and assist her, then leaned against the horse's heaving side.

"Oh, you've been here," Ryder commented.

Did he sound just a bit disappointed?

"No, I've heard about them, but I've never actually visited any." She looked around in the waning light at the steam rising from the ground and couldn't help commenting, "It's kind of eerie, seeing steam rise out of the ground like that, isn't it?"

"I like it." Ryder dismounted and moved around Midnight to help her.

You would, she thought, as he reached her side. "I thought it would be easier if I helped you, instead of bringing the crutch." He stood awkwardly, uncertain how to go about that and wondering if she was going to object to the idea.

"That's fine," she said, putting her arm through his and leaning on him as they made their way toward a smooth, flat-topped rock. It looked perfectly suited for use as a seat.

The sun had half disappeared over the tops of the mountains, and the sky was filled with a yellow-orange glow. Julia looked around and noted vegetation apparently didn't grow near the small geysers.

In most places, the ground around them looked uniformly gray, except for the tiny rivers of liquid flowing from them. In some places the rivers had dried up, leaving trails of colored minerals in their wake.

"The Indians have believed in the healing power of the water in this area for years," Ryder explained hesitantly. "I thought the warm waters might help your...injury." He was never comfortable discussing anything of a personal nature with her.

"Do they really work?" she asked, intrigued in spite of the uneasiness caused by the starkness of the area. A persistent voice at the back of her mind questioned the lack of evidence of any civilization in the area. They hadn't passed a house or seen a telephone or electric pole all the way there.

"See for yourself," Ryder told her, "that's why we came."

"I thought we came to hunt," she queried with a hint of a smile, pushing the uneasiness out of her mind. She wanted to enjoy this trip and use the time to get to know this man better.

"That, too," he agreed without an answering smile. "You wait here, while I make sure the baths aren't in use."

"In use?" she asked with a raised brow. Were there other people then, close by?

"By varmints," he explained, "the four-legged variety."

"Oh."

"I'll be right back."

Good as his word, she'd hardly got used to his being gone when he moved around a boulder and came into sight.

"Have we far to go?" she asked carefully, as he took her arm and made as though to lead her to Midnight. She was beginning to understand the meaning of saddle-sore.

Ryder grinned over the top of her head, guessing the reason for the question. Hours in the saddle could be rough on a body unused to it.

"The waters will take care of *all* your aches and pains," he assured her, then added, "If you feel like walking, it isn't far."

They rounded the large boulder and hadn't gone more than a few hundred yards, when Julia caught breath at what lay before her. It was a scene like she'd never imagined.

A body of water the size of a pool lay spread out before her, sunken a few feet below the surface where they stood. It was ringed by huge boulders on three sides, and steam rose from its surface like a soft white cloud. A series of rocks, like stepping-stones, led to its warm depths.

"Well, what do you think?" Ryder asked in deep tones somewhere near her left ear.

"It's...magnificent." She laughed self-consciously, in awe of her present surroundings. "Can't you just imagine a huge black caldron below the surface, filled with bubbling liquid, stirred by the Devil with pointed horns and a long, pointed tail?"

Ryder lifted an eyebrow and asked, "You have some imagination, haven't you? I need to hobble Midnight so he won't wander off. I'll be right back." He turned away, pausing with his back to her and suggested, "Why don't you get into the water while I'm gone?"

Julia felt her face flame. The thought of being naked in the water with this man standing a few feet away was enough to turn her blood to steaming bubbles.

When he'd gone, she raised her hands to her cheeks and stood without moving, thinking about this unusual dose of modesty she seemed to have acquired in the past week. Perhaps modesty bred modesty, because he was certainly modest himself.

For a long moment she stood undecided. Should she take off her clothes and get in the water as he'd suggested, or merely soak her leg up past her knee?

It was too tempting to resist. Disrobing quickly, carefully folding her underwear and placing it out of sight beneath the trousers and shirt, Julia moved onto the stepping-stones and drew slowly toward the steaming waters.

Ryder was in the process of rounding the huge boulder when she reached the water and paused to test it with the toes of one foot. He couldn't move. The sight of her bare, shapely back, rounded buttocks and long tapering thighs stopped him in his tracks.

She was the most beautiful thing he'd ever seen, and though he knew he shouldn't be spying on her like this, he couldn't seem to turn away. It wasn't until she'd lowered herself beneath the water to her chin that he was freed from his momentary paralysis and managed to turn away. It was several minutes before he could gain enough control over himself to round the boulder as though nothing had happened and present himself to the woman.

"There you are," she called in lazy tones. "I was beginning to get worried—is everything all right?" His face looked a bit strange, and there was an odd glitter in the dark eyes he kept turned away from her.

"Everything is fine, just fine." He placed a towel on the folded pile of her clothes and straightened. "How's the water?" He stood awkwardly at the edge of the stones, hands held stiffly at his sides.

"It's magnificent—" She broke off. There was that word again, he'd think she didn't know any other. "Are you coming in?" she asked abruptly.

"No, I don't think so. Someone has to keep watch—"

"Oh, please, do come in. I'll feel so guilty if you don't." She was playing with fire, but what better place than this, in the midst of the Devil's caldron?

"I'll turn my head while you get in, I promise."

Ryder made no further protest. Removing the gun strapped at his hip, he shed his clothes hurriedly, casting an uncomfortable eye in her direction every few seconds. He knew what he was about to do might lead to further trouble, but was unable to deny himself the pleasure of being with her like this ... just once.

He wrapped his gun in his shirt and laid it on the edge of the pool within reach, then lowered himself beneath the water's surface. Closing his eyes, he allowed every thought to leave his mind and simply enjoyed the sensation flooding his body.

"Euphoric, isn't it?"

Julia's soft voice coming from so close beside him jerked him back to an awareness of his surroundings. His eyelids popped open, and he found himself staring directly into her shining green eyes.

All at once he felt tongue-tied, unable to speak even the simplest of words. A tightness filled his chest, and a heaviness settled in his lower body. He drifted below the water, unable for the moment to keep himself afloat.

Julia ducked her head and laughed as he bobbed to the surface. Her hair was plastered against the top of her head, and beads of moisture caught in the dying rays of the sun sparkled like diamonds against her forehead. The smile on her lips looked warm and inviting.

He felt like a drowning man and wanted nothing more than to kiss the droplets of water from her red lips as he went down for the last time. Something in her expression seemed to say, *Do it*, and Ryder drifted closer.

Julia felt his rough hands cup her cheeks and let her eyes drift shut. Their legs collided beneath the water, creating minor explosions in every part of her body, and his warm breath bathed her damp skin a second before his lips touched hers.

The kiss deepened as Julia felt his thumbs stroke the sides of her jaw. Her hands reached for him, and they both sank below the water.

Her fingers touched his chest, slid up around his shoulders, and they clung together, bodies brushing intimately as they rose and their heads broke the water's surface. The kiss ended abruptly when Ryder wrenched his mouth from hers and pushed her away.

In seconds he was climbing out of the water, reaching for his clothes and hurrying out of sight.

Julia held herself still, moving only enough to keep from sliding below the water, and stared at his retreating back. What had she done? Feeling hurt and confused, it was a long time before she left the water.

Ryder was waiting for her on the other side of the huge boulder, fully clothed, the six-gun strapped to his hip and his rifle lying across his lap. He looked up at her approach, but his glance didn't quite touch her face.

"It isn't safe to camp too near the water, but I know a spot near here where it's safe. I've camped there a few times in the past."

It was over an hour later when they finally sat around a small camp fire and ate in silence. Again, the meal consisted of dried meat mixed with a little water from the canteen and heated. They washed it down with sips of tepid water from the canteen.

Supper was a lonely meal for Julia, but nothing compared to the long hours ahead. She'd never heard the sounds of night the way she heard them in the long hours of darkness. Every noise, no matter how loud or soft, caused the hackles to raise on the back of her neck.

The fire Ryder had laid was small. With longing, Julia sat looking across its diminishing flames at the face of the sleeping man. Drawing her knees up to her chin, folding her arms around them, she waited for morning, jumping at every unfamiliar clatter, eyes darting constantly around her in the dark.

Sometime in the wee hours of the morning she must have fallen asleep, because she awakened to the smell of roasting meat. Her gnawing stomach reminded her she'd eaten very little in the past twenty-four hours, and Ryder didn't have to get her out of bed.

They ate rabbit mixed with a few dried vegetables to form a stew and drank some of the sage tea he'd introduced her to on her first morning at the cabin. Nothing had ever tasted so good to her as the meal they ate that morning.

Though neither one mentioned the subject, the events of the night before were in both their minds. They were polite, too polite, to each other and very careful to see they didn't touch—not even fingers—as they passed the food and tea back and forth.

"You're moving easier this morning," Ryder observed abruptly.

Julia stopped gathering the bones from their meal and looked in his direction. "My knee feels fine this morning." Her immersion in the hot springs had certainly helped, but Julia knew they hadn't performed a miracle. The leg had been well on its way to being healed before the soaking, but she didn't tell him that.

"Are we heading back to the cabin now?" she asked curiously.

"No, I thought you might like to see how I caught breakfast. I learned to hunt from the Indians."

"I don't have to watch you . . . kill anything, do I?" she asked warily.

"No," he answered shortly. "If you don't want—"

"No," she interrupted him, "I'd like to know how you . . . do it," she finished awkwardly.

The first thing they did was to bathe, separately, and dress in a fresh change of clothing Ryder had hung out on bushes the night before. He explained to her that this was so the game they were tracking wouldn't smell them coming a mile away.

There were other rules, too. She had to avoid all conversation, keep as quiet as possible and think no song. Julia grinned at that, certain he was teasing her, but he explained seriously that the Indians believed that because animals love music, they listen for songs, even those that are thought.

She eyed him skeptically, thinking he was going to grin at any moment. The grin actually started around his eyes, became a faint twinkle in the dark orbs, then died before it reached his mouth.

"Where did you say you learned to track game?" Julia asked softly.

"From the Indians," he replied, moving away.

"Really?" She couldn't quite keep the note of skepticism from her voice as she followed him as quietly as possible, watching as he stopped to kneel and stare at the ground.

He turned to look in one direction, then another, before motioning her to follow behind him. When he did the same thing a little farther down the trail, Julia stopped where he'd stopped and hunkered down to stare at the ground. She had no idea what she was looking for and couldn't see anything unusual in the leaves, twigs, rocks and dirt.

"Do you see it?" Ryder asked very softly as he knelt beside her.

"See what?" She transferred her puzzled frown from the ground to his face.

"The way the leaves here have been disturbed." He pointed to the spot with one finger. "And here, see the way the soil has been thrown aside in small clots?"

Though he pointed out the signs, Julia couldn't really say she saw them. She guessed it took an experienced eye to see what he saw.

"What is it we're following?" she asked. "Can you tell?"

"Look at the tracks." He pointed at the gashlike dents in the earth. "See the way the front is wide with a rounded edge, then tapers back toward the end?"

Julia murmured, "Uh-huh," as she screwed up her eyes and concentrated hard on the unidentifiable marks.

"I'd say we're looking at the tracks of a pronghorn."

"Pronghorn?"

"Antelope," he explained.

"Really?" she peered closer, but still couldn't make head nor tail out of what she saw.

Ryder's eyes traveled over the side of her face nearest him, thinking how soft and rosy her cheeks looked in the early-morning light, forgetting for the moment all about his lesson in tracking. He was ashamed at the thought of what he'd almost done. Julia was a *lady*—not a woman of easy virtue—and if he was any kind of man at all, he'd be able to control his animal needs.

She'd braided her long, wavy red hair that morning while he'd doused the fire. He'd watched from the corner of his eye, noting how inviting she looked with her eyelids still puffy with sleep, a soft, vulnerable look to her mouth....

"I said, how far do we follow it?" Julia asked for the third time.

"W-what?" Focusing his attention on what she was saying, instead of on the shape of her mouth, he met her glance, realizing suddenly how near he'd drawn to her and instantly backing off.

"I asked if we were going to follow the antelope all day," Julia whispered, wishing he'd take advantage of their nearness to kiss her again.

"No," Ryder responded gruffly. "We'll camp in the same place we camped last night. That will give you a chance to soak in the hot springs again."

Mounted once more on Midnight's sturdy back, they made their way toward the hot springs. Ryder spotted something moving toward them in the distance and took cover until he could make out what it was. They moved downwind and sat hidden among the rocks as a herd of wild horses galloped by, their tails and manes streaming out behind them in the wind.

"How beautiful!" Julia exclaimed. "I had no idea horses still roamed free."

"Not so many as there used to be," Ryder told her sadly. "Times are changing, the old ways are dying out."

He didn't say much after that, but Julia sensed his distress. As the day wore on they traveled through a deep gulch and over wind-scoured buttes. Around midday Julia spotted what looked like a small dust storm in the distance.

Ryder pulled Midnight to a halt and sat studying it.

"What is it?" Julia asked worriedly, thinking it might be a dust storm. "Should we take cover?"

"Brown grass eaters," he murmured.

"Brown grass eaters," she repeated on a questioning note.

"Buffalo," he explained. "That's a herd of buffalo."

Julia was astonished at the size of the herd and how fast they moved. "I didn't know there were so many of them left," she whispered in awe.

"Not so many anymore," Ryder murmured.

"You love all this, don't you?" Julia made a sweeping gesture with one arm, indicating the animals and the countryside.

Ryder shrugged, tightened the reins and turned Midnight back in the direction from which they'd come. The sun was high overhead, and Ryder wanted Julia settled for the night before he left her to visit the Indian camp nearby.

He chose a very secluded spot for their camp that night close to the hot springs, but far enough away that he wouldn't have to worry so much about leaving her. He warned Julia against making any noise by telling her some kinds of wild animals were attracted to sound.

Later, before dark, Ryder took her fishing, only this time he didn't use a hook and line. Pulling off his boots and socks, unstrapping his gun belt, he rolled up his pant legs and shirtsleeves and waded into the shallow end of the stream where it flowed over deep rocks.

"What are you doing?" Julia asked in amazement.

"I'm going to show you how to catch fish with patience, instead of worms," he replied enigmatically.

"Is this a joke?" she asked with a smile.

Looking up from his bent position, hands held over the water a few inches apart, he answered, "Food is a serious matter. I never joke about food."

Julia didn't know what to make of him. She never knew where she stood with him, because she couldn't read his moods.

One minute he was angry with her and the next, worried about her safety. He was a modest man, careful of the proprieties, yet she'd sensed a leashed hunger in his kiss.

For a man of the twentieth century, he appeared well versed in the all-but-forgotten skills of the past. He was a man who attracted her and at times frightened her, but never failed to intrigue her.

She wasn't even surprised to see him catch a fish with his bare hands. She was beginning to think he could do anything, once he'd set his mind to it.

That night Julia bathed alone. When bedtime rolled around, Ryder placed his blankets on one side of the fire and indicated Julia was to put hers on the other. Reluctantly, she did as he bid, then lay awake staring at his sleeping form.

The same noises that had plagued her the night before returned in force, only this time they were accompanied by the feeling that eyes were watching her. The night grew chilly, and Julia huddled closer to the small fire. Wrapping her blanket around her, she sat cross-legged, shivering, staring from the prone figure across the fire to the dark, silent night surrounding them.

When the full moon began to dip in the night sky, an animal began to howl in the distance, softly at first, a low, mournful sound. Julia grew tense, wondering what kind of animal made such a sad sound.

After a few minutes it grew silent, then the sound came again, only louder this time. It echoed from mountaintop to mountaintop, causing Julia to scoot closer to the fire.

The sensation of eyes watching her grew stronger. The short hair stood up on the back of her neck and all along her arms and legs. Her glance fastened on the hat pulled low over Ryder's face. How could he lay there and sleep through all that racket?

On the point of demanding that he wake up and keep her company, she was surprised to see him lift an arm and use two fingers to push the hat back from his face. Sitting up, he met her accusing glance over the flames of the fire and asked, "Something bothering you?"

"N-no—" Now that she had his attention, perversely, she didn't want it. "It's just…so noisy tonight." She shrugged, wishing she had the nerve to move around the fire and spread her blankets beside him, angry with him for not suggesting it himself.

"That's only a coyote calling to his mate. The canyon walls make him sound close, but he's really a long way off, clear up in the mountains behind us," Ryder assured her.

Julia cocked her head in a listening attitude. "And that," she asked referring to the loud, harsh *cur-lee, cur-lee.* "What's that?"

"That's a curlew—a bird—it's nothing to be scared of, so why don't you lie down and try and get some sleep?"

Reassured by his matter-of-fact attitude, Julia spread out her blankets and lay down. She didn't want him to think she was a coward, and he appeared calm enough.

A short while later, the night grew quiet, and from the even rise and fall of his chest, Julia assumed Ryder had gone back to sleep. She was preparing to do the same when a loud howl erupted from the darkness directly behind her. Jumping as though she'd been shot, she climbed to her feet, clutching the blanket to her, and stared fearfully into the darkness outside the fire's small pins of light.

She began to back toward the fire, darting an anxious glance in Ryder's direction. It looked like nothing disturbed him. Well, that was fine for him, he was used to all this… wild life. She wasn't!

Gathering up all her blankets, she moved closer toward his side of the fire, still not quite daring to actually lie down beside him. Sitting with a blanket wrapped tightly around her shoulders, she rocked back and forth, eyes darting in every direction, prepared to wait for morning without closing even one eye again that night in sleep.

She kept the fire going by doing as Ryder had shown her, and placed twigs on the flames. It helped her to stay awake. Every now and then she threw an envious glance in his direction, wishing half angrily that she had his kind of self-possession.

Her eyes eventually became locked on the flames, and their hypnotic dance began to make her drowsy. Her eyelids grew heavy, her chin sagged onto her chest, and soon her eyes drifted shut. Head dropping forward, she dozed, only to awaken a few moments later with an alarmed cry. Her eyes flew toward Ryder.

He was awake and watching her.

Their glances caught and locked. What was that ellusive expression she saw far back in his dark eyes?

All at once, with a soft sigh of surrender, Ryder folded back the corner of his blankets. Julia stared at him without moving. Was he inviting her to share his bed?

She couldn't—*yes, she could!* Before he could change his mind, she was up and around the fire. Placing her blanket over his, she crawled beneath the covers and lay down against him. In seconds the heat from his body penetrated the icy chill of her flesh and she grew tense.

She felt an answering tension in him and realized she'd never be able to get to sleep now . . . not with his heart beating a strident tattoo against her left cheek. . . .

Ryder felt, rather than heard, the uneven sigh float through Julia's parted lips. All at once she gave a little moan and turned onto her side, throwing an arm around his waist and a knee across his thighs.

Apparently, she was comfortable at last. He was glad. He couldn't have borne much more of the stiffness. Yet now . . . with her knee so intimately close . . . her breasts pressing against his shoulder . . . the smell of her hair in his nostrils . . . sleep was impossible.

She smelled so good. He couldn't decide what it reminded him of, but it was a clean . . . womanly scent.

He dared to touch the side of her face with a gentle finger, and the feel of her soft skin had the same effect on him as would a kick in the stomach from a mule. It jolted through his whole body and left him feeling slightly sick.

He wanted to strip the clothes from her body and touch her all over. . . . Ryder moved uncomfortably against the knee prodding him, feeling like the worst scoundrel alive for having such lustful thoughts about her. She'd come to him because she was afraid, nothing more.

He'd brought her along on this trip for many reasons, not the least of which was to decide whether he believed her story about her sudden appearance in his life. And still he'd made no decision. All he knew at the moment was that it had been a long time since he'd slept with a woman, but that time would seem as nothing compared with the hours that now lay ahead of him until morning.

His visit to the Indian camp would have to wait. He couldn't leave her tonight.

Julia squirmed in her sleep, shifted her head until her cheek rested against Ryder's shoulder, her lips against his lower jaw. Ryder tried to ignore the disturbing sensations her closeness created inside him, but it was hard. The kiss they had shared at the hot spring had whetted his appetite for more.

He could feel her soft breath fanning his lips and knew he had only to move his head . . . just a little . . . and . . .

The muscles in the arm around Julia's shoulder quivered and grew taut as he unconsciously pulled her tighter against him. The weight of her knee resting across his thighs eased for a fraction, then shifted closer to his groin. It was all he could do to withhold a moan of pain—not the pain of injury, but the pain of self-denial. He wanted her so badly he literally ached with it.

Taking a deep breath, he looked at the huge black bowl of stars overhead. Every point where her body touched his throbbed with sensation. Sweat broke out along his hairline and above his upper lip. He licked his lips nervously, felt the sharp prick of his mustache and caught a strand of her hair on his tongue.

Lifting an unsteady hand, he swept the hair from his lips, hesitated, then smoothed it back against her cheek. His fingers lingered against her soft skin with a will of their own, slid slowly down the curve of her neck and stopped just above her right breast. He didn't have to stretch his imagination to recall how pink and white her body had looked at the hot spring the night before, or the way the tips of her small breasts had jutted toward the sky.

The muscles in his neck quivered with the need to turn his head toward hers. How sweet her lips had tasted....

All at once his fingers curled into a tight fist and he jerked his hand from her shoulder. Closing his eyes, he held his breath, trying to steady his breathing—hoping to push the image of Julia's naked body from his mind.

Snapping his eyes open, he stared at the brightest star within sight. Maybe if he counted the stars...

She moved against him. Her hand at his waist slowly crawled up his chest, slipped over the side of his face and stopped with her fingers threaded in the blond curls at the side of his head. Julia gently turned his face toward hers.

Ryder was breathing the same air she breathed as Julia raised herself on one elbow and pressed his head toward hers. Her mouth slid smoothly, hungrily over his, testing the strength of his lips, enclosing them in a damp warmth he felt throughout his throbbing body.

Julia's fingers tightened in his hair as Ryder strained his neck to accommodate her lips, his own mouth opening eagerly beneath hers. His arms moved to her shoulders, squeezing her up against his chest until he could feel her breasts flatten against him. The blood thundered through his veins, like the thunder of a herd of stampeding cattle as their hooves furiously pounded the ground.

Her lips drank of his, drawing the passion from deep within him. And when she let loose of his hair and quickly began to push the buckskin shirt aside as her hands massaged the muscles across his chest, Ryder couldn't withhold a groan of pleasure. Her palms covered his chest, her fingers became tangled in the wiry curls as their kisses deepened and her pelvis pressed ardently against his hip.

She felt like nothing he'd ever held in his arms. His hands moved up her back and into the red hair, pushed their way through it, till they spanned her head. His lips moved with hers, against hers, over and around hers, tasting her in a way he'd never tasted other lips. Breathing heavily, he pushed her head back until his lips could savor the soft skin on her long white throat.

His kisses moved to her ear, where he nipped playfully at the lobe and felt her shiver beneath his hands. Julia wrenched her face from his hands, pushed the shirt aside and bent to press wet, enthusiastic kisses against his breastbone.

Ryder couldn't stand it any longer. He wanted to see every inch of her beautiful body, wanted to touch it with his hands, pay tribute to it with his lips. Pulling at the back of her shirt, he lifted it up; she ducked her head and a moment later her satin smooth, mauve-tipped breasts were visible in the silvery moonlight. His hands reached out to them, cupped them gently, palms tingling as they smoothed across the taut nipples.

"So... beautiful," he murmured between gasps, leaning forward to press hot lips against the full curve of one breast. "So beautiful..." he repeated, burying his face in the hollow between them, drawing back to whisper, "like alabaster in the moonlight."

Julia's hand reached toward the laces at his waist and Ryder helped her. Together they removed his breeches and then hers. Finally, they lay close together on the blankets, naked.

"Make love to me, my wild cowboy," Julia whispered from beneath him. Her hands slid up his flanks and around to his chest, helping him straddle her quivering body.

"Make love to me," she repeated as he turned with her until she sat astride his prone body. The words seemed to echo on the air between them as Julia leaned toward him. Her long red hair fell across his face as he thrust into her, unable to withhold his need for release.

Ryder jerked sharply and woke up. For a moment he wasn't certain what was happening. He glanced toward the woman at his side, expecting—he didn't know what he expected.

It didn't matter, she was fast asleep. With a hint of disbelief, he realized that sometime during his calculations on the number of stars overhead, he must have fallen asleep. Julia now lay facing away from him, curled like a kitten in sleep. It must have been her movement, the feel of her hair on his face as she turned away, that had awakened him.

Ryder eased his arm from beneath her and slipped from the blankets. Cramming his hat on his head, he kneeled for a moment to raise the covers toward her chin, then stood and moved toward the fire.

He took a deep breath. He felt exhausted and weak. A fine sheen of perspiration covered his entire body and his heart was only now beginning to settle down to a normal rate.

From the far side of the fire, Ryder sat on his haunches and drank thirstily from one of the canteens. His eyes darted toward the slight mound beneath the blankets—*his blankets—his woman—*

No, not his woman! He stared into the fire and told himself, again, that he must have been dreaming.

Again, his eyes darted toward Julia's slight figure uncertainly, the taste of her lips lingering on his tongue. Pulling the hat low on his forehead, he added a few twigs to the fire, feeling a chill seep through his clothes to his damp skin underneath.

One hand lifted and unconsciously fingered a tender spot at the edge of his mouth. *It had all been a dream.* He'd have to keep reminding himself of that, no matter how real it had seemed. *It had all been a dream.*

Chapter 8

Julia was falling in love, and the thought scared her. She hadn't a clue about when it had happened, but sometime in the past week she'd come to care deeply for the tall, mysterious cowboy, and she didn't have a very impressive track record when it came to men. As a matter of fact, she didn't have an impressive record when it came to emotional involvements of any kind.

However, if Ryder's behavior last night was any indication of his own feelings, she figured she didn't need to worry too much about it. He'd run from her at the pool as though she was the devil incarnate and he the virgin sacrifice.

Considering her own reluctance, that should have reassured her, but it didn't. She wanted to know why he'd run and couldn't help wondering if it had something to do with his playing cowboy and acting as though for some reason she was out to get him.

It was obvious that he didn't trust her. She wondered if it was just her, or if his distrust stretched to encompass all women.

She supposed none of that should bother her since she'd be leaving him soon. All the same, she couldn't help noting a slight twinge in the vicinity of her heart when she remembered the tenderness and the hunger in the one kiss they'd shared.

The idea of trying to get him to agree to pose for her seemed ludicrous under the circumstances. She knew the desire to paint him had only been a thinly veiled attempt to justify her wanting to stay with him, in any case.

She recognized that now and knew if she were smart she'd put a stop to any feelings she had for him here and now, before they got out of hand. The idea of her helping him over whatever emotional trauma that had caused him to hide himself away in these mountains was quixotic at best. She wasn't capable of helping herself.

Last night that fact had been brought home to her as she'd fallen asleep in the cowboy's arms. She hadn't even been able to deal with the sounds of the mountains at night. It was a minor thing, but still it made her realize she wasn't ready for a new relationship and especially not one involving someone who appeared to be as big an emotional cripple as herself.

It was true that she'd found peace from the torment that had driven her like a wounded animal to make one rash judgment after another, resulting in even more pain and misery. But she still hadn't learned to weigh situations, or people, before making a decision.

She and Ryder could only hurt each other more, and because she had come to care for him, she didn't want that to happen. On the point of going in search of him, she glanced up and found him standing beside her. She'd been so engrossed in her thoughts she hadn't heard his approach.

He bent to drop two cleaned and gutted trout on the rock beside her, and against his will their glances met. They were so close he could see the light smattering of freckles the sun had brought out across the bridge of her small nose.

"Supper," he said shortly, straightening and turning away.

Julia closed her eyes for a moment to try and calm the furious pounding of her heart. He didn't even have to touch her, now all he had to do was look at her and she melted.

When she opened her eyes they landed on the accusing eye of a dead fish. "My turn to cook, huh?" she muttered in resignation.

"Your turn," he agreed, hearing the almost-silent whisper.

Well, at least he'd cleaned them, Julia thought, as she placed the fish in a skillet of fat Ryder had saved from an earlier meal and set it over the fire. The first time they'd fished together, he'd painstakingly showed her how to scale and gut them. When she'd protested, he'd told her she had to learn how to do it herself, because if she ever caught the fish, she'd have to clean them.

While they cooked, she mixed a small amount of water with a couple of handsful of ground corn the way she'd seen Ryder do it and fashioned small round balls. As she worked, she stole glances at her companion.

He'd dropped his hat on the ground beside his saddlebags and sat down with his back against a large boulder a little way from the fire. He must have taken a bath while he was fishing because his hair was slicked wetly back from his forehead and the sides of his face. She'd never actually seen him shave, but his face always appeared smooth and free of any beard except for the mustache.

For a moment she paused and pictured what it would be like to watch him shave. She bet he used a straight razor and lather in a mug with a brush.

"Somethin' wrong?"

Julia realized she was staring at him and glanced down at the corn dodgers waiting to be fried. "No, nothing."

Ryder finished cleaning his pistol, slid it into the holster at his hip and leaned forward to slide the knife from its sheath in his boot. For a moment Julia's eyes followed his movements as he reached into the saddlebag and removed what looked like a long gray rock.

A flash of sunlight off the blade drew her eyes back to the knife. She couldn't help thinking how dangerous it looked. The blade was long and broad along the spine, but tapered suddenly to a point. The main part of the blade was single-edged, but the tip was double-edged and looked razor sharp.

Ryder seemed oblivious to her scrutiny as he began to draw the knife back and forth steadily across the whetstone. The sound grated on Julia's nerves. When she didn't think she'd be able to stand it a second longer, he stopped to test the blade's sharpness against the edge of his thumb. Apparently, it didn't yet meet his standards, because he began the process all over again.

"When are we going back to the cabin?" Julia asked abruptly, hoping to still the nerve-racking sound.

Ryder paused and met her glance. "Not for a day or two. Why? Is there some reason you want to get back to the cabin?"

"No—I think it's time I left, that's all. My knee is almost as good as new—" she hesitated "—and I do have a life of my own to lead, you know."

"In California? Or Boston?"

"Neither." Her eyes rested on her hands as she dropped the corn dodgers into the pan of sizzling lard next to the fish. "I haven't decided where I'm going to settle. I might go south."

"Texas?" he asked with raised brows.

"Maybe."

"How you going to get there?"

"I'll manage."

"What's your hurry?" Ryder glanced back to the knife he held and began to move it against the stone slowly. "You meeting somebody in Texas?"

"No," Julia answered quickly. "I told you I was traveling alone."

"Then what are you worried about? Give your injury time to heal proper." He glanced up from beneath the black brows at her face. "That is, if you're sure you aren't keeping somebody waiting."

Julia found it almost impossible to keep from squirming guiltily beneath his stare, despite having no reason to feel guilt of any kind. She'd caught him staring at her strangely several times that day, and it added to her uneasiness now. She wanted to be angry at his insinuation that she was deliberately keeping something from him.

But instead of anger she becoming filled with a bitter disappointment. If she needed any proof that her idea of helping him through whatever kept him a prisoner in these mountains wouldn't work, there she had it. It would take more than her feeble efforts to make him regain his desire for human company. She was only wasting her time.

"The food is ready."

"Good, I'm hungry. This mountain air gives a body an appetite."

Julia picked at her food. It seemed the mountain air didn't have the same effect on her that it had on him.

As the evening wore on, as though in unspoken agreement, neither mentioned anything of a personal nature. Julia listened as Ryder talked about the mountains. He seemed to know a lot about them, but when Julia asked him where he'd gotten his information he only shrugged.

Earlier that morning they had moved camp at Ryder's insistence. The new spot Ryder had chosen was close to one of the smaller hot springs. He picked it deliberately because the Shoshone didn't frequent it much, preferring the larger, more easily accessible ones closer to their main camp.

Now night had fallen, and he knew it was time to do something about the real reason behind this trip north. He planned to visit the large Shoshone camp near the headwaters of the river.

Ryder glanced across the fire at Julia's sleeping form and knew he didn't want to leave her. The thought of what might happen to her should a Sioux brave stumble across her alone made him hesitate a long time over his decision.

He'd been surprised to see how readily she'd snuggled down in her bedroll and fallen quickly asleep. He supposed she must be tired after getting so little sleep the night before.

That thought brought to mind his own bout of sleeplessness and made him recall the dream he'd had of their making love. It had seemed so real. The dream had come back to him in vivid recall several times that day when he'd least expected it, causing him an agony of mental and physical confusion. Once, when he'd come suddenly across Julia at the pool bathing her face and hands, he'd gotten so caught up in the memories he'd nearly gone to her and lifted her into his arms to ease the torment.

He didn't want to leave her, in fact he'd have liked nothing better than to spend the night wrapped tightly in her arms, his body speaking to hers. . . .

But, in the end, despite his worry about her safety, he did leave her. He had to, because he had to know what the Indians were planning, especially if it meant he'd have to leave the only real home he'd known since his stay with the Shoshone.

Ryder placed his pistol and rifle on the blanket beside Julia, knowing she'd understand what to do if he didn't make it back. She might be from the East, but the instinct for survival was strong in man—and woman.

As he left their camp, he allowed himself one last glance at her sleeping figure. He carried only his bowie knife for protection, hoping he wouldn't need to use it, but knowing he would if the necessity arose.

The Indian signs he'd seen since reaching the hot springs surprised him. True, the Shoshone believed in the healing properties of the waters, but the signs were not only Shoshone. After what he'd seen around his own cabin, he'd expected to see Cheyenne, but he'd also spotted Blackfeet Sioux, Minneconjou, Oglala and Flatheads. And the gathering of so many nations together in one spot didn't bode well for the white man.

Their second day at the springs, when he and Julia had hunted together, Ryder had been uneasy about the signs. It had been a good thing Julia wasn't able to read them, or she'd have known they were surrounded by Indians.

After that first day, Ryder hadn't taken Julia with him to hunt. He'd left his pistol with her, instructed her to stay put, and hunted alone, using a bow and arrow he'd fashioned himself. He'd hunted quickly and quietly, keeping a close watch on his back.

Ryder had made plans to pay a visit to his old friend Washakie, chief of the Shoshone. The old chief was well into his seventies, but still a fierce leader when the need arose. He was proud of the fact that he was a friend to the white man, even though it had caused trouble among some of the more hot-blooded young braves in his tribe. Regardless of that, the old chief stood firm in his beliefs.

Ryder doubted his past ties with the tribe would help him if a young buck, bent on making a name for himself, caught him tonight and decided to lift his scalp. But he was more concerned with the thought that he might have to abandon the cabin upon his return. The Shoshone might not bother him, but the same couldn't be said for the Cheyenne and Sioux moving through the area.

He remembered well the location of the Shoshone camp and, employing what he'd learned from his red brothers, Ryder moved toward it on silent feet. He decided that if it wasn't possible to speak with the old chief without anyone else knowing, he'd nose around on the fringes of the camp and see what he could find out on his own.

He was about a mile from the Indian camp when his thoughts drifted back to Julia. He hoped he'd done the right thing in bringing her with him. If anything happened to her...

All at once a sixth sense warned him that he was no longer alone. Dropping swiftly and silently to his knees, he peered through the darkness with narrowed eyes.

He was closer to the Indian camp than he'd thought, and there were guards hidden among the trees up ahead. He should have realized the woods were unnaturally silent. The silence was broken suddenly by the soft hoot of an owl. Ryder listened closely and wasn't surprised a moment later to hear an answering reply.

It was a signal he recognized. One brave had signaled another, but still Ryder thought he was safe, until he heard a twig snap lightly somewhere in the darkness to the right of him.

The short hair stood up on the back of his neck as adrenaline pumped into his blood, bringing every sense sharply alive. He searched around in the darkness for a means of cover other than the tree behind which he now knelt. If he was caught this close to the camp in the middle of the night, the guards would make short work of him.

By morning, when Julia awakened to find him gone, he'd be little more than a memory. He hadn't taken the time to cover his tracks, because he was in a hurry. He knew the braves who found him would follow them back to camp and there they'd find Julia, alone and unprotected, completely at their mercy. She wouldn't stand a chance.

The trunk of a dead maple, felled by age or storm, lying a few yards away, caught his eye. Ryder scrambled quickly toward it on elbows and knees. He'd press himself into the slight hollow between trunk and ground and hope the Indians would simply step over it, never suspecting he lay hidden there.

Ryder was in the process of sliding as close to the trunk as possible when he realized the part lying next to the ground was completely rotted away. Pushing a hand into it, he discovered the inside was hollow. Hurriedly, he scooped out leaves and twigs and whatever else dwelt inside, then rolled inside scattering debris across the open side next to the ground to cover his tracks.

Seconds later, a moccasined foot thudded softly against the side of the tree, rocking it gently and startling Ryder. After a moment of silence the trunk rocked again.

Ryder held his breath, wondering what was going on above him. All at once the wood cracked overhead and his muscles tensed. He'd been caught! Expecting at any moment to be dragged from his hiding place at knife point, Ryder took a deep breath and prepared to do battle for his life.

The wood creaked louder and small bits of dead wood, termites, dust, and spiderweb showered his face and chest. Ryder held his breath to keep from coughing or sneezing and giving his presence away.

In the silence, filled with the uneven thump of his own heartbeat, the sound of voices carrying on a subdued conversation drifted to his straining ears.

He listened for a moment and then grinned in relief. It seemed two Shoshone guards were using the log for a place to sit and gossip, little knowing Ryder was using it for a hiding place.

Ryder sobered instantly when he realized the gist of their conversation. He understood enough of their native tongue to learn that the Cheyenne and Sioux were preparing for a large battle with the pony soldiers, somewhere to the north, at a place called Rosebud Creek.

Chief Washakie had left camp and gone to meet with the white soldiers camped near the creek to offer his assistance. The two braves didn't agree with the old chief's position. Along with several other young bucks, they planned to join the Sioux and fight with Sitting Bull and Crazy Horse against the white eyes.

They were drunk on thoughts of the forthcoming battle and chided each other good-naturedly on who would take the most scalps. They talked and joked about who was the bravest and who was better with bow and arrow, war club and knife.

Ryder listened for a while, smiling at their good-natured ribbing. Indians had a very well-developed sense of fun and liked to tell jokes and play practical jokes on one another. He'd been the brunt of a few himself when he'd lived in the Shoshone camp.

Eventually, worry about Julia began to take precedence over everything else. What if she awakened and found him gone? If she should happen to come looking for him and stumble into these two...

Eventually the two braves finished their conversation, sobered and left, but Ryder waited awhile before leaving his hiding place, just to make certain they were gone. He wanted to get back to camp, get Julia and leave. It wasn't safe for them to stay here any longer. Come first light, he intended for them to be long gone.

A few hours later, as he moved into the canyon where their camp was set up, his eyes went immediately to the spot where he'd left Julia. It took a moment for him to realize she was gone.

Julia made her way around the rocks and stood staring at Ryder's rigid back. So, he'd come back. He'd been gone for hours. She wasn't certain just when she'd realized she was alone, because the realization had come while she was asleep, but suddenly, she'd sat bolt upright, eyes going to his bedroll, and found it empty.

For a moment she'd been terrified, and then she'd heard Midnight nicker softly and realized that wherever he'd gone, he hadn't left for good. Ryder wouldn't leave his horse behind.

On the tail end of that thought had come panic. What if he'd gone to answer the call of nature and been bitten by a snake? She'd cast that fear aside almost as quickly as it had come, knowing how much in tune he was with his surroundings. Ryder was not the kind of man to get himself bitten by a snake.

Her mind had struggled with the fear that he'd been injured in some other way, and for a brief time she considered going in search of him, but knowing so little about this country, she figured she'd be more of a liability than a help, especially if he'd only gone somewhere to be alone for a time.

He'd already made it glaringly plain he didn't require the company of people. Maybe she'd been way off base in her assessment of his reasons for living out here by himself. Maybe he really liked being alone and her company was a trial to him.

No, she didn't believe that. If that were true, he wouldn't have been so willing to keep her with him while her knee healed. Whatever the reason for his absence, she'd been worried about him and just wanted him to come back unharmed.

In her anxiety she'd rolled over, and her arm had come into sharp contact with the cold steel of the six-gun. Wherever Ryder had gone, he hadn't wanted her to follow, that was why he'd left the gun. She hadn't touched it, but she hadn't moved it, either.

After a while, she'd drifted into a restless sleep, easily disturbed by the sounds around her. Sometime later she'd awakened to the call of nature. And now he was back.

Should she demand to know where he'd been? No—their relationship was already strained. He'd returned unharmed, and she hadn't suffered for being left alone. Some questions were better left unanswered.

Without saying a word, Julia moved up softly behind him. The firelight cast eerie shadows around the camp. Ryder turned at her approach, but Julia kept her eyes on the ground at her feet. Taking up her place beneath the blanket once more, she ignored him, turned onto her left side, facing away from him and closed her eyes.

After a long moment, she heard him move and bend over her. She knew he lifted the rifle and gun, and waited tensely for him to move away. He hesitated and her tension grew; she wished he'd say something or simply move away so she could relax. After what seemed like an eternity he moved, and Julia released her breath in a long, inaudible sigh. She didn't close her eyes the rest of that night and knew without looking that Ryder didn't, either.

The next morning, before the sun's rays had lightened the sky to more than a dull hue of gray, Ryder awakened her.

"What is it?" Julia flopped onto her back and stared up into his stern face.

"It's time to leave."

"Leave?"

"Yes, we're going home."

"Home?" she repeated faintly.

"Back to the cabin," he explained patiently. "It's time to leave here."

Julia sat up, holding the blanket to her chest fully awake. Her eyes searched his face, and she sensed there was something more he wanted to say, but he only straightened away from her.

"Ryder—" She prevented him from retreating by placing a hand on his arm. "I've...enjoyed our time together." There was more she wanted to tell him, but she couldn't find the right words. She'd never been what you could call shy, but he made her feel that way.

"Please." Her gaze traveled slowly from his chin to his eyes. "Can't we stay just a little longer? It's so peaceful here."

This was a last attempt on her part to get close to him, in the hope that he'd open up to her and share some of what he was feeling inside. She would still be leaving once they got back to the cabin, but she didn't want to leave with things so...incomplete, like a half-finished canvas, between them.

Their eyes locked, and Julia felt the world shrink until there was nothing but the two of them. Drawn toward him by that feeling, she rose on her knees and drifted closer. The blanket slipped from her grasp as she raised one hand and touched his face with quivering fingertips.

Ryder caught his breath. His jaw worked, but no sound escaped the stern lips as he cupped her hand in his, pressing her cold fingers tight against his rough cheek. He wanted her—needed her—badly. He'd wanted her since the instant he'd stumbled against something at the entrance of the mine shaft and lifted his lantern to see her beautiful, unconscious face. He'd needed her since the moment he'd held her naked, half-drowned, in his arms.

Everything in him was telling him to take her—right there—right now—yet, still, he hesitated, fighting the clamor of his senses. One question kept resurfacing in his brain, overriding everything else. *Was she a liar?* Was she lying to him, even now, not only with words, but with the soft, inviting look in her liquid green eyes?

Sliding her hand from his cheek to his lips, Ryder dared to plant a slow, warm kiss on its palm. Julia's pulse leapt at the gesture, but Ryder knew it was a kiss of regret. They were from two different worlds and nothing would ever change that.

She'd been born and raised in the East. Her mother was a society matron. By her own admission, Julia was used to servants and wealth.

He'd been born in the back room of a saloon and raised in one hellhole after another. His mother had been a whore, and he was a bastard. Before she'd taken up saloon work, his mother had once told him she'd been a ladies' maid in a fancy house, but the gentleman of the house hadn't been able to keep his hands to himself.

And if that wasn't enough, Julia was obviously well educated—while he . . . it didn't matter, it would never work between them. Perhaps in another time, in another place . . .

Loosening her hand, he put it away from him and stood. "It's time to go."

Julia watched in silent protest as he dismantled their camp. His attitude remained aloof, and when they were ready to leave he mounted Midnight with a taut, almost angry slant to his harsh-lipped mouth. He lifted her with a careless arm and held her on the saddle before him as they left the sheltered nook and passed between the steep canyon walls.

Julia couldn't help casting a regretful last glance at a place she'd remember for a long time to come. She knew that for a brief moment she'd touched him and he wouldn't soon forget their stay here together, either.

After the initial disappointment over his present attitude had worn off, Julia turned her thoughts to the reason for his sudden desire to leave the hot springs. Something was wrong, but under the present circumstances, she doubted he'd discuss it with her if she asked.

The journey to the cabin was made almost completely in silence. It seemed to take longer than the trip out, but then again, she'd been convinced they were traveling in circles part of the day. That only served to make her realize how unfamiliar she was with the area and didn't make her feel any better about the way things stood between herself and her silent riding partner.

It was late evening when they arrived at a spot about a quarter of a mile from the cabin. Julia was exhausted and looking forward to a visit to the outhouse. She'd thought about asking Ryder to stop, but his posture had been so unyielding, she hadn't wanted to.

Ryder brought Midnight to an abrupt halt on the crest of a hill overlooking the small valley where the cabin stood sheltered by mountains on all four sides. He dismounted and led the horse and its rider to a secluded spot among the rocks. There he stopped and handed the reins up to Julia.

She accepted them with raised brows and asked, "What's wrong?"

He didn't answer. Withdrawing the pistol from its holster Ryder checked to make certain each chamber was loaded, then held the gun out to her by its barrel.

Julia sat looking at it without making any effort to take it. "I don't want that."

"Take it. I'm going to have a look around the cabin before we ride down."

"Why?"

"Because sometimes it's smart to know what you're walking into before you walk into it. Here," he repeated impatiently, "take the gun."

"I don't want it," she repeated stubbornly, trying to pull her fingers away when he lifted her hand, turned it over, and tried to fold her fingers around the handle of the gun. If he wouldn't tell her what was going on, she decided stubbornly, she wasn't going to cooperate.

Paying no attention to her continued refusal, he forced the gun into her hand and closed her fingers over it. "If for some reason I don't come back, you'll be glad you have this." His glance locked with hers. "If that should happen, don't come looking for me, just head out of here as fast as you can. Go due east and ride like hell—don't stop for anything—you got that?"

Julia stared at him with startled eyes and didn't answer.

"You got that?" he asked again, tightening his hand over hers and giving it an insistent shake.

She nodded.

"After a while, you'll come to a town situated at the base of the mountains. You'll be all right there. Somebody'll help you get to wherever you want to go."

Lifting his rifle from its scabbard, Ryder turned away.

"Wait!"

Ryder hesitated a fraction before turning back. Laying the rifle across one arm and resting the other one along its barrel, he met her eyes steadily and waited for her to speak.

"Why are you doing this?" she asked with a frown. "What is it you expect to find down there?"

He wasn't going to tell her about the Indians. There wasn't any use in her worrying about trouble, before trouble knew her name. He'd seen the bravest of men turn weak-kneed when faced with a band of half-crazed, painted Indians on the warpath.

"Just do like I say," he answered dispassionately, "and don't worry about anything else."

The sun flared as it began to slide below the tops of the mountains at his back, bathing his tall figure in a glow of bright light. Julia blinked, and when she opened her eyes he was gone. For a moment she was filled with the darkest sense of apprehension she'd ever known, and then, like Ryder, it too was gone.

Time passed and she grew restless. Why wasn't he back? She was exhausted, and after the nights she'd spent sleeping on the ground, the thought of the feather mattress on the bed in the cabin was very inviting.

At first she had no intention of getting off Midnight's back, but as time passed and she got no relief from the pain in her tailbone by shifting her weight from one hip to the other, she decided she couldn't stand it a moment longer. She simply *had* to get off to relieve the agony.

Climbing gingerly off the horse, she stood for a moment looking at the reins, at a loss as to what to do with them. She started to drop them, then realized she'd never seen Ryder drop the reins when he dismounted. What had he done with them?

With a shrug she tied the two pieces of rawhide together in a granny knot and looped them over the saddlehorn. There, that would do, now they wouldn't drag on the ground and get caught beneath Midnight's feet.

Using both hands she rubbed at the sore spot on her lower back. When the pain had eased a bit, she walked around the horse, hoping to remove some of the kinks caused by sitting for so long. It also helped to get the circulation started again in her feet and lower legs.

The day had been hot and dusty, and on the ride home the canteen had been passed often between the two of them, but she was still thirsty. She didn't think she'd ever get the taste of dust out of her mouth. Lifting the canteen from its resting place, she unscrewed the lid and took a long satisfying swig.

The water was tepid and tasted slightly metallic, but as she let it trickle down the back of her throat a little at a time, she knew that nothing, not even the sparkling bottled water she was used to drinking, served chilled or over chipped ice, could taste any better at this moment. Replacing the lid, she wiped the back of one hand across her mouth, hung the canteen across the saddlehorn and turned away.

It felt so good to be on solid ground. She wandered away from Midnight, who was busy chewing on tufts of tall, purplish grass she'd heard Ryder refer to as needle grass, and looked for a comfortable spot where she might stretch out and wait for Ryder's return. Unable to find a place that didn't look as though it harbored things like spiders and snakes, she turned back after a few minutes.

Her eyes lifted to the spot where she'd left Midnight and Julia stopped dead in her tracks. Where was he? Scanning the immediate area with disbelieving eyes, she started to run. What was it about this country that had man and animal disappearing in the blink of an eye?

Julia searched frantically in the failing light without finding any trace of the horse. Even though she stumbled around boulders and past short, stunted trees and through the tall grass, forgetting her earlier fear of creepy-crawlies, it was no good. *He was gone.*

She looked down at the gun clutched in her hand and decided Ryder would probably turn it on her when he discovered the horse was missing.

"Midnight!" she called anxiously. "Where are you? Here, boy—here Midnight! Here, horse! Where have you gotten to?—damn it!"

What was she going to do?

Ryder kept well hidden as he moved through tufts of yellow foxtail, needle grass and timothy across the field toward the cabin. From the ridge it had looked deserted, but he knew that could simply be a guise to lure him into a trap. Keeping that in mind, he stayed low as he ran from the cover of rocks and bush to the back of the corral.

He quickly scanned the corral, saw it looked undisturbed, and moved around the side of the building, hugging the wall. His rifle ready, he inched his way toward the front of the cabin, listening for sounds that would indicate the cabin was occupied.

At the door, bracing himself for action, he threw the cabin door wide and leaped over the threshold. Knees bent and shoulders hunched, rifle level, he scanned the cabin's dim interior.

It was empty. Kneeling before the stones of the fireplace he pushed a finger into the ashes, searching for heat, but the ashes were cold. The cabin was safe—for the time being, at least.

Next he visited the mine shaft and the root cellar to make certain no one was lying in wait until night to make their move known. He found no sign of visitors, either white or red.

Stepping out of the root cellar, he looked toward the hills where he'd left Julia. He'd been gone a long time. He figured it was time to go and get her, before she decided he wasn't coming back and lit out on Midnight.

He returned via a different route, just to make sure he hadn't missed anything, keeping his eyes peeled for Indians. In the morning he'd take a better look around for fresh signs, but tonight he was worn out and it looked safe enough to stay in the cabin.

While he made his way to the hillside where he'd left Julia, his mind was busy with thoughts of what he should do in light of what he'd learned at the Shoshone camp. He realized that since Julia had arrived, he'd been entertaining thoughts of leaving the Wyoming Territory. He could head south across the border into Mexico, or go north into Canada.

Mexico was sunny and warm, and once he crossed the border the long arm of the law wouldn't be able to reach him there. But the weather in Canada was more like his home, or so he'd been told. He'd never been there; maybe it was time he gave it a try.

What about Julia? What was he going to do about her? He figured he was wrong to suspect her of being a bounty hunter or having anything to do with the law. It just didn't fit what he knew about her—or least ways, what he *thought* he knew about her.

He'd been plumb stupid to keep her with him at the cabin. If she'd been working with somebody to capture him for the reward on his head she'd have made her move by now, and he knew it. She made him think of a home with kids running in the yard, maybe a small herd of cattle....

Whoa! He put a bridle on such thoughts. Who was he kidding? He was a wanted man. The law wouldn't let him settle down and raise a family just as though he was like everyone else.

He'd busted out of prison, and a guard had been killed. Even though he'd had nothing to do with that, he'd been tarred with the same brush as those who did. The law would never let him be, not now.

Ryder came upon the spot where he'd left Julia with Midnight. He halted and turned this way and that, looking for them, but they were gone. Julia and Midnight were gone!

He couldn't believe his eyes. Hunkering down, he studied the signs on the ground where he'd last seen them, but it was getting dark, almost too dark to read them. From what he could make out, it looked as though Midnight had gone in one direction, while Julia had gone in another.

He had a choice to make. He could either go after his horse, or search for the woman. He hesitated, torn by the knowledge that if Midnight was captured by Indians he'd never see him again and the fear that Julia wouldn't survive a night spent alone in the mountains.

There was really only one choice he could make and he knew it, but that fact only served to make him angrier than he already was. The fool woman hadn't paid any attention to anything he'd taught her. She belonged back East, where she wouldn't get herself, or anybody else who had the misfortune of making her acquaintance, killed. And that's exactly where she'd go after this, if he had anything to say about it.

He found her a short while later wandering in the hills near the river. And with the kind of noise she was making, it was a wonder she hadn't been surrounded by the whole Sioux, Cheyenne and Shoshone tribes.

Circling around in front of her, he stepped out from the cover of a chokecherry bush and stood directly in her path. Julia let out a scream and Ryder grabbed her, jerking her up against him, smothering any further cries with a hand over her mouth.

When she'd calmed enough to realize who had her, she quit struggling and sagged against him, and Ryder removed his hand from her mouth.

"Oh, God, I thought you were—" She broke off to shake her head. "I don't know—I don't know—I'm so glad to see you!" She threw her arms around his waist and hugged him impulsively.

Ryder stiffened and pushed her away. "I thought I told you to stay put," he said curtly.

"I know, and I did—I was, but, Midnight didn't. I just turned my back for a moment, only a moment, and the next thing I knew—"

"Here, give me that," he said, taking the Colt .45 she was waving about in her anxiety, "before you shoot somebody."

"I can't understand it—honest—I only turned away for a second."

"Did you hobble him like I showed you?"

"Hobble him?" she repeated with a dawning sense of guilt. "No...I didn't think about it—but I tied the ropes together and put them over the saddlehorn."

"Well, that's just dandy," he interrupted her furiously. "If you looped those tied *reins* over the saddlehorn, he won't be able to lower his head far enough to eat or drink!"

"I'm sorry," she apologized in a tiny voice. "But he'll be all right, won't he?"

He wasn't backing down. She'd done an asinine thing, and it could cost Midnight his life. "I don't know. If he manages to find his way home, he might be. If not, he'll be easy game to a pack of hungry timber wolves or coyotes."

"You mean they might..."

"That's right, or he might break his leg—and then, if I ever do see him again, I'd have to shoot him."

"Shoot him," Julia breathed in horror.

"Come on," Ryder said, taking her arm in a rough grip.

"Where are we going?"

"To the cabin."

"But—" She hung back. "Aren't you going to look for him?"

"I'd have about as much chance of finding him tonight, as I'd have in finding a fly in a currant pie," he answered churlishly, throwing her arm away.

"I'm truly sorry," she whispered in a subdued voice, almost running to keep up with him. "I was only looking for someplace to rest . . . I didn't think—"

"That's exactly what you didn't do," he interrupted bitterly, "You didn't think!"

Back at the cabin, Julia sat on one of the wooden chairs, rubbing her right knee. The pace Ryder had set on their descent to the valley hadn't done it any good. She glanced at his figure kneeling before the fireplace and looked quickly away when he glanced up and caught her eyes on him.

He was attempting to start a fire with flint and steel. The sulphur-tipped matches he used very sparingly, because of short supply, were rolled in a piece of waterproof buckskin and secured in his bedroll somewhere on Midnight's back.

Julia glanced at him furtively, noting the tight lips and clenched jaw. He hadn't said anything more about her letting Midnight wander away, but his anger hung like a heavy pall over the atmosphere in the cabin. Every now and then he mumbled something to himself as he struck flint against steel without getting the desired result.

She'd made a mistake, Julia admitted to herself—a bad one—and she was sorry for it. If there was a way she could make it up to him she would. She'd buy him another horse—no, it wouldn't be the same. Midnight was more than just a horse to Ryder, he was a friend, and you couldn't buy friends.

When the fire was finally lit, Ryder made them some hot tea. He handed her a cup with a piece of dried venison to chew on and mumbled something about taking a last look outside before turning in for the night.

Left alone, Julia sipped at the aromatic tea, but didn't touch the meat. When the cup was empty, she took a pillow and blanket from the bed and laid them beside the bearskin near the fireplace. Ryder hadn't lit any candles, and Julia didn't bother to, either. In the light of the fire she dressed in the nightgown and climbed into bed.

Hours later, Ryder lay sleeping before the fire, and Julia lay watching him. She had really fallen in love this time; she knew that, because she wanted to stay here with this man, Ryder McCall. The old Julia would already be on her way, running from the mistakes she'd made, running from Ryder's anger, from his almost paranoid insistence that danger lurked all around them.

She knew all about running, she'd been running when she found the cabin and Ryder. She was good at it, because she'd done it so many times in the past. *But not this time*, this time she was going to stay and see things through to the end. Whatever Ryder needed from her, she was going to be there to provide it.

This time, Julia, a new and stronger Julia, had found her niche in life, and she wasn't going to give it up without a fight.

Chapter 9

"Bar the door after I leave, don't venture outside, and don't open it for anything till I get back. You got that?" Ryder tucked his rifle beneath his arm and waited for her reply.

Still half asleep, Julia wrapped the blanket more tightly around her and nodded. It was chilly this morning, even if it was somewhere in the middle of June, and her toes curled against the cold boards of the cabin's rough floor.

"I'll take the rifle, you keep this." Ryder used his free hand to remove the gun belt and lay it and the gun on the table. "Keep it close—use it if you have to. Shoot first and ask questions later, that's the only safe thing to do in times like these."

Julia glanced at the unwieldy-looking gun with its six-inch barrel and looked quickly away. She didn't believe in violence. There wasn't a problem in the world that couldn't be settled if people talked to each other. And that was what she and Ryder McCall needed to do, talk.

"Did you hear me?" he asked tersely.

"What—oh, yes, I heard you," Julia answered quickly.

"Then remember it." He made as if to turn away, paused and took a step closer.

Julia felt her heart accelerate at the fleeting expression in his dark eyes.

"I don't know how long I'll be gone." His gaze rested on the pale hand holding the blanket together at her throat. He couldn't look at her face because it was all soft and innocent-looking from sleep, and if he did he'd forget why he was angry with her and he didn't want to forget. Anger was the only thing keeping him from taking her in his arms that very moment.

"Not long, I hope," he added gruffly, turning without another word and striding firmly toward the door.

"Ryder!"

He paused, closed his eyes for a second and kept his back turned.

"Please, be careful." The words were dragged from her by the solemnity of the moment. Whether the implied threat out there was real, or only imagined, Ryder believed in it. She wanted him to know she cared about his safety.

After he'd gone, Julia barred the door dutifully as he'd instructed. She added a few sticks of wood to the fire and went back to bed. Snuggling beneath the covers, she found herself staring unblinkingly at the twisting flames in the fireplace. Soon her thoughts became unfocused. If she let herself go, she could imagine this was truly a hundred years ago and she and Ryder were pioneers eking out a living on the untamed frontier.

A sad, almost whimsical smile curled the edges of her lips as her eyes drifted shut. How wonderful it would be if that were true. That would mean that none of the mistakes she'd made in the past would have happened and she could start life fresh at Ryder's side.

Life must have been simpler back then...relationships far less complicated....

Julia awakened slowly to her surroundings with eyes still closed. She felt warm, too warm. She swallowed with a dry throat, her mouth feeling as though it were filled with cotton. She listened carefully, hearing only an occasional unidentified pop and snap.

One eye opened and fell immediately on the fireplace. The fire had burned down until there was nothing left but

brightly glowing red coals. The popping sound came again
as a pocket of air exploded in one of the logs and sparks flew
in all directions.

Her glance shifted lazily from the fire to the dark, shaggy
hair of the bearskin resting on the floor near the fireplace.
A shaft of white light streamed down onto it, and Julia
could see dust motes dancing in its glow.

Her eyes slowly followed the thin streak of light to its
source. The wood shutters on the window were closed, but
a gap between two of the uneven boards allowed the bright
ray of sunshine to spill into the room.

Shoving the blankets down to her waist, Julia pushed
sleep-snarled red hair from her eyes, yawned and stretched.
What time was it? Her eyes roamed the room, automatically seeking a clock, before she remembered that keeping
track of the time wasn't a necessary prerequisite for her
present style of living. There was no clock-watching done
here.

Loosening the tangle of blankets around her lower limbs,
she sat up on the side of the bed, then stood. The first order of business this morning was a trip to the bathroom—
rather, the outhouse. Ryder had introduced her to the
chamber pot kept beneath the bed, but Julia wasn't about
to use that, even if she was alone.

Without bothering to put on the moccasins he'd given her,
she hurried toward the door. Her hands were on the bar
across it when she remembered his warning to stay inside
while he was gone. But surely he hadn't taken into account
the amount of time he'd be gone, or her present need.

Lifting the bar, she opened the door cautiously and
peered through its narrow gap. The sun was high, she judged
it to be somewhere around noon. Ryder had left very early
that morning; he probably hadn't counted on being gone
this long when he'd told her to stay inside. If he had, surely
he'd have conceded her need to visit the outhouse—no, he'd
have expected her to use the chamber pot.

Well, she wouldn't do it! Why shouldn't she go to the
outhouse? It was daylight outside, and there wasn't a thing
in sight that might hurt her. She hadn't heard the sound of
another human voice, or seen any sign of another human

being, with the exception of Ryder, since she'd arrived. And she saw no reason to fear something she could neither see nor hear.

Pulling the door back with a flourish, thinking Ryder would never know, Julia hurried outside in bare feet. Skirts flying, she rounded the cabin and made a dash down the track toward the small wooden structure enclosed on three sides by tall rocks.

Her return a few minutes later was made in a more leisurely fashion. Her right knee was telling her to take it easy, unless she wanted to be hobbling around on a crutch again. As she drew near the garden she veered toward it and stopped to pick a ripe red tomato.

Wiping it on the skirt of her gown, she bit into its tender flesh with relish, tasted its tart sweetness, and felt the juice run down her chin. She wiped it off with a satisfied smile, lifting her face to the warmth of the sun.

Life here could be so wonderful if only Ryder could forget, as she was learning to forget, all the harshness in the modern world. It was he who had created this small haven of peace in the midst of a world filled with strife. Why couldn't he enjoy it? Why did he insist on filling it with demons from his past? That was what he must be doing, it was the only logical explanation for his fear.

Julia's gaze traveled from garden to corral, cabin to root cellar, and finally touched on the two graves in the distance. She liked it here and didn't want to leave, not ever. The determination behind that realization came as something of a shock. This wasn't the first time she'd thought about staying here, but always before, she'd centered her reasons for wanting to stay on Ryder and a desire to know him better. Now she realized there was more to it than that.

It wasn't only Ryder's presence making her want to stay; it was more. She felt a kinship with this vast land of beautiful rolling hills, sage-covered prairie and majestic mountain ranges. She belonged to this land in a way she'd never belonged to any other place. She'd found her home, her true place in life, and she wasn't going to leave without a fight.

Julia laughed self-consciously at such fanciful thoughts; no one was forcing her to leave. She shivered and slanted a glance around her, telling herself the feeling of eyes watching her was only in her imagination. If she was going to help Ryder, she couldn't succumb to such feelings of paranoia when she was alone.

Shrugging off the feeling, her steps grew lighter, and she did a little dance as she made her way back to the cabin. Her excitement grew at the thought of seeing Ryder again now that she'd made the decision to stay. And that was exactly what she'd decided. If Ryder would allow it, she'd stay... indefinitely.

One way or another she was determined to make him realize how wonderful life could be for the two of them ... if only he'd let it.

In the cabin, Julia poured hot water from a kettle hanging over the fire into the washbasin sitting on the corner of the table. With a smile for his thoughtfulness, she realized Ryder must have put it there for her before he left. She washed her face and hands and was about to throw the water out when she decided to make a more complete job of it.

She was going to fix her hair and wear something more feminine than the buckskin trousers and shirt he'd seen her in for the past few days. She wanted to make him take note of her as a woman. It would make the proposal she intended making to him a little easier.

She'd finished her bath and was dressed when she began to look for the comb and brush made of ivory Ryder had given her to use. They should have been lying on top in the trunk, but they weren't. She remembered she hadn't taken either of them with her on the trip to the hot springs because she'd been afraid she might lose them. So that meant they weren't tied up in Ryder's bedroll somewhere on Midnight's back—they had to be here.

Getting down on her hands and knees, she looked under the bed, paying special attention to the small space between the end of the bed and the back of the trunk. Something caught her eye, but she couldn't see well enough without more light to identify it.

If only she had something long, she could slide it into the small space and push whatever it was out into the open. Her eyes scanned the contents of the room and landed on a broom leaning against the wall near the tub. It wasn't a broom like she was used to—it looked more like the ones depicted in cartoons about witches, but it was a broom nonetheless and it had a long handle.

A moment later, using the rough wood handle, she pushed it into the narrow opening and shoved with all her might. After two tries, she finally managed to push the object from the gap and out onto the floor on the far side of the bed.

Dropping the broom, she climbed on the bed and scooted across it to hang off the other side. She was reaching toward what looked like a rope, not a comb and brush—when it moved!

Julia froze. Screwing up her eyes, she peered closer and saw it move again. A peculiar sound began to fill the silence, and every muscle in her body became rigid. She couldn't even breathe! She'd never seen one outside the movies or television, but that didn't keep her from recognizing that unmistakable sound.

Rattlesnake!

Ryder removed the saddle from Midnight's back and lowered it to the ground. He drew the halter down over the stallion's proud head and took the bit from his mouth.

"Okay, boy, now you can go get something to eat and drink." He patted the muscular flank and watched as the horse moved slowly toward the water trough.

Ryder was in a forgiving mood. He'd found Midnight easy enough, because the stallion had only wandered a few miles upriver. He didn't look as though he'd come to any harm, and Ryder was plenty thankful for that.

It was still early when he'd found the horse, so he decided to take the time and check some snares he had set in an area close to the cabin. Two of them had netted him a rabbit and a prairie chicken. And that put him in an even better frame of mind.

He'd tied the game together, slung their carcasses across the saddlehorn and headed back to the cabin. He hadn't gone more than a couple of miles when he'd run across a hunting party of Indians. Ryder had hung back in the cover of trees and watched and listened. They were Shoshone, but he made no attempt to attract their attention. After hearing the conversation between the two Shoshone braves near their large camp at the hot springs, he didn't want to take any chances that the fever of battle had spread this far south.

The fact of their being so close to the cabin continued to worry him. This time it was Shoshone hunters looking for wild game; the next time it could be a war party of Sioux. It was lucky he'd found Midnight when he had, otherwise they probably would have found him and Ryder would be without a horse.

He wondered if there was any news of the battle Chief Washakie had left to take part in, but he'd hung back in cover, even though the distance made it difficult to hear, and waited for them to leave. Ever conscious of the fact that if anything happened to him, Julia would be alone.

Julia . . . just thinking her name gave him pleasure. It just might be that he'd have to take the chance of getting caught and take her to town, where she'd be safe. He'd been thinking about that since the night he'd kissed her at the pool.

Once the Indians had left, Ryder had ridden hell-bent-for-leather straight back to the cabin. He told himself it was because he had worried about her safety, but he knew deep inside it was more than that. He couldn't wait to see her sweet face again, or hear her say his name with that breathless little catch, the way she'd said it that morning.

Ryder left the game he'd caught on the tree stump beside the ax sticking in it and quickly made his way toward the cabin.

Julia's eyes darted from the snake coiled at the edge of the table leg to the top of the table. She could just make out the shape of the gun and holster lying beneath the towel she'd used for her bath.

It seemed as though she'd been crouched on the bed for hours watching the snake, waiting for it to move and fearing that when it did, it might move toward the bed. Finally it moved, and her worst fears came true as it slithered out of sight beneath the bed. She had a terrible few seconds wondering if the flat head would appear over the edge of the bed. But Julia breathed a sigh of relief when it moved slowly into sight and made its way toward the table.

She thought about it and realized it must have gotten inside when she'd gone to the outhouse. She'd left the door standing open, and the snake had probably come inside looking for relief from the midday sun.

Her eyes moved toward the gun. She'd never fired a gun in her life. If she tried she'd probably only miss and end up making the snake more nervous than it already appeared. She'd heard somewhere that rattlesnakes could attack without provocation.

"Miz Southern—ma'am!" Ryder's deep voice bellowed softly, suddenly, into the silence.

Julia gave a startled little yelp and jerked a glance toward the heavy door. He was back!

The sound of Ryder's voice appeared to have startled the snake, too. The gray, brown-splotched head lifted, and small, beady eyes stared at Julia coldly, unblinkingly. The tail, consisting of four—no five—joints waved back and forth hypnotically. Julia found she could hardly take her eyes off it.

"Miz Southern—Julia—are you in there?" He thought he'd heard her voice, but now there was only silence.

Julia drew herself up on the bed in consternation and stared from the snake to the closed door. She'd forgotten to bar it! What was she going to do? All he had to do was push on the door and—

"Don't come in!" she called sharply, glancing again at the snake's rattle as it began to quiver faster.

"Are you ill?" Ryder asked in quick concern.

"N-no, I'm fine. I—" She didn't know what to say. She didn't know what to do!

"Are you . . . decent?" he asked diffidently, thinking the breathless sound of her voice might be caused by embarrassment at being caught without clothes.

"Yes—no—that's it. I'm dressing!" Maybe if he thought she was dressing he'd go away for a while and the snake would get tired and go to sleep and then she could sneak past it.

"Oh, well—I'll just take care of Midnight and come back when you're done."

"F-fine—Midnight! Did you say you found Midnight? G-good, good. Is he all right?" She was talking to keep him there, because despite her idea of making a run for the door, she didn't want him to go away and leave her alone again with the snake.

Ryder was on the point of leaving, but something held him back. "Midnight's fine. Are you sure you're all right?" he asked uncertainly.

When she didn't immediately answer, he put a hand against the door, felt it give, and made a quick decision. "If you don't have any clothes on you better cover up, 'cause I'm coming inside."

"No!" He wouldn't stand a chance against the rattle-snake. It was much too close to the door, and she knew they were quick and dangerous. "You can't. There's a snake—a rattlesnake—in here!"

"My God, woman!" he bellowed. "Why didn't you tell me before now? Are you snake bit?"

"I was afraid to tell you," she admitted in a weak voice.

"Are you snake bit?" he repeated tensely.

"No—no, I'm not."

"Where's the snake?"

Julia bunched a corner of a blanket in her hands nervously. The snake was getting jittery. The coil it had made of its body became tighter, and it had raised its head at least a foot off the floor. The rattle quivered faster.

But that wasn't what frightened her the most. Somehow, it seemed to sense *she* wasn't the threat. The snake's unwavering attention had become focused on the cabin door.

"It's by the table," she answered in a loud whisper, "just below the leg nearest to the door—and I think it knows you're out there," she added fearfully.

"Keep back, I'm comin' in!"

Ryder shoved against the door. Julia leapt from the bed and without giving a thought to what she was doing, threw the blanket she held clutched between cold, shaking hands over the deadly snake covering it completely. Grabbing one of the wooden chairs hurriedly, she tumbled it over on top of the blanket. By the time Ryder had slammed the door back on its hinges and entered the room with his rifle at the ready, the danger was over.

"Where is it?" he whispered tautly, pointing his gun at the floor as he peered around cautiously.

Unable to speak, Julia pointed toward the wriggling lump beneath the blanket. She was sitting on the rungs of the overturned chair, her arms wrapped around the quivering knees she'd drawn up to her chin.

"You're sitting on the snake?" he asked incredulously.

Julia nodded. "A b-bite can be d-deadly," she explained shakily. "I was afraid it would strike you before you could shoot it.

"Besides," she confessed with trembling lips, "it's my fault the snake got inside. I left the door open. The snake shouldn't have to die because of my mistake."

Ryder shook his head as he lifted her off the chair and carried her to the bed, where he sat her down gently. Striding to the chair, he gathered the snake up in the blanket and took it outside.

A few moments later, he returned empty-handed. "I left the blanket outside on a bush."

"The snake—"

"Is somewhere in the grass out back."

Julia nodded. Her limbs were still shaking so badly she didn't think she'd be able to stand if she had wanted to.

"Are you all right?" he asked with quick concern, seeing the state she was in.

"I'm fine. I was never in any danger—not really."

"Where's the gun I left you?" he asked abruptly, his face wiped of all expression.

Julia averted her eyes and pointed to the table. Now she was in for it.

"Why is it on the table, instead of in your hand? I told you to keep it with you—didn't I?"

Julia nodded silently.

"And why was the door left open?" He was becoming angrier by the second and suddenly suspicious. "Where did you go?"

"Nowhere."

"Nowhere! You don't leave the door open so a snake can get inside if you don't go nowhere! Don't you pay any mind to anything I tell you?"

"I had to go to the outhouse," she explained in her defense.

"You had to go to the outhouse," he repeated slowly.

"Yes." All at once Julia's glance challenged him. "You said not to go outside, but you didn't take into account certain... functions one must perform."

Ryder's glance slid from her sparking green eyes to the toe of his boot. His discomfort about discussing such intimate details with a lady returned full force, but this time he was too angry to back down.

"You could have used the—"

"No, I could not!" She knew he'd mention the chamber pot.

"You could have died before I got back," he persisted doggedly. "If I hadn't found my horse—*damn it*—that's another thing, I wouldn't have had to go looking for Midnight if you had done like I told you yesterday and stayed put!"

"Well, really," Julia exclaimed in a fed-up voice, "I suppose *everything* is all my fault now. It's my fault Midnight got away, my fault you had to go after him, my fault I had to visit the john, and my fault the snake was looking for a cool place to rest—"

She was running out of breath. "My fault I left the *damned* door open, my fault—*all my fault!*" She felt like throwing something at his head.

"Why didn't you use the gun?" Ryder persisted mulishly. He'd never argued with a woman before, and her quick changes of mood confused him.

"I didn't use it," she rounded on him furiously, "because I don't know how to use the damned thing!"

"Don't know how to use it?" he repeated in consternation, shocked at her use of profanity. Cussing was a man's thing, not a lady's.

"Is that all you can do," she asked irritably, "repeat whatever I say?"

"I don't understand you," he told her with a frown. "You knew I left the gun—I've *been* leaving the gun—so you could protect yourself. If you didn't know how to use it, why didn't you just say so?"

"I . . ." She shrugged, at a loss all at once for words. "I didn't want to," she finally admitted. "I didn't want you to think I was—ignorant."

"You didn't want me to think you were ignorant," he repeated with deceptive mildness, moving up behind her and taking her by the shoulders, turning her to face him.

"Have you any idea what can happen to someone alone in this country without a weapon? Any idea at all? Ignorant!" He laughed without humor. "No, I don't think you're *ignorant*—I think you're just plain *dumb!*"

Julia gasped and jerked away from him. "Dumb! Why you—you—hick! Don't *you* dare call *me* names!"

"What would you call risking your life and the lives of others without reason?" He took a step toward her, pointed a finger beneath her nose and answered his own question. "I call it *dumb,* plain, ordinary, common, *dumb!*"

"Get out!" Julia screamed. "Get out of here—before I use the gun on *you!*" Hurrying toward the table, she swept the towel aside, grabbed the gun from its holster and whirled toward him, waving it in the air.

But he was gone. The door stood open, attesting to the fact he'd taken her at her word—he'd gotten out.

Julia looked from the empty doorway to the gun in her hand, realized what she held and felt tears clog the back of her throat. Very carefully, she laid the gun down on the table and backed away.

Moving numbly toward the rocking chair, she dropped down onto the hard wooden seat, put her hands over her face and cried. This is not how she'd pictured their first conversation on his return, not how she'd pictured it at all. . . .

Ryder stood in the doorway and stared at the woeful picture she made. He hadn't meant to make her cry. True, she'd acted foolishly in the past couple of days, endangering not only her own life, but his and Midnight's, too. Still, he hadn't acted any better just now, when he'd argued with her. What she needed was to be taught the proper ways of the West, not yelled at.

"Stop crying and come with me," he demanded abruptly. He didn't like to see her in tears, but didn't know how to apologize. He'd never had the need to apologize to a woman before now.

Julia wiped both cheeks with the palms of her hands, sniffed, and denied haughtily, "I'm not crying. And why would I want to go anywhere with a man who thinks I'm stupid?" she added huffily.

"I didn't say you were stupid, I said you were *dumb*. And you are," he maintained stubbornly. "Least ways, it looks like you are about guns, and what it takes to survive in this country." He wanted to make it plain that he wasn't starting another argument with her before she could get her dander up again. Then he couldn't help adding, "I wonder how you got this far, without getting yourself killed."

"Well, *excuse me,* but life in Boston, or California, for that matter, didn't prepare me for *you,* or any of this," she gestured with one hand toward their surroundings.

"I understand that. That's why I've decided to teach you how to shoot."

"What?" Julia was on her feet in an instant. "I don't want to learn how to shoot."

"Why not?"

"Well . . . because I haven't any need to learn. I refuse to kill anything."

"What if you come across another rattler, one who ain't so patient this time?"

"That's easy," she grinned cheekily, "I'll simply call for you."

"And if I'm not around?"

She could tell by the stubborn set to his jaw he wasn't going to let this go. She might just as well cooperate, or at least *pretend* to cooperate, and save time. After he saw how inept she was at it, maybe he'd be happy to forget all about any more shooting lessons.

"All right," she said, giving in. "Let's get this over with."

Outside, on the hill near the front of the cabin, Ryder had placed a row of empty cans from the root cellar as targets. He must have been sure of himself, she thought, as she screwed up her eyes and peered at them in the distance.

"Surely you don't expect me to hit any of those from here?" she asked in amazement.

"This is easy," he answered. "When you get good, you'll be able to hit all of them dead center from the doorway of the cabin."

"I doubt that," she muttered beneath her breath. "I doubt that very much."

"You ready?" he asked from behind her.

"As ready as I'll ever be," she replied tartly.

Ryder moved up behind her, put his right arm around her shoulder, with the Colt in his hand, and lowered it so she could look down the barrel at the sight. "You see that?"

Julia felt his mustache brush against her right ear and couldn't control the sudden shiver that raced down her spine. She took a deep breath to help get herself under control and found herself more aware of him than she'd ever been. He smelled like sunshine, tobacco, horseflesh and man-sweat. And she'd never known a more potent aphrodisiac.

"Are you listening?" Ryder asked testily.

"Y-yes, of course I am. You said..."

"I asked if you can spot the target down the end of the barrel, just above the sight."

Julia raised herself on her toes and answered, "Now I can."

Ryder lowered the gun in disgust, took both her hands and clamped them around the handgrip. He took hold of her right index finger. "This finger is the one you use to pull the trigger. You got that?"

His cheek was so close to hers, she could almost feel the brush of his whiskers. "I g-got it." She swallowed tightly.

"Okay, now straighten out your arms like this."

He proceeded to put his hands on the underside of her upper arms and his knuckles brushed against the sides of her breasts. Julia smothered a gasp as her nipples tightened into hard knots, and she felt the muscles in her arms begin to quiver.

"No, no," Ryder told her impatiently, "hold the gun steady. You're liable to shoot your foot off, or kill what you aren't aiming at, if you don't."

"Right," Julia murmured, taking a deep breath, "steady." He was so close she could feel his chest move in and out with each breath. His knees fit into the curve at the back of her legs, and if she lowered her hips just a tiny bit she could almost be sitting on his lap. The thought made her knees feel weak.

All at once a vivid memory of the kiss they'd shared sprang into her mind and her knees gave way. Ryder caught her back against him, and the curve of her buttocks molded itself to his groin.

"S-sorry, it must be the heat." Julia fanned her face with one hand, the gun dangling heavily from the other.

"What are you doing?" Ryder asked, trying to pretend he wasn't aware of her soft curves. "Don't wave a loaded gun around like that!" He reached for the gun, and it went off. The bullet whistled past his head and landed in the bush somewhere behind him.

"Oh, my God!" Julia let go of the gun and it fell to the ground. "Are you all right?" Her hands reached for his face, but Ryder was bending down to pick up the gun.

"I can see teaching you how to shoot is going to take some time," he commented dourly. "All right, let's take this from the start. First, you need to stand like this." He showed her how to stand with feet slightly apart, arms lifted to shoulder level, the gun held between both hands.

"You think you can do that?" He shifted his attention from the target to her face.

Julia nodded. "How's this?"

"Good, good," he answered approvingly. "Now, here, you take the gun—and remember, it's loaded and dangerous."

"Loaded and dangerous," Julia repeated. "I won't forget."

Once again Ryder took up a stance behind her, placed his arms around her shoulders, and showed her how to hold the gun in the correct position. This time his hands lay along-side the back of hers with his fingers curled around her wrists.

"All right, take aim. You looking down the sight?" he asked softly, knowing she was looking up at him from the corners of her eyes.

"Yes," Julia murmured, turning her face toward the targets and closing both eyes, aware only of the warmth of his body surrounding hers.

"All right, fire when you're ready."

Julia pulled the trigger, unprepared for the resulting kick. The gun jerked in her hands, the shot went wild, completely missing the targets, and she catapulted back into Ryder's waiting arms.

Ryder gazed down into her face. It figured. "You can look now," he said in disgust.

"Oh, sorry," Julia murmured guiltily, opening her eyes and staring up into his face.

"It's all right...." His voice trailed off as he became aware of just how close they were standing. Unconsciously, his breathing became timed with hers. She was so beautiful, even up close like this. His eyes moved from her long, gold-tipped lashes, down over the freckles across the bridge of her nose to her lips.

He'd felt that mouth beneath his once, and he'd never forgotten the taste of it. He'd tried, but it was impossible, she haunted his dreams like a ghost.

"I think you've had enough for one day," he murmured deeply, remembering the night she'd slept curled around him like a kitten seeking warmth and the resulting dream.

No! Julia could see him distancing himself from her, the way he'd distanced himself from her since the night he'd kissed her, and she knew she couldn't let that happen again. She had his attention now, and she wasn't going to give it up so easily again.

"*Not yet!*" She spoke the words aloud.

Ryder looked startled, and she explained, "I'm not ready to stop just yet. Give me another chance. I'll do better—much better, I promise. Just show me one more time how to hold the gun."

He studied her for a moment, then moved behind her and lifted his arms. Julia could feel his hands shaking as he placed them alongside hers. So, he wasn't as immune to her as he pretended.

Did his blood burn with the same wild rush of passion burning in hers?

"Is this good?" she murmured softly, brushing her hips back against his stomach as she pretended to shift position. "Am I doing it right?"

"Y-yes, that's...good," he whispered in a strained voice.

"And this," she asked in soft suggestive tones, resting her head back against him and turning her face so their lips were only a whisper apart, "is this the way you...like it?"

"Yes," he breathed unsteadily. He was on fire for her. His face swung slowly toward hers, and the brim of his hat touched her cheek. "Just...like...this."

Julia lowered the gun slowly, aware of nothing but him as his hands slid up her arms to her shoulders and turned her into his chest. The forgotten gun dangled from one hand as his lips came down hard on hers. But somehow, she continued to hang on to it, even as she raised herself on her toes and lifted her arms up around his neck.

She'd never been kissed by a man with a mustache until Ryder, and she liked it. The short stiff hairs made her lips tingle; they tickled her skin when he brushed his mouth against hers, then trailed his lips down to the side of her neck.

One of Julia's hands moved to the back of his neck, ruffling the short hair, making him quiver, as she strained against him standing on her toes. She felt his hands move to her waist, and then he was pulling her closer.

Sliding her fingers through the soft curls at the back of his neck, she knocked the hat from his head. Her sudden open-mouthed kiss shocked him, and when her tongue pushed its way past his teeth to his gums Ryder felt as though his insides caved in.

He couldn't believe the depth of this woman's passion. He felt one of her hands slide down his neck, across the front of his shirt, to his waist. A moment later she had pulled the shirt from his trousers and slipped her hand up his naked belly to his chest.

Julia molded herself to him, rocked her hips against his pelvis and kissed him until he felt as though the ground was being torn from beneath his feet. That was when he knew he had to have her. Lady or not, he knew he'd never rest until he'd had her naked beneath him, and not in a dream this time, but in reality.

Lifting her high in his arms, Ryder strode purposefully toward the cabin. Julia kissed his chin, took hold of his face with one hand and tried to draw his mouth down to hers for another kiss.

"Wait, woman, wait," he half muttered, the corner of his mouth against hers. "Let me get you inside...."

But Julia couldn't wait, she'd wanted him for days and her desire for him had long since grown past the bounds of patience. Forcing his mouth to hers, she enfolded his lips with hers and kissed him deeply.

Once inside the cabin, with their lips still locked together, Ryder slid her slowly down the length of him until her feet touched the floor. He was learning fast.

Capturing her face between his palms, he opened his lips over hers and touched her mouth experimentally with the tip of his tongue. He liked it. He liked the freedom this woman offered him with her love-making. He drew her bottom lip into his mouth and sucked gently on it, his groin quickening as he heard her give a soft moan.

Julia began to slide the suspenders down his shoulders. "Hurry," she murmured between kisses. "Oh, hurry—I want you!"

A moment later, Ryder put her abruptly from him. While he thrilled at the streak of wildness in her, a part of him was shocked by it.

Julia stared up at him with passion-glazed eyes. "What is it?" she asked in growing bewilderment as he continued to hold her aloft. "Is something wrong?"

"You—you're so...wild...."

"I want you." She tried to press closer, but his hands tightened on her shoulders, keeping her at bay. "Don't you want me?" she asked when he failed to respond.

"Y-yes . . . but . . ."

"But what?" The look in his dark eyes was almost one of censure.

Why was he holding back? Ryder asked himself. Was he going to deny himself the pleasure of loving this woman who tied his insides up in knots because her eagerness reminded him of the past—of his mother?

"Have I done something wrong?" Julia asked hesitantly. "I only want to make you happy." She withdrew slightly. "If you don't want me—"

Ryder's head dipped, and his mouth took the words from her lips. Bunching his fingers in her hair, he pushed them through the long, curly red strands, spreading them against the sides of her face.

He loved the silky softness of her hair, he wanted to feel it next to his skin. His hands glided down her back to her waist, his palms cupped her derriere and pulled her hard against him, removing any lingering doubt she might have about whether or not he wanted her.

Kicking the door shut, Ryder let her go only long enough to drop the bar into place, then he was moving with her toward the bed. Julia stood where he'd left her, waiting impatiently as he lifted the smock over her head. She wanted to be in his arms with his mouth pressed hotly over hers.

Beneath the smock Julia wore the delicate lace underwear she'd almost lost her life trying to save in the river. Ryder felt his heart stop, then kick against his ribs as the enchanting beauty of her full, sienna-tipped breasts, narrow waist, and long tapering thighs were revealed to his hungry eyes.

"I've wondered what you'd look like in these," he whispered thickly, touching the lacy bra with one finger, "ever since I first saw them."

"Oh, Ryder." Julia melted against him, lifting her arms as though to put them around his neck, but Ryder stopped her.

"I don't think we'll be needing this." A smile crinkled the corners of his dark eyes and his mustache twitched with humor as he removed the forgotten gun clutched in Julia's numb fingers.

Placing the gun on the trunk at the foot of the bed, he turned back to her and enfolded her in his arms. "I wanted you the moment I first laid eyes on you in the mine shaft," he confessed with his lips against her hair. "I wanted you even more at the hot springs."

Julia drew back to kiss the corner of his jaw and asked, "Why did you wait so long to tell me? Didn't you know I wanted you, too?"

"I do now," he answered, seeing her passion for him flare in her green eyes.

Julia climbed on the bed and waited for him to join her, an anxiety growing inside her as the moments passed. What if she disappointed him?

Unaware of her fears, Ryder removed his own clothes with hurried movements and dropped down on the bed beside her. He felt humble just looking at her and could hardly believe she was his to love.

"Come," Julia whispered gently, afraid that if he didn't touch her soon she'd lose her nerve. Motioning with both hands, she lay back against the fluffy down pillows and added, "Come to me—make love with me."

Ryder turned and slid the naked length of his quivering body alongside hers. Lying on his side, he reached out to smooth a curl back from one cheek and let his fingers glide down the ivory skin of her neck to the hollow between her breasts.

Julia closed her eyes and raised her taut breasts, heavy with desire, to his touch. Ryder made her feel beautiful, unlike her ex-husband, who had always complained she was lost in her painting even when they made love, and he made her feel desirable.

She felt the palm of his hand skim over the taut nipple of one breast, and then he was cupping it gently in his palm. A moment later, his head dipped and she felt the gentle prick of his mustache stab sensitive skin as his lips closed over the nipple.

Julia's eyes opened wide, she caught her breath, and her glance fell on the top of his head. Leaning forward, she planted a kiss against the soft cap of blond curls.

Ryder lifted his eyes so he could watch the excitement fill her face as his tongue circled the puckered nipple, then rubbed gently across it. The dark pupils of her green eyes dilated with mounting passion. She could hardly lie still beneath the onslaught of his tongue and lips as she offered her other breast up for his hedonistic torture.

Ryder held one soft globe in each hand, covering them with hot kisses. All at once his face dipped to the hollow between and he pressed a deep, fervent kiss against her breastbone.

"I've never had a woman like you," he couldn't help murmuring as his lips moved lower.

"What do you mean—like me?" Julia asked, touching the sun-streaked curls at the base of his neck.

Ryder smoothed a hand down her side to her hip and thigh before answering slowly, "You're different from any woman I've ever known."

"Is that *known* in the biblical sense?" she asked with a raised brow.

Ryder slanted her a look from beneath level black brows before touching the tip of his tongue to the depression in her navel. One hand came to rest on the inside of her thigh and Julia caught her breath, unable to think about anything but the sensations he was causing inside her.

"Well . . . I've never before *known* a man like you, either," she finally managed to get out. "So that makes us even—oh! Don't do that," she whispered breathlessly.

"You mean that?" he asked, watching her face.

"Oh, yes," she moaned lifting her hips to his touch, "Yes!"

The sensations spreading through her body were all at once too intense to bear. Shoving against his chest with a firm hand, Julia forced him over onto his back and raised herself to lie half over him.

"What's this?" she suddenly asked, frowning, running a finger along a deep scar that started low on his side before curving down toward his pelvis.

"Bull."

"Bull?" she asked in a puzzled voice, letting her fingers glide along the cratered edge.

"I was gored by a—bull," he gasped as her fingers walked their way to his manhood.

"How awful!" Julia sympathized. "Thank God you're all right. I never realized working on a ranch could be so dangerous."

"You," he answered, rolling her over onto her back, lifting a leg between hers as he mounted her, "are dangerous."

"Do you like it?" she asked softly, waiting tensely for his reply, keeping her eyes locked with his as she massaged him gently.

"I..." He leaned forward until her breasts were squashed against his chest. "Like . . . you . . ."

His lips covered hers, as hardness pressed against softness. Softness yielded and he felt her welcome him inside.

Julia's fingers bit into his shoulders as she felt him move against her, quickly taking her to a height of passion she'd never even imagined. She surrendered herself to his mastery and rode the tide of his mounting desire quickly catching fire.

Their bodies fused together and moved as one, giving pleasure, taking pleasure, igniting a fire that raged quickly out of control between them. It consumed the both of them, rendering them to ashes, destroying all they'd once thought and believed of life and love.

And still the fire wasn't finished with them, because as the passion flared, then burned low, their dreams were rebuilt. Out of the ashes of what was once two separate human beings, there emerged what was now and would always be two parts of one whole. They were joined together forever.

When the loving was finished, each felt as though something momentous had taken place between them, but neither understood its significance. And so they lay, hands clasped tightly between their quivering bodies, each filled with a sense of rightness, a sense of peace, and in complete accord.

A little later, Ryder moved slowly from the bed to place a log on the fire. They'd loved the afternoon and evening away. Night had fallen and the cabin had grown chilly.

Ryder knelt on his haunches before the fireplace, stoking the blazing fire. His body ached in a hundred places, but there was a new sense of strength inside him—and a glow, a glow that made the aches pale by comparison. His glance drifted toward the bed. This time he knew for a fact that it wasn't a dream. She was really there and she was his. Getting to his feet, he moved silently toward the bed to look down on her sleeping face.

He didn't want to awaken her, but couldn't resist the lure of her soft skin. Gentle fingers explored her face, a breast, the concave hollow of her belly. Just for a moment, he dared to imagine that soft skin stretched taut, her belly filled with his child.

Such thoughts were foolish under the circumstances, he knew that, but he couldn't stop them from forming in his head. Neither could he stop the voice that kept reminding him she was his . . . *but only for a short time*.

Chapter 10

"What is it?" With heavy-lidded eyes, Julia gazed up into the face of the man standing beside the bed. She'd been dozing, lost in memories of the love she and Ryder had shared a short time ago, deep in the afterglow of remembered passion when something had awakened her. Julia stared in surprise at the look of profound regret in Ryder's dark eyes.

"You..." Ryder dropped to his knees and buried his face against her stomach. "You...are...so...beautiful," he whispered against her soft skin. Drawing back, he took one of her hands between both of his, and raised it to his lips.

"I always want to remember you like this—with your skin all soft and dewy, like a brand-new morning, your eyes shining like you know a secret no one else knows."

"You sound as though I'm going to be leaving soon." Julia rose and leaned toward him. "I want to talk to you about that—"

"Make me a picture of you, like the one you did of me," he interrupted her quickly.

"W-what?"

"Please, draw yourself for me—now—looking like you do right this minute. I want to remember you with your lips

swollen from my kisses.'' He touched her lips with a gentle
fingertip. ''I want to remember that expression in your eyes,
the one that says you've just been made love to by a man—
by me.''

''I...''

''Will you do it?'' he asked her eagerly. ''Will you do it
for me?''

''Yes...all right.'' Julia leaned forward to plant a soft kiss
at the corner of his mouth. ''I'll do it for you.''

Ryder found her pencils and drawing paper and held his
shaving mirror for her so she could see her own reflection.

''Is that me?'' she breathed slowly. ''I've never had stars
in my eyes.'' She looked at the man holding the mirror.
''You put them there.''

''Draw,'' he whispered, holding up the mirror.

The next few days passed without incident. The days were
filled with hunting, fishing, bathing in the river and learning to shoot a gun. At night they made love and Julia slept
in Ryder's arms.

The sketch Julia had done of herself sat propped against
the wall next to the fireplace, beside the one she'd done of
Ryder. Neither of them mentioned the eventuality of Julia's leaving. They didn't discuss their past, or their future.
It was as though both were afraid to trust in anything but the
present, and by an unspoken mutual consent had agreed to
make time stand still for as long as possible.

Julia was learning to cook on an open fire, not always
with the greatest success, but Ryder was patient and very
tolerant of her misjudgments. He never complained of over-
cooked rabbit or undercooked vegetables.

Julia was aware of his patience and silently blessed him
for it. But as the days passed, she began to feel the strain.
The only conversations they had were about the most innocuous of subjects.

She still wanted to paint him, but didn't mention it again
after one unsuccessful attempt at trying to talk him into going to town for painting supplies. He'd listened without expression to her request and then simply walked away.

Outside, he'd saddled Midnight and ridden off into the hills, staying away until twilight.

Julia had been angry at first, but as the day had worn on she'd grown concerned and at evening she was terrified he wouldn't return. When he finally did, apologizing for being gone so long, she'd wanted to run into his arms and tell him it didn't matter, nothing mattered as long as he was safe. But she didn't run to his arms, because his attitude of aloofness had returned, making her shy of him.

That was the night Ryder went back to sleeping on his saddle in front of the fire. A new strain had entered their relationship, putting a wedge between them. Julia was at her wits' end for a solution to the problem, but afraid to say too much, in case he became angry or fed up and told her to leave.

She hung on doggedly to what they had, convinced that sooner or later he'd break down and tell her what was bothering him. In the meantime, she consoled herself when he wasn't around with long glances at the sketches she'd drawn of him and of herself. Surely, she kept telling herself, the expression of love she'd observed and sketched on her own face the night they'd first made love was a reflection of the emotion she'd seen on Ryder's face that night.

One day, after he was satisfied that she knew how to use the pistol, he insisted she wear it all the time for protection against wild animals. Julia hadn't bothered making any protest, suspecting it wouldn't do any good. After that, she began to dress in the buckskin trousers and shirt all the time, because it was easier with the gun and holster, and it didn't seem to matter to Ryder what she wore, anyway.

And then one night Julia awakened to find him gone. The bedroll lying before the fireplace was empty. At first she thought he must have gone to answer the call of nature, but as time passed without his returning, she became worried.

What if he'd met with an accident? She remembered the rattlesnake, and the fact he'd cautioned her about bears only the other day. The thought of his lying helpless, bleeding from wounds inflicted by a wild animal, filled her with fear for his safety and remorse for the anger she'd begun to feel toward him lately because of his continued indifference to her.

Julia began to reflect on how Ryder seemed overly cautious about taking his rifle wherever he went. True, it might be prudent in this country to use extra caution because of wild animals, but Julia sensed it was something more.

What did he fear? She'd come to know him during this time they had spent together, and she no longer entertained the idea that he might be mentally unbalanced.

If Ryder believed there was danger, then there was danger. And that thought opened new areas of concern for her. What if someone had come sneaking around the cabin in the middle of the night looking for money or weapons? Things like that happened all the time, even in remote areas like this one.

Could that be where Ryder was now?

If anything happened to him...

On the point of crawling out of bed, Julia heard a sound she couldn't immediately identify. Her glance shifted toward the table. The gun and holster Ryder had insisted she keep close at hand for safety was lying on the table in the same spot as the last time she'd needed it.

The sound came again and this time she recognized it. Someone was at the door. Pulling the cover up to her chin, she peered at the door with one eye.

The door burst open suddenly and Ryder's tall frame filled the doorway. Julia's heart leapt at the sight of him. She breathed a long heartfelt sigh of relief. On the point of letting him know she was awake, she hesitated, something in his manner stopping the words in her throat.

Ryder closed and barred the door with the utmost care to keep from making any undue sound. Julia felt warmed by the thought he did it out of consideration for the fact she was sleeping. A few moments later, he found something on the heel of one boot and Julia quickly revised that thought as she saw him direct a furtive glance toward the bed, get to his feet and hurry outside, taking the offending boot with him.

When he returned a short while later, his glance went first to the bed. Julia's curiosity was aroused, but a cautious voice warned her not to let him know she'd witnessed his actions a few moments ago.

She pretended to be asleep and continued to give that impression until the room grew silent. Finally, feeling slightly foolish for playing possum, Julia opened her eyes a mere slit and saw he'd gone to bed.

All at once, Ryder raised himself on one elbow and cast a long look toward the bed. Julia's heart fluttered and stood still. She was a fool to doubt him. He yearned for her just as she yearned for him, it was there in his glance.

She was on the point of letting him know she was awake when Ryder's head shifted slightly. Julia's breath caught at the back of her throat. Firelight now glittered in the dark eyes, revealing their true expression.

Julia shivered and closed her eyes in denial of what she'd seen. She wished now she had been asleep when he'd returned, so she wouldn't have witnessed that last look, a look that said he knew she was playing possum and he could play the game, too.

All the next day, Julia was aware of Ryder in a way she'd never been. He watched her and she watched him. But despite the fact they hardly spoke to each other and were obviously uncomfortable in each other's company, neither seemed anxious to put any great distance between them.

Bedtime rolled around, and as had become his habit of late, Ryder went outside to smoke. He used that, or a visit to check on Midnight, as an excuse to leave while Julia got ready for bed. His ventures outside took long enough to ensure she'd be soundly sleeping by the time he returned.

Tonight, Julia fooled him. When he came back inside after what must have been an hour, she was ready for him. She was resolved to find out if he disappeared every night after she'd gone to sleep.

She didn't dare allow herself to speculate on where he went, what he did…or who he saw. Despite her feelings for him, she knew very little about him. He'd made certain of that. What if he had someone—a girlfriend—or a wife? He'd told her he wasn't married, but he could have been lying.

* * *

The minutes dragged by slowly, and Ryder made no move to leave his place by the fire. The crackling and popping from the fireplace were the only sounds in the cabin. Occasionally, Julia heard an owl hoot or a coyote howl outside. She began to get drowsy.

She had no idea of the time, but it was beginning to look like she'd gotten upset and suspicious over nothing. Every time she peered cautiously toward his bedroll, she could see Ryder's chest rise and fall rhythmically in sleep.

She had just about decided she was ready for sleep, too, when Ryder stirred. Julia caught her breath and held it, then realized if she didn't breathe normally, he'd know something was up.

Forcing herself to breathe slowly and evenly, she waited for another sound, any sound that would tell her what he was doing. All at once she could hear a muted rustling and then a soft thud as the door was unbarred. He was leaving.

A moment later, when she opened her eyes, sure enough, he was gone. But where?

It was hours later, some time just before dawn, when he returned. Julia had slept and awakened several times by then, and when he opened the cabin door, she was wide awake.

All day she watched him without appearing to as they went about what had become for her the normal routine of everyday life in this country of untamed beauty and freedom. And that night she lay tensely, waiting for him to make a move.

Again, as before, just when she'd concluded he was staying in that night, Ryder silently gathered his things and made for the door.

It was closer to sunrise when he returned this time. How long would he keep this up? The strain, caused by too many sleepless nights, was beginning to tell on the both of them.

By the fourth day, Julia was living on the edge of raw nerves. They'd been lovers, shared the most intimate act two people could share, and yet he kept this secret from her. She was beginning to suspect it was this, and not his past, that kept them apart.

While she lay tensely through the long hours of night unable to sleep, wondering what he was up to, she began to imagine all kinds of reasons for his strange behavior. The worst of which involved another woman and a passel of kids.

Out of that fantasy grew a sense of fear that quickly turned to anger, and Julia began to ignore Ryder, keeping to herself as much as possible. She toyed with the idea of leaving in the middle of the night, while he was gone on one of his nightly appointments but common sense kept her from doing it. Ryder had once told her, if something happened to him to head for a town that lay at the base of a mountain range to the east. But he hadn't said how far away it was, or how long it would take her to get there and even if she headed back to her car and found it hadn't been stolen or towed away, unless this country harbored good fairies, it would still be without gas.

A part of her urged her to face her fear and suspicion and tell Ryder she knew he left each night. *Go on,* the voice whispered. *Ask where he goes, what he does and whom he sees.*

Something always held her back. She didn't want to admit it, but knew it for what it was—fear. She was afraid that when she confronted Ryder he'd admit there was *someone* or *some thing* that prevented them from being together.

Wondering if there might be something in the cabin she'd missed up till now that would explain his strange behavior, Julia decided to have a look. Ryder was in the garden pulling weeds and she figured this was as good a time as any.

An hour later, feeling greatly disappointed at having found nothing pertaining to Ryder's past or present, Julia sat on her knees beside the trunk and stared at what she had found. She'd unearthed a small, thin volume of verse buried in a bottom corner of the trunk. The poems were handwritten and unsigned.

Julia wondered if they could be the work of the woman who lay buried in one of the graves out back. The verses were about love and obviously written by a woman who had lived a long time ago.

The poems portrayed life in the untamed frontier. They were all beautifully written, sometimes a little sad, but always full of the deep abiding love she obviously felt for her man. Reading them made Julia feel guilty. In her heart she professed to love Ryder, yet she doubted him, even feared him at times.

Bowing her head in sudden shame, she clasped the thin volume against her and—

"What are you doing?" Ryder asked from the door.

Julia raised her head slowly, all the love she felt for him shining in her luminous green eyes. "I was looking through the things in the trunk...and I found this." She held the small, clothbound book so he could see it.

"What is it?" he asked, without making any effort to inspect it closer.

"Poetry—a book of beautiful love poems." Getting to her feet, she moved toward him. "I wonder if they could have been written by the young woman buried out back."

"Why?" Ryder asked, setting his rifle in the corner by the door.

"They're very old and obviously written by a woman, but none is signed. There is a signature on the last page, but it's gotten wet at some time or another and the letters have run together."

She turned to the last page. "Here, take a look, see if you can make it out."

Ryder didn't even bother to glance at the book. Moving around her, he went to the fire and bent to lay a few sticks of wood on it.

"You've about let the fire go out, and there's a wind coming up, clouds on the horizon. We're in for some rain before evening, and from the chill in the air, it's like to get mighty cold tonight."

"Aren't you going to look at the book?" Julia asked, following to where he knelt before the fireplace.

Ryder kept his back to her for a couple of beats, then turned to look up at her. "Why? What good would it do me to look at something I can't make head nor tail of?"

"How can you know that until you look?" she asked in a vexed voice.

"Because I can't read!"

Julia fell back a step in surprise. "You . . . can't read?"

"That's what I said." Climbing to his feet, he brushed past her and made for the door.

"Wait!"

Moving close to him, Julia laid a comforting hand on his forearm and said, "There isn't any shame in being unable to read. I admit it comes as a bit of a shock, but—"

"Is that right?" he cut across her words angrily. "Well, I'm real sorry about that, yes sir, I'm might sorry to be the one to shock such a *lady*," he mocked her. "Maybe I better get myself out of your sight till you get over the shock."

Jerking his arm from beneath her hand, he stormed from the cabin, leaving Julia to stare after him in sadness. Why hadn't he let her finish, instead of immediately taking umbrage at her words? She'd been about to add that his being unable to read meant nothing, compared with the other skills he possessed.

The afternoon wore on, and as Ryder had predicted, the wind brought rain, a cold, bone-chilling rain. Julia combined a pot of vegetable stew with leftover chicken and rabbit.

She left it simmering over the fire, and its appetizing aroma filled the cabin, yet she couldn't work up an appetite for it when she sat down to eat alone. Ryder still hadn't returned. She'd gone to look for him just before the rain began to fall, but his saddle was gone and Midnight's stable was empty.

She'd really hurt him. Her eyes moved for the hundredth time toward the rifle standing upright in the corner of the room. He'd gone off without his rifle.

Leaving the bowl of stew untouched, she lifted the quilt off the bed, wrapped it around her shoulders and went to sit in the rocking chair before the fire. Wind whistled around the eaves of the cabin, sounding like a multitude of lost souls calling in the distance. Rain drummed on the roof, and in the corner by the cupboard water began to drip from the ceiling.

Julia stared at the flames and rocked, back and forth, back and forth. The rocker made a slight noise, and after a few minutes it began to sound like a name—Ry-der, Ry-der, Ry-der.

Her chin sagged onto her chest, the room took on a damp chill, and a thin stream of water made its way slowly toward where she sat in the chair.

The cabin door opened slowly. "I could smell that stew cooking clear on the other side of the meadow." Ryder loosened the rawhide ties beneath his chin, took off his hat and shook it out the door, casting a quick look toward Julia's unyielding profile.

"It's unseasonably cold out there—more like winter than summer," he added into a silence broken only by the rain beating against the cabin. He removed the yellow oilskin slicker and hung it on a nail on the back of the door, darting short, quick glances toward the silent figure in the rocking chair.

Julia turned her head and followed his movements. He looked wet, tired and hungry.

Rubbing his hands together, Ryder turned toward the fireplace, muttering, "It's cold in here."

He was glad to have something to do to keep his eyes off Julia. Putting some wood on the dying embers, he stirred the coals until bright yellow flames began to leap toward the chimney.

Holding his hands out to warm them, still on his haunches, he swiveled to face her. She wasn't looking at him, she was staring at the flames, and every few seconds she shivered.

Ryder's glance moved down over her pinched face to the quilt around her shoulders. His eyes shifted lower and he saw bare feet peeking out from beneath the edge of the blanket.

Scooting toward her, he reached out and lifted one of her small feet in both hands. He looked up as she made to withdraw it and whispered, "Sit still—you're near to frozen."

Julia stopped trying to pull her foot from his grasp and let him place it on his thigh. He began to rub it gently between the palms of both hands, warming it. A few moments later, he lifted the other foot and gave it the same treatment.

Eyes on the delicate contours of her feet, he spoke in a low, contrite voice. "I'm sorry about running out on you like that. I shouldn't have said what I did. I've never been what you'd call sensitive about not having any book learnin'." His voice faltered. "And I didn't mean it when I implied you weren't a lady. You are, every inch a lady—"

Julia's fingers against the damp curls on his forehead stopped his words. He glanced up slowly, swallowing tightly at the expression on her face.

"I accept your apology... and I must make one to you. I didn't mean to sound... when I spoke of your..."

"Ignorance," he filled in for her.

"Lack of formal education," she corrected him. "Anyone can learn to read," she added quickly.

He shrugged and looked away. "You're different from the women I've known. You're educated, genteel... I feel... unworthy when I'm around you."

"That's ridiculous! Being able to read doesn't make me any better than you," she insisted quickly. "I could teach you to read—"

Ryder set her feet on the floor and stood, suddenly feeling very uncomfortable. "I... don't know." He shook his head. Having her see him struggle to learn would be mortifying. He didn't know if his pride could stand it.

Realizing something of what he was feeling, Julia wisely let the subject drop for the time being. She hadn't won him over, but at least they were talking again. "If you'll sit down at the table, I'll fix you a bowl of stew."

"I'd be obliged."

Julia was bending over the fire, ladling soup into a bowl, when she felt a light touch and looked down to see the top of Ryder's blond-streaked head. He was holding the moccasins so she could slip her feet into them.

A little later, Julia sat down in the rocker and watched Ryder hungrily tuck into his food. Her heart swelled with emotion. He was a proud man, but he'd humbled himself to her a little while ago and she knew that must have been very hard for him.

Ryder McCall was what most people would call a man's man. But he was also gentle and sensitive, a very complex man by anyone's standards. She felt as though she knew him a little better now, after this latest disagreement and she felt very proud to know and love him.

Yet for all the things she knew, or thought she knew about him, there were at least twice as many she couldn't even guess at. He hid his true self from her, revealing only bits and pieces at a time, keeping her always just a little confused.

Later, after she had gone to bed, she watched him sit in the rocking chair and smoke, his eyes on the flames. What was he thinking? Were his thoughts about her?

After a while Julia dozed, but her sleep was uneasy. She couldn't guess at how long she'd been sleeping when she awakened abruptly, knowing instantly she was alone.

Her eyes fell on the empty blankets. He'd left her again to do whatever it was he did at night, while she slept. All at once, she couldn't stand it any longer. She was angrily determined to find out what his nocturnal wanderings were all about.

Climbing from the bed, she hurried to the door and peeked outside. She was just in time to see his dark figure, lantern in hand, disappear into the old mine. Without waiting to put on shoes or grab a wrap, Julia darted out the door, through the muddy yard toward the mine.

It had stopped raining, but the sharp wind continued to blow. It ripped at her hair and pulled at her nightgown, trying to strip both from her body. Julia fought it, fought to keep her footing in the thick mire and struggled on toward the mine.

As she all but fell inside the entrance, Ryder's figure disappeared around a bend in the tunnel ahead. Without a light of her own, she stumbled down the narrow passage, running her fingers along the right side to help feel her way.

She must have traveled faster over the rough terrain than she realized, because as she rounded a curve, she nearly caught up with him. Stopping abruptly, she pulled back behind a slight outcropping of rock to catch her breath and waited to see which tunnel he'd take. He didn't even hesitate as he passed the shaft to the left, but continued toward the large cavern at the tunnel's end.

Julia leaned against the cold rock and closed her eyes, breathing heavily. She jumped all at once, barely containing a startled yelp caused by the abrupt noise coming from inside the cavern ahead.

What was he doing?

Julia swallowed quickly, took a deep breath and moved closer to peer around the jutting edge of rock wall. She watched for a long moment in confusion. If she didn't know better, she'd think he was mining....

Mining? What? Silver? Gold?

No, it couldn't be, she was thinking as Ryder picked up an odd-looking tool with a point at the end, held it against the wall and struck the flat end of it with a heavy wedge-shaped hammer. A small avalanche of rock and dust fell to the floor.

There was no doubt about it, he was mining something. Julia wished she could get a closer look, but didn't dare move into the cavern. Whatever it was, he didn't want her to know about it.

She'd read about gold fever and how it affected people's minds. Could that be what had Ryder under its spell? She remembered what she'd read in the history books while she was in school about the California gold rush. It had started in January of 1848 when James Wilson Marshall, a man hired by John Augustus Sutter, intent only on building a mill on the American River, built a damn across the water, and discovered gold.

But that had been in California, not Wyoming. She'd never even heard of gold being found in Wyoming. And besides, she'd always pictured the men who hunted gold these days standing in a river, with their pant legs rolled up to their knees, dipping large flat pans in the water, swirling it around, letting it spill out over the edge a little at a time, looking for shiny bits of yellow dust and rock.

Ryder appeared to be taking his directly from the wall itself. The words, *mother Lode*, popped into her head. If she remembered correctly, that was a pure vein of gold found in some kind of rock—quartz, or something like that.

My God, if that was what this was, the man was probably as rich as Croesus! *That's what he'd been hiding from her all this time.*

He'd found a gold mine and didn't want anyone to know about it. That explained his living as he did. No one would suspect him of being wealthy—just slightly crazy. One look at the way he lived no doubt sent visitors quickly on their way, thinking he had a screw loose.

It was hard to say just how long she waited and watched, a deep sense of disappointment growing inside her as the hours sped by. Ryder seemed tireless as he worked well into the night.

Julia could understand his wanting to keep others from trying to steal his gold, but why hadn't he explained things to her? Did he think she was after it, too?

The thought hurt, even though she tried explaining his actions away by telling herself he didn't know her any better than she knew him and it was her own fault if he didn't trust her.

In the beginning, keeping her past a secret from him had been a kind of defense mechanism. Later, she'd been afraid that a man who lived as simply as Ryder, wouldn't understand what had caused her to live the kind of life she'd lived in California. She'd been afraid he'd condemn her for it.

Lost in her own unhappy thoughts, Julia didn't at first notice when Ryder finished his work for the night. He was kneeling on the floor emptying what he'd labored so long for into a small sack with pull-string ties. That's when she realized he'd be heading out of the mine directly toward her in a very short while.

Making her way through the tunnel as swiftly as possible in complete darkness was a terrifying experience. She kept remembering the underground river as icy fingers of fear played up and down her spine, convincing her she'd somehow got off track and was heading directly for it.

Eventually, she came to the entrance and made a dash for the cabin knowing Ryder wasn't far behind. She made it only as far as the tree stump near the end of the cabin when his tall figure exited the mouth of the tunnel and came into sight.

Hiding in the shadow of the stump, Julia prayed Ryder wouldn't head directly for the cabin. How would she explain being outside? Her panic subsided somewhat when she realized she could always say she'd been on her way to the outhouse. But even that wouldn't explain why she was crouched beside the stump.

Ryder passed so close to her she could have reached out and touched his leg. He moved past the stack of wood at the end of the cabin, and headed into the darkness behind it.

Julia waited a moment and then followed. She saw he carried a shovel, and she had a feeling she knew its purpose.

Climbing over the corral fence, Ryder strode toward the shelter where Midnight stood nickering softly. He stopped a couple of yards inside the corral, along the cabin's back wall. There he dug down about a foot, picked up the sack of gold he'd dropped to the ground beside him while he dug, placed it in the hole, and began covering it up.

Julia's eyes darted over the ground inside the corral. How many more sacks lay buried there?

She had to admit it was a clever idea. With Midnight constantly moving over the area, no one would suspect someone had been digging there. And, too, if a stranger came snooping around, the horse would give Ryder plenty of warning before he could find the gold.

Julia saw he was finished and hurried back to the cabin with him following so close behind she didn't even think to wipe her feet. She made a dash toward the bed, and her head had barely touched the pillows when Ryder strode soundlessly inside.

Julia peered from between slitted eyes as he made himself comfortable on the floor. His saddle was outside. He hadn't brought it in when he'd returned that evening, probably because it was wet, but that didn't stop him from falling immediately to sleep. And she knew why. He must be exhausted by his labors.

Julia didn't find sleep that easily. Even though a few of the questions plaguing her about him had been answered, there were plenty left to confuse her. And yet that made no difference to how she felt about him, nor the wish to have him lying close beside her at this very moment wrapped in her arms.

Chapter 11

The storm was only a memory the next morning when Ryder awoke to a cold cabin. He rose and put a few sticks of wood on the fire, thinking it was time for another hunting trip.

If they were going to stay in the cabin much longer, they'd need something more than the meager supply of wood on hand to keep them warm on nights like the one just past. And they needed more meat, too.

He still hadn't decided if he was going to be here this winter. It depended on a lot of things.

Snuggling back beneath his blankets, he glanced toward the bed at Julia's face in repose. Mostly, it depended on her.

He'd treated her badly yesterday. It hadn't been fair to get all riled up at her because of his own shortcomings.

Raising himself on an elbow, his hand cupping the back of his head so he could see her better, he noticed how her skin glowed in the firelight. Just looking at her tied him all up in knots inside. He'd like nothing better right this minute than to slide beneath the covers and awaken her with...

His eyes rested on her full, pouting lips. They moved, and he realized she must be dreaming. He wondered if he figured in her dreams. Probably not, he grinned wryly, unless they were nightmares.

He made a quick decision. Last night was the last of the gold—at least as far as he was concerned. He'd had enough. He was going to tell her who he was, all about where he'd been and what he'd done. If that didn't make her run away screaming, he was going to tell her he wanted her to stay with him, explain what that would mean to her, and *then* he'd tell her about the gold.

He had a gut feeling, one that had been growing inside him since the night he'd found her lying at his feet that he should trust her. He'd fought the idea, but all along he'd known it was no use. She got under his skin right from the first, and from that moment on, the importance of the gold had dulled by comparison.

True, he'd been suspicious of her, even tried to convince himself she wasn't who she said she was, but he knew that was only fear talking to him. He was afraid of the feelings simply looking at her provoked inside him.

Even before his mother had died, he'd learned to keep to himself. All his life he'd watched people use each other. The men in the saloons where his mother worked used her, and occasionally tried to use him to get to her and his mother had used them and their money until her death.

His time spent living with the Shoshone had been a time of discovery. For the first time in his life he'd lived with people who weren't after what he had. The Indians wanted nothing from him because they didn't think he had anything worth taking. He was a white boy who didn't know enough about how to live in the world around him.

The land, the creatures of the forests, mountains, prairies and plain, were gifts to man from the gods, red or white, it didn't matter. Man had only to use what the gods had provided for food, pleasure and shelter.

The Shoshone knew the secret of living in harmony with their surroundings. They freely offered that knowledge to Ryder, but it was up to him to accept or reject it. It made no difference to them or their way of life.

Ryder had accepted it and thought he'd learned well—until he returned to the white man's world. As a boy he'd learned intolerance and greed from his own people. And on his return to the white man's world he learned nothing had changed. White men listened to no one, took what they wanted, whether it was theirs to take, leaving only destruction and chaos in their wake.

Because it was the world he'd been born into, Ryder tried once again to fit into it. He trusted the word of a man he thought was a friend, and that put him on the wrong side of the law.

Ryder told himself he wasn't like them—like the men who had condemned him without just cause. He didn't lie and cheat, or steal. Nor was he greedy. At least he hadn't been up to now. And that's why he'd decided it was time to move on. He had all the gold one man could spend in a lifetime, and there was still plenty left for somebody else who might come along needing it.

Julia stirred on the bed, drawing his attention as her eyelids fluttered open. She saw him watching her and smiled lazily.

"Good morning." In those first few moments of awareness, she forgot his deceit.

"Good morning," Ryder murmured deeply.

Julia's glance slid from his face to the firelight glinting off his hair, burnishing it with gold. Her smile on her face became arrested. Her eyes wavered toward his face. He watched her with a puzzled slant angling the black brows.

"I'm hungry," she murmured abruptly, at a loss for something to say, yet needing all at once to speak. Her tummy growled, prompting her to ask, "What's for breakfast?"

Ryder rose to a cross-legged position, still watching her. "How about leftover stew?"

Her nose wrinkled at the thought. Ryder's eyes flickered, and Julia looked hurriedly away.

"If that doesn't tickle your fancy, then how about fresh fish? I'll do the cooking," he added as he stood.

Julia sat up, thinking about the first meal they'd shared. It had been a breakfast of fried fish. At the time she'd thought him odd, now she understood—or at least thought she understood—the reasoning behind his living as he did.

"Is that frown for the fish—or my cooking?" he asked
with a gleam in his eye. It seemed he remembered that meal,
too.

Julia pushed her feet from beneath the blanket and smiled
obligingly at his rare attempt at humor. "Fish sounds fine,"
she answered, noting the taut way he stood with arms
hanging at his sides. "And you don't have to do the cooking."

"I want to," he murmured stiffly.

Her eyes focused on his face. What was the source of the
expression she saw there? Julia felt her pulse begin to hammer. Was he about to reveal the secret of the gold?

"I'll fish, while you dress," he murmured in a constrained tone, shifting his glance from her motionless figure and heading for the door.

Julia's shoulders sagged in disappointment. Just for a
moment she'd thought he was about to reveal the secret of
the gold. She'd been wrong, it was the sight of her getting
out of bed that had made him nervous. Pushing the covers
aside, Julia stood, forgetting the gold as she was struck anew
by Ryder's old-world sense of propriety.

He was the most modest man she'd ever known and she
had to admit she found it charming. She liked his gallantry.
He granted her all the privacy she desired; not an easy thing
to do, living as they were in such close quarters.

She was in the act of removing her nightgown when she
noticed its mud-splattered hem. Remembering her trek of
the night before, she lifted the bottom of one foot and in-
spected it. She hadn't worn shoes last night! Her foot and
the spaces between her toes were stained brown with mud!

For a moment she was overcome with panic. Had Ryder
noticed? If he had, why hadn't he mentioned it? And what
might he do if he had?

Obviously, he didn't want anyone to know about the
gold—and now she knew. Had he guessed that? She was
filled with a sense of impending doom. She should never
have followed him. It was his secret—his gold.

Wait! She was letting her fears get out of control. He
couldn't have noticed the mud, or he'd have mentioned it.
He might be reluctant about displaying his body, but the

same certainly couldn't be said about his letting her see his anger.

Besides, even if he had seen the mud, there was nothing to connect it with a visit to the mine. She could have gotten muddy going to the outhouse last night in the rain.

Julia bent to straighten the covers on the bed. If he hadn't noticed, then she'd better get rid of the evidence before he returned so she wouldn't have to answer any questions. She didn't want to have to lie to him. A quick wash in the basin, just as soon as she'd tidied the bed, would take care of that.

She pulled hurriedly at the covers, giving a quickly smothered gasp of dismay when she spotted a telltale dark stain. Throwing back the blankets she saw twin trails of brown mud spreading halfway down the sheet.

In her ignorance, she hadn't considered the obvious. Muddy feet ultimately led to a muddy bed. Julia brushed frantically at the thick crust of dried mud with her fingernails.

When the crusty top was gone, she used a damp cloth to remove the dried stain. Once all traces of the stain were gone, she spread the quilt and blanket over the top of the damp sheet. Tonight she might be a little uncomfortable, sleeping on a damp bed, but at least Ryder would be none the wiser about her late-night venture.

Ryder baited his hook and threw it into the water with unnecessary force. Julia knew about the gold!

There was mud on her feet! And even though she could have soiled her feet by going to the outhouse during the night, he knew she hadn't. If she'd awakened and found him gone, this morning, first thing, she'd have asked him where he'd been.

He knew she'd followed him, just as surely as he'd known she was playing possum when he'd returned to the cabin early this morning.

He ought to go back, right now, and force her to confess the deception—no! He couldn't do that. He wasn't ready to let her go—not yet!

In his anger, Ryder clutched the fishing line so tightly it snapped in two. He blinked and stared down at it in surprise. Busying himself with repairing the fishing line, he considered her reasons for being there. He'd cast aside any thoughts about her working with the law. She didn't handle herself well enough to have been trained for that kind of work.

But, what if someone else knew about the mine? What if *he'd* sent Julia to find out if there was any gold in it? Or worse yet, maybe whomever it was knew about the gold and sent her to find out where he kept it hidden.

Ryder knew he wasn't the first to mine the gold. Someone else had dug out the mine shaft, maybe from a cave that was already in the mountain. It was more than likely that over the years others had come to know about it, too. He just hadn't figured on any of them still being attached to their hair because the mine was so near Indian land.

A few years ago, the Indians didn't understand the white man's obsession with the yellow rock. But it hadn't taken long before for them to learn it could buy them things, like guns and ammunition—and whiskey.

It also made the white man do crazy things to get their hands on it. Indians weren't all that interested in digging for the yellow rock, but they weren't above stealing it whenever they got the opportunity. Or killing the whites who searched for it to keep them from overrunning their lands.

Ryder had got away with living this close to Indian land because the Shoshone knew him. And too, he did nothing to anger them. He didn't kill the game for pleasure and took only enough to live on. He didn't trap and kill large numbers of animals for their fur pelts, leaving the meat to rot in the sun.

But most importantly of all, as far as they knew, because he mined the gold only at night, he wasn't scratching the yellow rock out of the earth. His being there didn't threaten them with the possibility of word of the gold leaking out and bringing droves of whites, crazy with the lust for the yellow rock, down on their heads.

Ryder had deceived his red brother as badly as Julia was deceiving him and he felt guilty for it. Everything pointed to the fact it was time for him to pull up stakes and light out of there. The tribes were gathering for a big battle and this place was no longer the safe haven from the law it had once been.

And as for Julia...everything had happened so fast between them.... A part of him felt guilty about hiding the gold from her. He didn't want to believe she was there to steal it from him...but he'd been wrong about people in the past....

Almost from the first, he'd known she was hiding something. And even though that had made him leery of her, in a way he'd understood. He had never liked people pestering him about his own past, even before his little ruckus with the law.

For a time, when she showed no interest in the mine, he'd let it be. He couldn't forget the fact she'd saved his life when the rattler had got in the cabin. Still, if she'd been after the gold, she wouldn't have wanted him dead before she found out where he hid it.

There was no denying she'd been sniffing around the mine looking for something the day he'd caught her at it. She'd been mighty interested in everything she saw. Was that so she could report back to someone?

Ryder pulled in another sucker fish and added it to the growing pile at his feet. He could put his fears to rest by asking her a few questions. And if the answers weren't to his liking...

He'd been a fool to consider keeping her with him. The gold was all he'd had before she'd shown up out of nowhere; it was all he'd have when she was gone.

But could he take a chance on letting her go, when she knew about the gold?

Julia's head was swimming with questions. Once she'd taken care of the mud and finished dressing, she'd prepared everything Ryder would need to cook the fish. Now, with that done, she had nothing to do but wait for his return.

With chin on hand, she found her glance resting on the inevitable gun lying on the table only inches from her fingers. Ryder was not the person he pretended to be, of that she was certain. But then, who was he?

Why did he shun people and hoard gold? He had told her he didn't go to town. So, what did he do with his gold? Did he distrust everyone—or only her?

A sudden wave of horror seized her. What if she wasn't the first to learn what he was doing? What if there had been others?

Those graves out back didn't look as though they'd been there over a hundred years. And then there was always the underground river. That would make an excellent place to dispose of bodies—wait! What was she doing?

Did she really think Ryder capable of...cold-blooded murder?

She didn't want to. She didn't want to doubt his sanity or his morals. It was just...fear? Was it fear for her own safety making her think such awful things about him?

She ought to feel ashamed at the thought. Hadn't he taken care of her? He didn't have to, he could have got rid of her any time, especially when they'd gone to the hot springs.

Julia climbed to her feet and paced the room nervously, telling herself she was going crazy. Ryder was just an ordinary man who happened to live—her eyes slowly scanned the room—in an *extraordinary* fashion.

She dropped into the rocking chair and began to rock furiously. There was an explanation for all this, a logical explanation, there had to be, and all she had to do was find it.

The rocking chair slowed. Julia glanced at the rough furniture, the stone fireplace, the bearskin rug. If there *was* a logical explanation, then she didn't know what it could be. The only one that came readily to mind was too preposterous to be believed.

Why didn't she simply admit she was in love with the guy? If she saw him shoot someone dead right before her eyes she'd try and find a good reason for it.

She knew it didn't matter what he'd done—*she loved him*. She'd found a tender, gentle side to the man she'd never found in any other, except for her father.

Still, she couldn't help wondering if there had been a woman who'd loved Bluebeard; one who had known about his crimes and still insisted he was innocent right up to the end.

When Ryder returned a little later with more fish than they could eat for breakfast, Julia still hadn't decided what to do. The meal was prepared in mutual silence with each tiptoeing around the other warily, until, as they were sitting down to eat, Ryder suggested a hunting trip.

For a moment Julia couldn't speak or breathe. Was this it? Was he going to take her hunting and make sure she had a little accident?

Almost immediately she realized that was a ridiculous thought. Why go to the trouble of taking her someplace else, when he had ample opportunity to do it here and dispose of her body in the mine without anyone knowing?

Ryder mentioned the trip again and suggested they leave the next day if she was agreeable. They would only be gone a couple of days. It would be the perfect opportunity for her to show him how well she'd learned to handle a firearm.

Julia agreed, unable to silence the small voice inside suggesting she was being led like a lamb to the slaughter. A part of her wanted to believe the trip was a prelude to his telling her about the gold, but that dissenting voice continued to urge caution.

As the day wore on, it became more than obvious he was avoiding her and the voice of caution gained precedence over the other, saner part of reason.

The next morning, Julia was awake and ready to get started the instant Ryder moved. She hadn't slept much all night. Visions of the past, the night her friend Mariette died, had come back to haunt her.

She was more than anxious as they prepared for the trip, because she'd reached a decision. She was going to confront Ryder with her fears and questions. It was time to get them out into the open. She had grown to care for him, and there was reason for her to believe he'd come to care for her, too.

Surely, based on that, there was sound reasoning behind the questions she needed answered. Ryder would see that for himself. There must be total honesty between them.

Tying her red hair back firmly with the silk scarf she hadn't worn in days, Julia decided to make an opportunity while they were gone to tell him about her background, all of it, from birth to the present. There were many aspects of her past she didn't particularly like remembering and dreaded to speak about, but for Ryder, she would do it.

They rode south, taking a route in the opposite direction from the one they'd taken to the hot springs. Julia found herself wondering if they'd see anyone else on this trip. It still amazed her to see no signs of civilization, no signs of life, except for animal life.

As a matter of fact, now that she thought about it, they hadn't followed any actual roads on the first trip they'd made, only paths. She wondered, and not for the first time, how Ryder knew where he was going. She decided to ask. It would be the first spoken words between them since leaving the cabin.

"I'm never certain where I am in this country. How do you stay on course?"

"I mark the trail by the position of the sun—"

"What if it's cloudy?" she interrupted.

He was very aware of her in his arms, of her hair blowing against his chin. His arms tightened involuntarily around her. It would have been better if she'd kept silent, then he could continue to pretend he wasn't aware of her with every beat of his heart.

Clearing his throat, he pointed in the direction they were riding and said, "Take a look out there. What do you see?"

Julia looked hard before answering. She had started this conversation to keep a sense of normality between them. If she didn't keep talking, she'd be turning around in the saddle any moment now and offering him her lips.

"Sagebrush, bushes, trees, rocks, hills—snow on the mountains," she replied slowly.

"That all?"

"Yes," she answered doubtfully, wondering if there was something she should see and didn't.

Ryder halted Midnight and pointed to one particular mountaintop. "Do you see that mountain peak? See the way it sort of spreads out on either side as it climbs upward? Doesn't it look like the head of an elk?"

"Elk? No—I—" She started to shake her head, then hesitated. The longer she looked at it, the more it began to take on the appearance he'd suggested. "Well...maybe," she finally conceded.

"And there—" He pointed in another direction off to the left. "Do you see that lonely stand of tall pines?"

"Yes," she was quick to answer this time.

He pointed in another direction and asked, "The rock, just there, do you see how it's shaped like a tall beehive?"

"Okay," Julia said, managing a grin, "you've convinced me. You know how to mark where you're going."

"Not only where I'm going," he corrected her, a hand hovering near her cheek, "but where I've been."

"Where you've been?"

"That's right. An Indian looks at all sides of a trail, so he knows it coming and going. That's how I do it, I learned it from the Shoshone."

Julia barely heard his words. She turned to look at him, and their eyes had met. Despite the matter-of-fact tone of his voice, a deep hunger burned in the dark eyes locked with hers.

She couldn't resist him. The same hunger she saw in his eyes had been steadily growing inside her. She tilted her head for his kiss and let her eyes drift shut.

All of a sudden, a striking change in the landscape over Ryder's left shoulder caused her eyes to pop open again. They widened in surprise.

"What is it?" Ryder asked gently, noting her change of expression.

"Indians," she murmured slowly. "A bunch of men on horseback...dressed in feathers and paint...right behind us. We must have inadvertently blundered onto a movie set."

Her eyes crinkled in amusement as she thought about the way she'd been living for over two weeks. "How appropriate," she murmured with a laugh. A few minutes ago she'd

been looking for signs of civilization. What could be more
civilized than a movie company?

It took a moment for her to realize Ryder's whole attitude had changed. His head swiveled toward the left. There
were at least ten Indians, mounted on sorrel or pinto ponies, sitting on the other side of a deep gorge running down
the length of the canyon.

The leader was a young buck with an eagle feather
braided into a lock of black hair hanging at the side of his
face. The tobiano pinto he rode had a blood mark, an up-
side-down, red handprint, on its left shoulder. That was the
highest honor a warrior could receive.

Zigzag streaks, denoting thunder and lightning, ran from
the horse's rump down its legs. Those were signs of power
and speed in battle, believed to be delivered from the god of
war. The ponies of the other warriors were painted simi-
larly.

"Sioux, war party," Ryder muttered tautly, hoping the
Indians hadn't yet spotted them. "Hang on tight, we're
gonna make tracks."

"Make tracks?" Julia asked in bewilderment. "Why?"

"Because I want to keep my hair," Ryder answered,
hauling back on Midnight's reins, urging him forward with
the light use of his heels.

Running was an area in which Midnight excelled. He
outdistanced the short-legged, broad-chested, Indian ponies in moments, even carrying a double load.

The stallion came from excellent English riding stock.
He'd been imported expressly for stud purposes. The government intended to breed a horse to be used for a remount
program designed for the U. S. Cavalry. The man Ryder had
won him from in a poker game had bought him in England
and had him shipped to the U.S. for that purpose.

"Come on, boy!" Ryder urged him on as his arms tightened around the bouncing woman, riding astride the saddle, in front of him. "Let's put some distance between us
and them!"

"What-are-you-do-ing?" Julia yelled, grabbing hold of
the saddlehorn with both hands and hanging on for dear

life. Her words came out in uneven segments as the wind was forced from her lungs with each jolt from the saddle.

"I'm trying to keep that red hair of yours from ending up on some warrior's lodge pole," Ryder replied, turning his head for a quick glance over his shoulder.

"Are you crazy?" Julia shouted. "Stop this horse, right now, and let me off!"

Ryder met her angry eyes with flintlike determination. "Either keep still and let me get us out of here, or I swear I'll drop you on the trail and let the young bucks take their turns with you, while I get away."

Julia gasped in shock at the crude picture he painted. "What are you saying—are you telling me this isn't a...performance?" she shouted above the sound of the horse's hooves hurling over the hardpacked ground.

A volley of arrows whistled past their heads. Julia ducked instinctively, then turned to cast a glance of shocked indignation behind her. "Well, really, that is carrying things a bit too far."

"Performance?" Ryder repeated, whipping Midnight to a faster pace. "I don't know what in blazes you're blathering about—but if you mean you think they're only chasing us for exercise, just give a listen to those war cries."

Julia twisted in the saddle to stare up into the rigid planes of his face. "You're serious, aren't you?" she asked in stunned amazement. "They're chasing us...because they want to...kill us?"

Ryder didn't bother answering. He was too busy turning his horse toward a possible escape route.

A fifty-foot chasm divided the mesa from the valley floor. If he could get across the valley and into the mountains on the other side, they could hide in one of the hidden caves located there. The caves were inaccessible to those who didn't know how to reach them and they'd be a perfect place to lay low until the Indians were gone. These mountains and valleys weren't the natural hunting grounds of the Sioux; he was counting on their not knowing about the caves.

An arrow sliced through the sleeve of Ryder's shirt. Julia cried out in alarm, twisted toward him, and ripped it from his shirt, tossing it away in anger.

"We'll be out of range in a few minutes," Ryder reassured her. "Just keep your head down till then."

They heard the sound of a rifle crack behind them and Julia grabbed at his arm in fear. "Are we going to be out of range of that, too?"

Ryder shook his head. "Not quite—what are you doing?"

"I'm getting the rifle," she replied, hauling it from the sling with difficulty. She was terrified. She didn't understand what was happening, but she understood getting shot at, and she wasn't about to sit still and let "Indians" get away with it.

"Keep your head down," Ryder warned again as she raised up to cast a quick look behind.

Julia ducked her head immediately, leaning away from Ryder and raising the rifle to take aim and fire. She slammed back against Ryder's strong arm. She'd forgotten about the weapon's recoil.

"What are they doing?"

Julia peered around his shoulder. "I don't know, they're gone."

"No." Ryder shook his head. "They're moving down off the rim of the canyon. In a few minutes, they'll be on this side of the ravine and we won't be able to outrun them."

"What are we going to do?"

"We've only got one chance. We have to hide in those mountains." Ryder pointed to the cliffs ahead of them.

Julia looked and shuddered. "I can't climb up there."

"You have to, it's our only chance."

Searching for a way out, she insisted, "Midnight will never be able to manage the rocks."

"Midnight isn't coming," Ryder replied, slowing the horse and glancing behind. "Still no sign of the war party—good. This is what we do. When I tell you, you jump and roll when you hit the ground. I'll be right behind you."

"What do you mean, Midnight isn't coming?" she asked worriedly. "You can't mean you're going to leave us stranded out here without transportation!"

"You said it yourself, he can't make the climb. Besides, he's going to keep going so our friends back there think they're still following us."

"But—"

"Now!" Ryder gave her a push. "Remember—roll!"

Julia landed on her rear with a hard jolt and an angry cry. Letting momentum carry her forward, she tucked her head down between her shoulders and did as Ryder had said; she rolled in the dirt.

When she finally rolled to a stop, she lay panting, expecting an Indian to appear at any moment and grab her by the hair of the head. A sudden hand on her shoulder startled her into whirling around with clenched fists.

"Whoa—it's me." Ryder's palm came up as she let fly with a fist. "Come on—hurry. I can hear the sound of horses."

Using a branch from a bush, he brushed at their tracks as they backed toward the shelter of rock. From a hiding place, they watched the band of Indians unknowingly pass them by.

"We're safe," Julia panted, brushing the hair back from a dusty forehead and cheeks.

"No." Ryder shook his head. "It won't take long for them to run Midnight down. When they do, they'll begin backtracking. Soon as they see where the hoofprints get lighter, they'll figure out where we are."

"What do you mean, lighter?"

"A horse carrying a rider—or two as the case may be—makes deeper gouges in the earth than one running light."

"Oh, God. This is a nightmare!"

"Let's go." Ryder motioned for her to follow him. "We got a long climb before us. We ain't out of this yet."

"Well, what now?" Julia asked, sitting on the hard floor of the cave. They'd been climbing for what seemed like hours when Ryder had spotted whatever sign he was looking for and they'd found this cave.

The valley below looked so far away, it made her dizzy to look over the edge of the cliff. Every muscle in her body

ached, and there wasn't a spot she could name that wasn't
either bruised or scraped raw.

"Now we wait," Ryder replied, sitting back against the
wall just beyond the entrance. From there he could see the
trail dropping away from the side of the mountain. He knew
the cave was invisible from below and so was the trail, but
you could never tell with Indians.

"How long?" Julia shuddered. She was hungry and
thirsty and completely out of patience with everyone, including Ryder.

"As long as it takes," came his inflexible reply.

"Do you think they'll search these mountains for us?"
she asked with arms clasped around quivering shoulders.

"They'll search. Just like a dog on a scent, they won't give
up till they catch us—or get tired of the hunt."

"So we just sit here and wait for them to find us?"

"You got a better idea?" he asked shortly.

She glared at him before dropping her head to her chest,
too tired to hold it up any longer. Her eyes fell on the canteen lying on the floor between them. She eyed it thirstily,
but couldn't seem to make the effort to reach for it.

Ryder scooted till his back was against the rock forming
the mouth of the cave's opening, laid the rifle across his
thighs, and kept his eyes trained on the empty stretch of trail
outside. That's how he wanted it to stay, empty.

Julia looked up and watched as he made himself comfortable. She had a lot of questions she wanted to ask him.
But at the moment, it was an effort just to keep her eyes
open.

She'd close them for a moment . . . just till her heart
stopped thumping as though it was trying to beat its way out
of her chest . . . and then she'd ask him . . . what this was all
about. . . .

Chapter 12

Julia shifted over onto her side, pulled the cover up to her chin and tried to get comfortable. This was the hardest bed she'd ever slept on. What had happened to the feather mattress?

"Are you awake?"

Lifting an eyelid, she stared with one eye across the cave at the blond head of the man turning something on a spit over a fire.

"I thought it was all a dream," she whispered softly.

From her tone of voice, Ryder could tell she was disappointed to learn it wasn't.

"Are you hungry?"

Julia stared at the meat on the stick and felt her stomach cramp with hunger. "Yes," she answered, sitting up and pushing the hair back from her eyes and feeling for her scarf. Her eyes grew round as she realized it was gone. When had she lost it? Where?

Ryder caught the movement out of the corner of his eye, saw her sudden expression of fear, and knew immediately what she was thinking. "It's gone. Your scarf is somewhere out there." He nodded toward the entrance to the cave.

"I'm sorry," she whispered in remorse. "I didn't realize—"

"I know," he said, cutting her off. It was too late to worry about it now. He'd realized it was missing when he'd carried her sleeping form into this second, larger chamber of the cave. He had liked seeing her wear the scarf, its rainbow of colors had looked real nice next to her red hair.

"Forget it," he told her, "it's too late to do anything about it now. Come over here and get yourself something to eat."

"The Indians," she whispered, scooting closer to the fire and lowering her voice, "what if they find it?"

Ryder shrugged.

"Are they gone?" she asked hopefully.

"I don't know. They weren't awhile ago, when I went hunting for supper."

"You mean—"

"I mean they're camped below us. Don't worry," he added, seeing her sudden fear, "they'll never find this cave."

"How did you find it?"

"You know that bearskin rug on the floor in the cabin?" She nodded.

"Well, I tracked that wily ole varmint to this very cave— got him, too." He nodded in satisfaction.

"But the smoke from the fire," Julia protested. "Won't the Indians see it?"

"Look up." He gestured upward with the point of the knife he'd been using on the meat.

Julia saw a thin trail of gray smoke rising slowly toward the top of the cave. "How do you get it to do that?"

"I don't." He grinned wryly. "There's a vent hole up there somewhere."

"Why did those men chase us?" Julia asked abruptly, watching him slice the meat away from the bone and into small pieces, laying them on a flat piece of rawhide. "Why were they dressed like that? Do you know them—are they after the gold?"

Ryder sat back on his haunches, his face an expressionless mask, and met her baffled stare. "I wondered when we'd get to that."

"Then it is the gold they're after—isn't it?"

Ryder shook his head and began to saw at the meat again. "Like I said before, you ask a lot of questions—" he stopped and considered her taut figure from beneath lowered brows before adding "—for somebody who doesn't cotton to answering questions about herself."

"You know who I am—"

"I know who you *said* you were," he corrected her, wiping the knife blade on the leg of his trousers before laying it down. He reached for an object on the floor beside him and Julia followed the movement.

She frowned. "What's that?"

She'd seen that small pouch, or one very like it, somewhere before.

"This?" He weighted the soft doeskin pouch in the palm of one hand.

"Yes, where did you get it?"

"I've had it a long time. It's my medicine bag." He closed his fist around it and pushed it out of sight beneath the neck of his shirt.

"Medicine bag?" she asked with a frown.

"That's right. It was given to me by my adoptive father, the man who took me to live with him when I lived among the Shoshone."

"I suppose there must be a lot of those things around . . . with that same design—"

"No. The markings on every medicine bag are different." And so was what lay inside. His bag contained things from his youth: a bird's feather that had landed in his hair on his first hunt; a sign from the gods, his adoptive father had said, that he was blessed; a stone he'd used to kill a rabbit, proving his aim was sure and swift; the tail from a buffalo he'd killed to save another's life during a hunt; and a small glass bead from the dress his mother had worn to be buried.

"But . . . you must be mistaken . . . I know I've seen it before."

"You might have seen it in the cabin."

"No—" Julia shook her head decisively. "That isn't it." She was certain she'd seen the bag, with the unusual sunburst design and stick figures around it before, but it hadn't been in Ryder's possession at the time.

Where? Where had she seen it?

And then she had it—a bar in California—*the night Mariette had died*.

She'd gone to the bar alone, depressed about her inability to work. She hadn't touched a paintbrush in months. She began to drink. The hours passed, and the noise in the crowded bar faded to a dull roar in the background of her mind, dulled, along with her emotions, by the quantity of alcohol she'd consumed.

After a while, she had gotten up and left the booth at the back of the bar to go in search of a bathroom. When she'd returned, the waitress had cleared her table, taking the drink she'd ordered just before leaving.

Julia was a frequent customer at the bar and was on friendly terms with the bartender. She went to him and complained about the drink she hadn't touched.

He'd given her another, and they'd talked for a few minutes. He asked if she was waiting for someone, and she'd told him no. Then he asked if she knew the guy who'd been sitting in the corner watching her for most of the evening.

Again Julia had told him no and started to turn away. But he detained her, took something from below the counter and laid it on the bar next to her glass.

"Whoever he was," the bartender said, "he left this behind. I thought if you knew him, maybe you'd see he got it back."

Julia had looked at the bag with bleary eyes. It was unusual, both in color and design. The artist in her forged to the surface through the alcohol-induced fog in her mind.

She reached for the bag. Long fingers snaked out and picked it up before hers could touch it; the bag was weighed in the palm of a broad hand for a moment; then the fingers closed around it.

Julia lifted her head, but the man's face wouldn't come into focus. All she saw was one big blur just a moment before her eyes closed and she sank slowly to the floor, unconscious.

She awoke some time later lying on a couch in the back room of the bar. A young, attractive waitress was with her. She told Julia a customer had picked her up when she passed out and the bartender had told him to carry her in here and lay her down. The bartender, Pete, had instructed her to stay with Julia until the latter woke up.

Julia asked what time it was, saying she had to get home before it got too late. The young woman had grinned and said it was almost dawn. Pete had closed the bar, but had found plenty of work to keep him busy, so he'd let her sleep undisturbed.

The young waitress then went to get Pete, and Julia climbed shakily to her feet. While she was gone, Julia used the phone on the desk to call a cab. She was worried about Mariette. When either of them was planning to be gone overnight they always let the other one know ahead of time. Her friend would be worried sick.

As Julia was climbing into the cab a short time later, the waitress stopped her with a question. "What's the name of the guy who carried you into the back room?"

Julia looked back over her shoulder and shook her head. "I don't know, I wasn't with anyone last night."

"Well, he sure seemed to know you," the other woman replied with a knowing wink. "He was some hunk," she'd murmured enviously, closing the cab door, "a real cowboy."

The words echoed inside Julia's brain now as she looked up at the man seated across the fire from her. "Who are you?" she whispered in a voice devoid of air. "Where did you come from?"

"Ryder McCall," he answered stonily.

"How did you get me here? What's this all about? Have you been following me?" Her voice rose higher and higher as the hysteria inside her built.

It didn't make sense. Somehow she knew this man was the same man who'd been in that bar all those months ago on the night her best friend had taken her own life. But what could he have to do with that?

How could he have known she'd go to Wyoming? How could he have known she'd go to the cabin? The light! Of course, she would follow a light . . . but that still didn't explain any of the rest of it—the cabin and its contents, the gold, the Indians. . . .

She must be going crazy—that was it! The alcohol had affected her mind. She was insane!

Julia got to her feet in a daze and stalked nervously around the cave. What was she going to do? How did she get out of *this* mess?

Pushing her hands through her hair, pulling at it, she began to whimper. She stumbled against the cold, rough wall of the cave and slid slowly to the floor on her knees, clasping her arms around herself, whimpering, rocking back and forth.

Ryder watched her in growing concern. He knew it, he'd expected something like this to happen when she learned about the Indians being on the warpath. He figured the best thing he could do as long as she didn't do anything foolish like trying to run out of the cave, or start screaming, was to leave her alone and let her get over the worst of her fear.

Pushing a piece of meat into his mouth, he chewed slowly, keeping his eyes on Julia. It wasn't that he didn't want to go to her, take her in his arms and comfort her—he did. But, once again, he sensed this wasn't the right time to offer her comfort. There was more to this . . . more to her strange behavior . . . than met the eye.

"W-where are we?"

The fire had gone out and the cave had grown cold. Julia had no conception of time in this dark, soundless void she'd awakened to only a few minutes ago.

"In a cave." Ryder's deep voice came to her from out of the blackness.

"Where?" she asked urgently. "*Where are we?*"

Ryder frowned, wishing he could see her face. He was saving what little wood they had because he didn't know how long they might be stuck in this cave.

"Wyoming Territory," he answered carefully.

"Territory?" Julia asked, picking up on that word, feeling her stomach turn a flip-flop. No, it couldn't be!

Some time during the past few hours, since remembering having seen the medicine pouch, she'd thought of and discarded several explanations for the events going on around her. Events she couldn't explain.

"Did you say Territory?" Her voice quivered. "Don't you mean State—Wyoming State?"

"Wyoming isn't a state—not yet."

No, what she was thinking was impossible! Things like that didn't happen—maybe on television . . . but not to real people . . . not in the real world. . . .

"W-what—" she licked suddenly dry lips "—what is to-day's d-date?"

"I don't know." Ryder scratched his head, wondering where all these questions were leading. "Somewhere around the middle of June, I 'spect. Why?"

"The year?" Julia swallowed tightly, feeling as though an icy hand had her in its grip. God, this was crazy, but if what she suspected . . . everything—all the confusion she'd felt over the past couple of weeks—would make sense.

"Eighteen-seventy-six."

Julia held herself stiffly, almost afraid to acknowledge what he'd just said. "D-did you say eighteen-s-seventy-six?"

"That's what I said," he answered, lighting a match and setting the wood to flame. He had to see what was going on in her face.

Julia sagged against the wall. Her teeth were chattering so hard she could barely get the words out. "Th-that's what I th-thought y-you s-said."

"Are you all right?" Ryder asked, coming up onto his knees.

Julia tensed at his movement, raising her eyes to his face. "I'm fine," she answered warily. Something in her expression must have told him she wouldn't welcome his touch, because after a moment's hesitation, he settled back on his side of the fire.

"Will you tell me s-something about yourself?" she asked, watching him.

"I have done—"

"No, not that," she interrupted him quickly. "Where did you get that pouch?"

"I told you, I got it from my adopted father, when I lived with the Shoshone."

"H-how long did you live with them?"

"Six years. My mother died when I was twelve. She was sick a long time and the woman who ran the... place where she worked... didn't like having a kid around." He shrugged. "I left—took off across the territory—right after Ma's death."

Julia listened with a growing sense of unreality. Could she really be sitting here, listening to a man who had probably died close to a hundred years *before* she'd been born?

Ryder's glance moved toward the fire's rippling flames as he continued to speak. It seemed now that he'd started, he couldn't stop. "Chief Washakie and his band found me half dead from starvation in the mountains up north where we visited the hot springs. They took me in—he made me his son."

"How did you get there?"

"I hired on to a wagon train going to California. I was supposed to help tend the stock. The man who hired me thought I needed reminding, every now and then, who was boss—"

"He hit you?"

"Among other things." Ryder's bitter expression turned lethal. The beatings weren't the worst of it, but he wouldn't speak of that.

"Were you happy with the Shoshone?"

He nodded. It had been the best six years of his life, or so he'd always thought... until now.

"Why did you leave them?"

Ryder shrugged without answering, but in the flames he saw the face of a young Indian girl. He'd left because of her, because she was falling in love with him, and though he cared about her, he didn't love her.

After the life his mother had led, he'd decided he'd never do what his father had done to his mother. He'd never get a woman pregnant then leave her to raise the kid all alone. But he also knew he wasn't the kind to stay in one spot very long. It seemed like he was always looking for something he never found.

When he'd told Julia about his mother, and the fact of his own birth, it was because he wanted to shock her. He had expected to see the same look on her face he saw on the face of everyone else when they learned he was a bastard.

The truth of the matter was that his mother *did* know the name of his father. He'd been a family man in the town where Ryder had been born. He'd wanted children but his wife refused to conceive.

Years later, when Ryder's mother told him the whole story, she hadn't tried to make herself sound innocent in the matter. She'd told it honestly and concisely. She'd worked as a seamstress for the wife of the man who'd fathered her child.

She admitted she'd deliberately allowed herself to become pregnant in order to lure the man away from his wife. She loved him and had thought he loved her.

But her ploy hadn't worked. When the man's wife learned about the baby, she immediately set about getting pregnant herself. Ryder's mother had never recovered from the blow she'd received when the man had told her he loved his wife and denied fathering the child she carried.

Still, she hadn't been able to leave the town, or Ryder's father, for a long, long time. And when she did, she'd taken up the life of a prostitute. Ryder always blamed the man; he never thought of him as his father, for that. He'd made her a prostitute by coming to her in the first place and then throwing her away when he was through with her.

"What did you do after you left the Indians?"

Julia's soft voice brought him back from a very painful past to the present. "I worked as a drover for some of the big cattle ranchers. When I got tired of that, I took up gambling. I'd learned to deal a fair hand of poker while my mother was alive and I never forgot how."

"What brought you to the cabin?"

Ryder shrugged.

"What keeps you there?"

"The gold," he murmured deliberately, meeting her eyes for the first time since he'd begun answering her questions.

"G-gold?" Julia repeated. He heard her smothered gasp of surprise.

"That's right. The vein you saw me working a few nights ago is a vein of the purest gold I've ever seen. I mine it at night—"

"Why at night?"

"The Shoshone leave me alone, because of my friendship with Chief Washakie, but that might change if they thought I was mining gold. They know the news of gold spreads fast, and it would bring hundreds of white men onto their land, hunting their game, polluting their water, killing their people. To keep that from happening—they'd kill me and anyone else involved."

"Is that why the Indians below chased us today?"

"Those Indians aren't Shoshone, they're Sioux. I started noticing a large movement of Cheyenne and Sioux passing through this area a couple of weeks ago. One night at the hot springs, while you were asleep, I sneaked close to their camp. I heard two young bucks talking about a place to the north where they were going to fight the pony soldiers."

"Battle?" Julia tensed. "Can't you stop them?"

Ryder looked at her. "How?"

"Where is this battle going to take place?"

"A place called Rosebud Creek."

Julia bit her lip. "I don't suppose it's possible to change the past," she whispered dismally, thinking not only of the famous battle that had taken place on June 25 in 1876, but about the battles she'd had in her personal life, too. "No matter how much you'd like to," she added softly.

"What did you say?"

"Nothing." Shaking her head, she shivered convulsively.

"You're safe here with me," he assured her.

"I don't feel very safe," she murmured faintly, thinking not only of the Indians outside, but of the world she'd left behind.

"This mountain is catacombed with caves. There's a small underground pool of clear water in the next chamber—we have food and wood for the fire. We'll get out of this."

A sudden question popped into Julia's head. "The two graves behind the cabin . . . do you think the Indians . . ."

"I don't know." Ryder shook his head and stirred the fire.

A silence fell between them neither seemed to want to break. Julia lay down and turned away from the fire. This whole conversation seemed totally beyond the bounds of reality. She was lying in a cave talking to a man about Indian medicine, war parties, dead settlers and gold mines, as though they were a part of her everyday life.

She had to be crazy! She'd seen painted Indians, been chased and fired upon by them, yet in her heart of hearts she knew that wasn't possible....

Was all this nothing more than a figment of her fevered imagination? Had she ever really left Los Angeles? Or was she still in the city, confined to a padded cell in some mental hospital, living this dream that seemed so very real?

Julia raised her head, tempted to test reality. What if she told Ryder all about herself—about her real self? Maybe facing the nightmare head-on would cause it to dissipate.

No, she couldn't! What if this wasn't a nightmare? What if it was real? What if, somehow, impossible as it seemed, she really had stumbled into a time warp and tumbled backward in time?

That would explain so much that had been puzzling her about her surroundings—and Ryder.

Turning over onto her side, facing the fire, she glanced at him through partially closed lids. He was real, he had to be. She'd lived with him...spoken to him...touched him... made love with him....

Would speaking about the future bring the past to an abrupt end? Would all this, the cave, the Indians, Ryder— disappear?

She couldn't take that chance! Because whether this place was real, whether Ryder really existed or was only a dream, Julia had fallen in love with him and that's all that mattered. If it was a dream, please, God, she prayed silently, let me never awaken.

For the first time in her life, she had purpose, and a real sense of the person she could be. She couldn't lose that feeling—or Ryder—not now...not now!

Ryder lay by the fire darting glances toward Julia's closed eyes and pale face. She was acting very strange, more strange than ever before.

She'd disappointed him. He'd expected her to own up to knowing about the gold and about following him last night. He'd hoped she'd tell him more about her own past.

The crackling fire drew his attention, and as he stared into the bright flames, he looked inside his own heart. He remembered the day they'd loved the afternoon away. He could see the sketch she'd drawn of herself at his request, and he wished they were back in the cabin right now.

He'd never expected to feel like this about any woman. Thoughts of his mother's wasted life, spent loving a man who didn't love her, had made him determined to keep that from ever happening to himself.

Julia had once said how surprised she was that he didn't seem to be affected by his childhood, and he'd always thought that, too. But now he doubted the truth of that. Perhaps, like being unable to read or write, he'd simply refused to admit it. If he didn't admit it, or think about it, it had no power to hurt him.

Julia had made him start facing the truth about himself. She was a totally unexpected element in his life. He didn't know what to make of her. She had turned his life upside down. Yet, these days spent with her...

The passing years were just something he got through on a day to day basis with little change from one to the next, until *she* came into his life. Time had never been precious to him, not until a little while ago, when he thought it was about to run out before he'd had a chance to tell her what she meant to him.

"Julia."

The deep timbre of his voice whispered across the space separating them. Julia lay without moving as the vibrant sound played over her nerve endings. For the first time since she'd met him, he'd actually spoken her name in something other than anger or fear.

Julia lifted her head after a moment and looked up into his face; into those magnificent dark eyes.

"Ryder?"

He was moving toward her. At her side, on his knees, he drew her up before him. His glance moved over her face and body.

He couldn't get his fill of looking at her. If he looked at her till the end of time, it still wouldn't be long enough. She was beautiful beyond anything he'd ever seen and more precious than the breath of life.

His hands cupped her cheeks and lifted her face up to his. Slowly, reverently, while the firelight danced on the walls around them, his head descended toward hers.

The touch of his lips came as a shock to both of them. A powerful surge of feeling flashed between them, turning the air electric.

Ryder didn't fully understand what was happening, but it didn't matter. Nothing mattered, not even the answer to whether or not Julia had only sought him out for the gold. Nothing was important but the powerful feeling of love she'd brought into his life.

Whatever she wanted was hers for the asking. Until she'd arrived, he'd had nothing. If she wanted the gold, it was hers, if she wanted his life . . . he would gladly lay it at her feet.

He tried to restrain the powerful fires of hunger burning him up inside. He didn't want to frighten her, but he wanted her to know what he was feeling. Yet, he was no good with words. And then, as she bent to his will, he knew words weren't necessary. He could show her, better than any words could ever convey, what he felt inside.

He tasted her lips, drew them into his mouth, ate them, sucked at their sweetness, while his hands glided across her shoulders, moved down her back and up beneath his own shirt to rest flat against her bare skin. And that wasn't enough—touching her wasn't enough. He wanted to feel her naked in his arms, he wanted to be inside her, spilling his seed in her, filling her with life—his life.

Circling her waist with his hands, he drew her up tight against his chest. They rose together on their knees, arms locked around each other, lips fused, a passion raging between them hotter than the fire at their backs.

Julia felt his heart thudding beneath the muscled wall of his chest, and her own pulse echoed the riotous tattoo. Her hands began to pull at his shirt, found the suspenders and shoved them aside impatiently.

Ryder slipped the suspenders down over his shoulders and let her pull the shirt loose from his trousers. He felt her mouth, wet and hungry, slide from his lips to his chin down the side of his jaw, leaving a trail of hot kisses.

He couldn't wait any longer. He fumbled with the buttons on her shirt, trying to keep their mouths fused. Julia was as eager as he and just as determined to help rid them of their restricting clothes. They ripped and tore at each other's clothing, starving for the sight and feel of each other's flesh.

"Touch me," Julia moaned, lifting Ryder's hand to her breast.

His palm cupped her warm flesh massaging it slowly. "You're so soft," he breathed, bending to draw a taut nipple still encased in a lacy bra into his mouth. "I've never known anything as soft as you feel in my hands."

Julia's head fell back. She used both hands to press his face against her. "Yes—oh—yes—like that..."

Ryder's hot, hungry mouth traveled from one breast to the other, his tongue rubbing softly against the sensitive flesh through the lace. Julia stood it as long as she could, before pulling his mouth back to hers.

They kissed deeply as she pulled the shirt up over his chest, their lips parting only long enough for him to shed it before fusing again.

Julia propelled herself against him, her weight carrying him back against the floor. She spread herself over him like a second skin, touching him through his trousers, feeling him hard against her palm.

Ryder's hands glided up her naked back, up the ridge of her spine, to her shoulders. He massaged them, moved his hands up to her neck beneath her hair and kissed her all over her face.

When his mouth once more locked with hers, his tongue slipped between her teeth, touching the tip of hers. Julia moaned and captured his tongue against the roof of her mouth, sucking it gently, as she pressed her hips against him.

In a frenzy of desire, Ryder sat up, stripped the trousers from both their bodies and pulled her onto his lap, wrapping her legs around his waist. He entered her quickly, bringing a gasp of surprised pleasure bursting from Julia's lips.

Grasping his hair in both hands, she held his mouth to hers as he moved against her, rocking them, creating a rhythm of love. Ryder's hands slipped up and down her back, around to fondle her breasts, rubbing the pebble-hard nipples against the palms of his hands, and then back to her hips. He drew her closer and locked her tighter against him as the rhythm of their lovemaking increased in tempo.

As though trying to hang on to something precious, yet fleeting, they drew strength from each other, tried to steal time and prolong the ecstasy.

"Now!" Julia gasped. "Oh—yes!" Grasping his shoulders, she arched back, feeling his face press against her bare breasts as the world ripped apart. It exploded into a million tiny pieces and flew in all directions, taking Ryder and Julia along with it.

As before when they'd made love, each felt as though they had become part of the other. But this time they acknowledged it by look and touch. From now until the end of time, nothing could separate them.

Sometime later, Julia realized she was hungry. Ryder offered her some of the meat. After she'd eaten some, she asked how he'd managed to capture a sage hen right under the Indians' noses without their knowing.

Ryder grinned. "Remember the rattler that came visiting not long ago?"

Julia nodded with a puzzled air.

Ryder gestured toward the meat she held in one hand. "That's his cousin."

"C-cousin?" The flush on her cheeks disappeared, leaving them pale. She swallowed, gagged and swallowed again.

"Here, drink some of this." He handed her the canteen filled with water. "And don't think about it. We can't afford to pass up food, any food, right now."

Julia knew he was right, but she hoped snake meat wouldn't be the main item on their menu. She washed the meat down with a large drink of water, telling herself it tasted like chicken. And anything that tasted like chicken couldn't be bad for you.

When they settled down to sleep, Ryder held Julia clasped tightly against him throughout the long night, wondering what the morning would bring.

Chapter 13

The next morning, Ryder left the cave to check on the Indians. He returned to tell Julia they were gone. Apparently, they had gotten tired of waiting as he'd predicted and moved on to easier game.

Their manner toward each other as they prepared to leave was warm, yet subdued. Last night, they had both made some devastating discoveries about themselves. Yet neither knew how to broach the one subject uppermost in both their minds.

Julia still couldn't quite believe in the idea that she'd somehow traveled backward through a whole century of time. Nor did she understand the significance of her having seen Ryder's medicine bag in a bar in her own time. None of it made sense.

She wanted to tell Ryder what she was thinking, but again the fear that she might somehow lose him if she did, kept her silent.

Under the circumstances, the hunting trip was canceled. If Ryder needed proof that the area had become dangerous, he now had it. The trip back to the cabin was a slow, uncomfortable journey, until they reached the banks of the river and found Midnight happily munching on manna grass.

Ryder decided to wait until they were at the cabin to sort things out between them about the gold. He no longer cared why she'd come to him. He believed she loved him as much as he loved her and that's all that mattered. They hadn't yet spoken the words, but the feelings were there.

He still needed to tell her about being wanted by the law, and that worried him, because when he asked her to share his life, he'd be asking her to live it on the run. They'd always be looking over their shoulders, worried someone might find out he had a price on his head. It would take a special kind of woman to be willing to give up a life of peace and security to live in constant fear with the man she loved.

This time, unlike their return from the hot springs, they rode to the cabin together. Ryder wasn't aware they had a visitor until the last minute, an indication of his frame of mind.

"Good day, ma'am." The tall, dark-haired stranger, dressed in Levi's, chambray shirt, wool vest and bandanna, lifted his Stetson and nodded to Julia.

Still seated on Midnight's back, Julia returned the nod diffidently and glanced at Ryder, who had dismounted and stood close to her side.

"Who are you?" Ryder asked coldly, moving away from Julia and taking up a stance familiar to their visitor. His right hand rested on the butt of the gun at his hip.

"Name's Whitson," the other man answered, eyeing Ryder with a lazy smile. "Delroy Whitson." He moved toward Ryder with a raised hand, but dropped it when the other man made no attempt to take it.

Transferring his gaze to Julia, he said, "I sure hope you folks don't mind that I spent the night inside. I could tell someone lived here—you keep a fine house, ma'am."

"What's your business in these parts?" Ryder asked, still in that unfriendly tone.

"I was on my way to Fort Bridger when I…lost my way," Delroy answered with a slight laugh.

Something in the expression in the man's unwavering blue gaze put Ryder on edge.

Scratching at the thick black beard on his chin, Delroy continued, "It's the damnedest—oh, pardon me, ma'am." He shot a look of apology in Julia's direction and offered her a slight bow before continuing. "It's funny how that happened, my getting lost, and all. I'm not usually one to get turned around."

His eyes slid back to Ryder's poker-faced expression. "I'd a probably been fine if I hadn't happened on a war party about then."

"War party?" Julia repeated faintly.

Delroy shifted his glance to her face. "That's right, ma'am. Sioux, they was, a bunch of young buck all decked out in feathers and paint lookin' for trouble."

Feeling a sudden kinship with someone who'd suffered the same scare as themselves, Julia offered him a small, uncertain smile. There was something in his expression when he looked at Ryder that made her uneasy, but he was the first man—white man—besides Ryder, she'd seen in over two weeks and she was willing to give him the benefit of the doubt.

"You're welcome to stay—"

"The night," Ryder cut across her invitation, glaring at her darkly.

Julia frowned, but accepted his decree and continued, "With us and rest up, before continuing your journey."

"Why, thank you, ma'am," Delroy replied, removing his hat. He ran a hand through the long black strands and sighed. "It's mighty nice of you to be so hospitable to a stranger. I haven't had home cooking in—" He hesitated and dropped his eyes to the hat he held in one hand in embarrassment. "Sorry, I didn't mean to jump the gun. Maybe your invitation didn't include a meal."

"Of course it did," Julia answered quickly, giving Ryder's closed face an unflinching look of resolve. "You're more than welcome to share our food."

"I didn't catch your name." Delroy looked at Ryder.

"McCall," he replied. "What's your business at the fort?"

"I breed horses for the army," Delroy answered. His attention moved to the horse beneath Julia. "I'm workin' to develop a breed of horseflesh that can carry a rider over a long distance before he has to change mounts. That's what country like this—where the people are spread far and wide—really needs.''

Delroy stepped forward and touched Midnight's forelock. The horse jerked his head and shied back a few steps, surprising Julia and causing her to lose her balance.

"Oh!" She forgot everything Ryder had taught her about staying on a horse and threw her hands up in the air. Her fear sparked a like fear in the animal and Midnight reared up on his hind legs, unseating her.

Ryder made a sharp move in her direction, but the stranger got there first. He caught the frightened Julia in midair, holding her for a moment before setting her on her feet. Even then, he stood close to her, his arms staying around her waist longer than was strictly necessary.

"Are you all right?" Delroy asked, looking deeply into her eyes.

Julia was flustered. She'd made a fool of herself, and this man's solicitude only made matters worse.

"F-fine." She backed away, loosening his arms from around her. "I'm fine." Cheeks flaming, she looked toward Ryder, saw the chiseled expression on his set face, and glanced at the other man still standing much too close.

"I—I'll just go inside and—" She made a fluttering motion with both hands. "I'll just go inside."

Ryder stepped between her and the stranger, took her elbow, and walked her to the cabin door. Inside, he stood with her a moment, body rigid, and asked, "Are you sure you're all right?"

"Yes." She met his eyes and couldn't seem to look away.

"I don't care who he is, I don't like him touching you," he whispered from between clenched teeth. Drawing her up against his chest, he said, "If he touches you again, I'll kill him." Slanting his mouth over hers, he kissed her hard, put her abruptly from him and left the cabin.

Julia raised a confused hand and touched light fingertips to her throbbing lips. What was that all about? Who did he think Delroy Whitson was? She felt as confused as Alice must have felt when she tumbled through the looking glass and landed in Wonderland. She remembered what had occurred in the cave and realized she had as much reason as Alice to feel that way.

The meal that evening consisted of smoked venison in gravy, corn on the cob, fried potatoes and bannock. They ate in silence, and even if the food wasn't up to gourmet standards, Julia noted the two men ate with hearty appetites.

As for herself, she picked at her food rather than ate it. She kept casting worried glances between the two men, as though she feared at any moment they might jump to their feet and start throwing punches.

The atmosphere between the two continued to be strained, to say the least. Ryder didn't try and hide his dislike for Delroy but instead of angering the man, it appeared to amuse him, and that only made Ryder angrier.

At first Julia had looked on Delroy's presence as a kind of respite from the strain of the last few days. But now, she realized asking the man to stay overnight hadn't been a good idea. The atmosphere around the table was so thick you could cut it with a knife.

Since he'd given her that rough kiss right after they'd returned to the cabin to find Delroy waiting for them, Ryder had hardly spoken two words to her. He kept her within sight, never leaving Delroy alone with her for an instant, but he didn't look happy about it.

While she was preparing the meal, Delroy had insisted on adding something to it. He removed a sack of coffee from his saddlebags, and Julia boiled a pot of coffee. It was the first cup of coffee she'd had in many days and she enjoyed it, even if it was stronger and more bitter than she was used to drinking.

Ryder had refused the coffee, saying he preferred the sagebrush tea. But Julia had seen the way he'd inhaled the air teeming with the aroma of fresh-brewed coffee, when he thought no one was watching. It was childish of him to refuse it because it had come from Delroy Whitson, but instead of making her angry with him, it only endeared him to her because it made him appear more human.

Obviously Ryder didn't trust Delroy. She assumed it was because of the gold, but he cared for her and yet he didn't trust her, either. Didn't he trust anyone?

True, she was keeping things from him, but they had nothing to do with the gold. She had a sound reason for her reluctance to discuss personal matters—or at least thought she did.

She could hardly believe what had happened herself, and she was an intelligent, modern woman of the twentieth century, a woman used to technology that would seem like magic to someone born over a hundred years ago. How could she expect him, a man from the past, to believe she'd come to him from out of the future?

She caught Ryder studying her with puzzled eyes and guessed he was probably wondering if her silence had anything to do with the gold. She should have discussed her knowledge of it with him in the cave, but at the time there had been other, more important, considerations to think about.

She wished she could share her thoughts with him about this strange thing that had happened to her, but the fear she'd felt in the cave was still with her. What if she spoke of the present, her present, of which Ryder could have no part, and suddenly lost him?

"Ah, me—" Delroy pushed back from the table and patted his trim waist. "That was a fine meal, ma'am, the best I believe I've ever eaten."

Julia gave a slight start, brought back to her present surroundings with a bump. "Th-thank you, Mr. Whitson. I'm glad you enjoyed it."

Patting his upper right-hand vest pocket, the man withdrew a long, thick cigar and asked, "Do you mind?"

Julia shook her head. He'd bathed, shaved and changed clothes while she prepared the evening meal and looked rather attractive at the moment.

She'd learned, though, not to make eye contact with him, because every time she did, a flurry of chill-bumps erupted on the skin of her arms and legs. She couldn't put her finger on what it was about him, but some fleeting expression far back in the depths of his eyes unsettled her.

"You, sir?" Delroy offered a cigar to Ryder.

"No, thanks." Ryder stood abruptly and left the table. He returned with the makings for a cigarette.

"Have the two of you been here long?" Delroy asked no one in particular.

Julia shot a quick glance at Ryder before replying, "No, we—"

"Yes." Ryder raised his voice to cover hers. "Been living here more than a year now."

"That so?" the other man asked, puffing on his cigar. "Ever have any trouble with the Indians?"

"No," Ryder replied shortly.

"I noticed two graves out back when I rode in. Indians?" He glanced sharply from Ryder to Julia and back.

Ryder shrugged. "They were here when we got here. Don't know how they died. Could have been a fever."

"I noticed there's an old mine shaft here, too. You been inside?"

"I been inside," Ryder answered.

"Any gold?"

Ryder laughed contemptuously. "What do you think?"

"Yeah," Delroy answered with a sardonic grin, "that's what I thought."

While Julia cleared the table, the two men smoked in what might have appeared to a stranger as a companionable silence, but there was nothing friendly in the air between them.

"I expect you'll want to be on your way at first light," Ryder said abruptly, breaking the thick silence.

Delroy took a long drag on his cigar, blew out the smoke, and tilted his chair back on its hind legs. His eyes slid to Julia. "You get to town much, ma'am?" he asked, deliberately ignoring Ryder's comment.

"N-no, I don't," Julia answered uncomfortably.

"Where would the nearest town be?" he asked, considering the end of the cigar.

Julia shook her head without answering.

"A long way from here," Ryder answered sharply, pushing back from the table and ending the conversation.

"Here, ma'am, let me." Delroy jumped to his feet as Julia lifted the heavy bucket of water she'd used to wash the supper dishes and started toward the door. "A little thing like you shouldn't have to lift a heavy bucket like that. It's a man's job," he emphasized, taking the bucket from her hands.

He'd barely left the cabin when Ryder slammed a fist against the table in anger and muttered, "That's it! He goes!"

"Ryder, please—he'll be gone in the morning. Don't send him out into the night—remember the Indians."

When the other man returned, Ryder said, "It's getting late. You can put your bedroll outside, beneath the porch roof."

Delroy eyed the cozy fire in the fireplace. It got cold in the mountains at night. "Thanks," he replied laconically.

He moved around the room until his eyes found the sketch Julia had done at Ryder's request. Moving closer, he picked it up and studied it carefully.

"This is very good," he commented, looking at Ryder. "Did you do this?"

"No," Ryder replied stiffly. He didn't like the man looking at the picture, because it had been done immediately after they had made love. Julia's expression was too open, and though she'd only drawn as far as the tops of her breasts, Ryder didn't like another man seeing her bare bosom.

"Well, ma'am, you're good. But then, you got to know that already." Picking up the sketch she'd done of Ryder, he studied it, too, but made no comment about it.

"Thank you." Julia folded her hands together at her waist and smiled uncomfortably.

Ryder took the sketches from the man's hands as he was about to put them back, strode across the floor, lifted the lid of the trunk and dropped them inside.

Delroy watched him before making his way to where Julia stood. Lifting a hand, he brushed his lips lightly against the back of it. Ryder was on the point of jerking him away from her by the scruff of his neck when he straightened and dropped her hand.

"I just want you folks to know, in case I'm gone before you get up, it's been a real pleasure to make your acquaintance." The words included both of them, but Delroy's glance rested on Julia's face.

Julia flushed a deep red and nodded, looking everywhere but at Ryder's angry face. "Thank you," she whispered again. "Have a safe journey."

That night Ryder barred the door and spread his blankets on the floor in front of it. His rifle, loaded and ready to fire, lay across his chest.

A slight sound awakened Ryder some time in the middle of the night. His hand went immediately to the rifle. Grasping it firmly, he lay tensely waiting and listening.

The creak of saddle leather met his ear and he relaxed. Delroy, or whoever he was, was leaving, and *good riddance*!

Looking toward the bed, Ryder smiled grimly. It was time he put an end to the questions between himself and the woman he loved.

For a time, after they'd found the man at the cabin waiting for them, Ryder had wondered if he was Julia's partner in a scheme to get the gold. But in his heart of hearts he'd never doubted her, and within the hour he'd known he'd been a fool to even suspect such a thing.

Ryder heard the sound of a horse's hooves leaving the yard, and still he didn't rest any easier. He'd seen plenty of men like Whitson in prison. They were back-shooters, the kind who'd share your camp fire and grub, then knife you in the back for your horse. Every time the man had gone near Julia, he'd wanted to riddle him with lead.

Knowing he wouldn't sleep anymore that night, Ryder got to his feet and stood warming his hands before the fire. His glance strayed toward the bed. What he wouldn't give to climb beneath the blankets and lay her...no, he'd made his decision. He wouldn't touch her again, until she knew the truth about him. And he couldn't tell her that until he'd made a decision about their future.

He'd thought he had it all figured out. Because they loved each other anything was possible, but then Whitson had showed up and now he wasn't so sure anymore. Delroy Whitson was the kind of man they'd have to deal with every day of their lives if he took her with him.

Julia was fixing breakfast the next morning when Ryder removed the drawings from the trunk and placed them where they rested on the low table near the fireplace. He looked up and caught her watching him.

"I didn't believe his story."

"What story?" Julia asked.

"That he was lost and stumbled across this cabin."

"Why not?"

"I think he knew *exactly* where he was and what he was looking for."

"What?"

"Gold, maybe. Did you notice him messing around the mine at all yesterday?"

"No. Besides, you told him there wasn't any gold." Julia poured them each a cup of the coffee made from the bag of beans Delroy had left and shook her head.

"No, I didn't," Ryder denied. "I just let him come to that conclusion for himself." He picked up a cup and took a sip, realized what it was and gave Julia an annoyed look. Taking the cup to the fireplace, he threw its contents into the flames.

"I don't trust him," he muttered half angrily. He wasn't angry with her, but with himself. He had to come to a decision soon about the two of them and he was getting nowhere.

"He's gone," Julia reminded him softly, wondering at the repressed violence in his voice.

"That doesn't mean he isn't hiding out in the hills somewhere, just waiting for the opportunity to sneak back in here and steal the gold."

"The gold," Julia repeated slowly. "Is that all that's important to you—*the damned gold?*" Slamming her empty cup on the table, she whirled around and made for the door.

Ryder started after her, but changed his mind at the last moment. The gold was important—to both of them. If she knew the truth, she'd understand just how important.

They couldn't continue to stay in the cabin. Now that Whitson had found them and was headed to Fort Bridger, word of their being there would spread like wildfire. People kept track of things like that in this country.

Sometimes, especially in winter, when the snow was waist-deep, knowing where a cabin was located, or where a squatter had built a sod hut, could keep a man from starving or freezing to death.

Ryder knew their days here were numbered. All he had to do was tell Julia the truth—all of it. The only thing that kept him from doing that was fear—the fear of losing her.

"Where are you going?" Julia slowed her rocking and watched as Ryder lit the candle in the lantern, using a twig from the fire.

Turning on his haunches to face her, he answered, "It's been three days since Whitson left. I figure it's probably safe to work tonight."

Julia clamped her lips together and looked away. She was very troubled. Ryder had been acting very strange ever since their night spent in the cave. He'd kissed her only once in all that time and that had been the day they'd found Whitson waiting for them upon their return. After that, he'd kept his distance.

Sometimes, she found him looking at her with an unreadable expression in his dark eyes. Those were the times she wondered if he'd finally come to realize how inept she was in her present surroundings. Surely, he'd noticed her awkwardness, just as she'd noticed his odd behavior. But the days passed and he asked no questions of her.

The strain was getting to her, something had to happen soon to break this veil of silence, or she was going to go mad.

"Don't go." A sense of impending disaster forced the words from her lips.

Ryder stood and moved away from the fire. He picked up his rifle. "You'll be safe—I'm leaving the gun."

"Don't go," she repeated with her eyes on the flames because she couldn't look at him and let him see the desperation in her eyes.

"I have to."

"No," she refuted softly, "you don't have to."

"You don't understand, the gold is—" He hesitated. "It's all I have."

Julia felt her heart skip a beat. "What do you mean, it's all you have?"

"I'm nothing without it," he muttered in a low strained voice.

"You're a man!" Julia insisted, "A good, hard-working, decent man. You don't need the gold!"

The word *decent* echoed in his brain. "You don't understand—"

Placing her hands on the arms of the rocker, she raised herself to her feet and stood facing him. "Then explain it to me."

Ryder frowned. "Why are you angry?"

"I'm not," she insisted coolly.

"What have you got against being rich?"

Julia turned away. "You don't need the gold." Money had never brought her happiness.

"Don't I? How would you know what I need? You've had everything you want all your life," he accused her without realizing he was going to. Did he resent her for that? "I've had just the opposite. I came into this world with nothing, but when I leave it, it won't be with nothing."

Shouldering his rifle, the lantern in one hand, he moved toward the door.

"What if I told you I'll be gone when you return?" she asked abruptly.

Ryder stiffened. She was trying to force him into making a decision he wasn't ready to make. *He wouldn't be forced.* The door slammed behind him.

Julia sat down in the rocker and began to rock, keeping her eyes wide so the tears filling them wouldn't spill onto her cheeks. Hours went by and the cabin grew cold.

Julia shuddered and gave her head a slight shake. How long had she been sitting here, staring into the fireplace without moving?

Her limbs felt stiff, her body bathed in gooseflesh. Getting pneumonia wouldn't help her present situation. What she needed was a roaring fire, maybe a hot drink, and bed.

The cabin door creaked and opened abruptly, creating a stir in the air around her. Julia felt her heart leap. He'd come back! Ryder had come back!

She spun to face him, a smile of welcome on her cold lips—the smile froze.

"W-what do *you* want?"

"Gold." Delroy Whitson grinned from behind the barrel of the Winchester aimed unwaveringly at her chest.

Chapter 14

Ryder felt the fresh wind push at his back and glanced up at the sky. Clouds scudded over the moon, blocking its light. A storm was on its way, he could smell it in the air.

He hadn't worked in the mine after all. He'd spent the time sitting in the second tunnel, staring down at the black water, thinking about Julia. He knew he'd dithered back and forth long enough, it was time for action. Keeping that thought in mind he headed back to the cabin.

As he started to open the door, Ryder lifted the glass top on the lantern and blew out the candle. He didn't want to awaken her. Let her sleep, she'd need a clear head for what he was going to tell her later this morning.

"That's far enough."

Ryder gave a start and automatically jerked his rifle toward the man seated on the trunk pulled before the fire.

"Don't try it," Delroy Whitson warned in a hard, ruthless voice. He nodded toward the trunk beneath him and placed the tip of his gun-barrel against the wood. "If you even think about it, I'll pull the trigger."

"Julia—" Ryder began.

"—Is in the trunk," Delroy said, supplying the rest.

"If you've hurt her, you polecat, I'll rip your heart out and eat it."

"Drop the rifle."

Ryder bent at the knees, keeping his eyes on the other man, and laid the rifle on the floor. "I had a feeling you'd be back—if the Indians didn't get you first."

"Well, now, ain't you a prize?" Delroy asked sarcastically.

"Let her out of there, so she can breathe." Ryder nodded at the trunk.

"She's fine, don't worry about her. The one you ought to be worryin' about is yourself. You're the one with the price on your head—for murder." Kicking the side of the trunk with the heel of his boot, Delroy asked, "You hear that, missy? Your boyfriend here is a killer."

"That's a lie!" Ryder made a sharp move in the other man's direction.

Delroy cocked the hammer of the gun and grinned coldly. "Go ahead, try it. Maybe you'll make it, maybe you'll get me, and get to her—before she dies."

Hands knotted into fists, Ryder forced himself to relax and think calmly. "I'm not a killer. I had nothing to do with killing that guard."

"No? Well, that isn't what this here wanted poster says." Pulling out a folded piece of paper, Delroy shook it open and threw it on the floor at Ryder's feet. "You're worth a thousand dollars to me—dead or alive."

"What do you want?" Ryder asked coldly.

"Why, what makes you think I want anything but your hide?"

"If it's me you wanted, you had plenty of opportunity to back shoot me when you were here the other day."

"Now, that's true enough." Delroy nodded. "Maybe it ain't you I'm after."

"Then who?" Ryder asked quickly, his eyes going to the trunk.

"Not her, you blockhead. It ain't *who* I'm after," he explained in exaggerated patience, "but *what* I'm after."

"I don't know what you're talking about." Ryder played dumb.

"Oh, I think you know all right."

Standing away from the trunk, Delroy lifted the lid and pulled Julia up so Ryder could see her. She was bound hand and foot, and gagged.

"Pretty little thing, ain't she?" Delroy asked, smoothing a hand over her hair, while he covered Ryder with the gun.

Ryder ground his teeth. "Keep your filthy paws off her!"

"Now, now." Delroy let his hand slide down the back of her head, around to her shoulder, and across the front of her dress. "She's good in bed, ain't she? I'd bet on it, 'cause she's got red hair and that means plenty of spirit, plenty of passion."

"Why you—" Ryder lifted the lantern he still held and made as though to throw it at him.

"I wouldn't do that if I was you," Delroy warned. "If I shoot you, who's going to protect her from me? You know," he muttered thoughtfully, "maybe that's what I ought to do, anyway. I'll bet she could tell me where you got the gold hid."

"I told you, there ain't any gold."

"You're a liar!" the other man snarled, lifting the gun and jamming it against Julia's head. "I'm fast losing my patience, tell me where the gold is, or she dies! Quick, where's it at?"

Ryder stared into Julia's frightened eyes. She was trying to tell him something with her eyes. He thought she was begging him to tell Delroy about the gold and save her life.

"Look, I ain't an unreasonable man," Delroy said suddenly in a calmer voice. "I tell you what, we'll make a deal. You decide which you want, the gold . . . or the girl. The decision is yours—but you can't have both.

"I been a bounty hunter most of my life, and I ain't never gonna be a rich man if I stay in this line of work. Now, I figure a few sacks of gold would take care of that.

"'Course, I'll have to forgo the pleasure of taking in your dead carcass, but if you make it worth my while, I can stand that. Besides, I think the gold would help ease my conscience some about lettin' you go. I'm tired of bein' saddle sore from chasing scum like you all over the countryside."

"All right," Ryder agreed, his eyes on Julia.

She began to shake her head and try to speak through the gag. Delroy shoved her down in the trunk and started to shut the lid.

"No!" Ryder took a step toward him, stopping when the other man jerked the barrel of the gun in his direction. "Let her out—or you can forget the gold."

"You makin' the rules now?" Delroy asked with narrowed eyes.

"Yeah...I am...if you want the gold." Ryder refused to back|down.

"All right," Delroy conceded after a long pause, "I'll let her out, but she stays tied up and gagged."

"No." Again Ryder spoke up. "I want you to turn her loose. Put her on my horse and let her leave. Then, and only then, I'll tell you where the gold's hid."

"You think I'm a fool?" Delroy snarled angrily.

The air grew thick with tension. Julia's glance slid from Delroy's twisted face to the gun in his hand. His knuckles grew white as his fingers tightened on the grip.

"Then shoot me," Ryder told him calmly. "But let me warn you—" he nodded toward Julia "—she doesn't know where I've hidden the gold.

"Of course, you can always stay and take my place, work the mine. There's one thing maybe you ought to know, the Indians in these parts know me, that's how I've managed to keep my hair. You're a stranger, and they don't cotton much to strangers minin' gold near their land."

"I could shoot you, both of you, and look for the gold myself," Delroy threatened.

"Sure you can, and you might even find it...before one of the war parties passing through these mountains finds you."

Delroy rubbed at his beard, his eyes on Ryder's calm face. He'd seen plenty of Indian signs while in hiding in the area the past few days. And he'd heard before leaving Fort Laramie there was trouble brewing between the Sioux, Cheyenne and the cavalry.

"All right," he conceded at last. "I'll let the girl go."

"I have your word on that?" Ryder insisted.

"Yeah, my word," Delroy agreed.

Ryder breathed an inaudible sigh of relief, only to tense again at the man's next words. "But not till I get the gold in my hands."

"No—"

"Yes." Delroy turned on Julia, took hold of her hair and pulled her head back till he could put the tip of the gun below her chin. "One shot is all it'll take."

Ryder knew the palavering was at an end. He'd gone as far as he dared with Julia's life hanging in the balance. He had no reason to trust the man, but he had no reason to think the man would kill them if he got his hands on the gold. After all, he was wanted by the law. It wasn't like he was going to run to the nearest lawman and complain he'd been robbed.

And why would Whitson want to kill Julia? She had no part in any of this. Even if he shot Ryder after letting her go, at least she'd be safe.

"All right," Ryder agreed, "but first we saddle Midnight, so the minute the gold is in your hands, Julia can go free."

They moved outside where the storm Ryder had predicted was gaining force. Wind howled through the trees, whistled around the rocks and did its best to knock them off their feet.

In the corral, Delroy held a gun on Julia while Ryder saddled the horse. Lightning lit up the sky, making the light from the lantern sitting on the ground beside them unnecessary.

Thunder crashed overhead, and Midnight turned skittish. It took all Ryder's patience to calm him so he could get the saddle and bridle on the horse.

Julia kept a close eye on Delroy. She didn't trust him. She kept remembering the night he'd spent with them and the expression she'd seen in his eyes every time he glanced at Ryder and thought no one else was watching.

It had been a shock to learn Ryder was an escaped convict wanted for murder. She'd listened to Delroy's accusations with a growing sense of incredulity. And when Ryder hadn't refuted them, except to say he wasn't a killer, Julia had waited for a feeling of revulsion to fill her at the thought of what he'd done. But all she'd felt was a deep sense of sadness for Ryder's sake. It didn't matter to her if he was wanted by the law, justly, or unjustly accused. She loved him and that's what really counted.

"There, he's saddled." Ryder led Midnight across the corral to the gate and looped his reins to the top rail.

"Okay, now take me to the gold," Delroy insisted impatiently.

"You're there."

Delroy lifted the lantern and looked around. "What is this, some kind of trick?" Hard eyes locked on Ryder's face.

"No trick. The gold is buried over there." Ryder pointed to a spot beneath the overhang at the back of the cabin.

"Go get a shovel," Delroy told him. "But remember, I got the girl."

"No need," Ryder answered, moving inside the darkness and returning with a shovel. "I keep one handy."

An hour later, twelve bags of gold lay at their feet just as the storm brewing overhead hit with a vengeance.

"Quick," Delroy yelled over the sound of thunder, "get my saddlebags and stuff the sacks inside." He motioned with the gun for Ryder to do as he'd said.

Julia was tempted to throw herself against the man while his attention was centered on Ryder, but fear of reprisal against Ryder stopped her.

The knot of fear in her stomach, growing ever since she'd looked up and seen Whitson standing in the door of the cabin, had become a heavy rock, weighing her down. She knew instinctively that Whitson was not a man of his word.

"That's the last of it," Ryder said, fastening the flap on the bulging saddlebags. "Now let Julia go."

"Just one more thing," Delroy said as rain began to pelt them from all directions at once. "I want you to show me where the vein of gold is located, just in case I decide to come back some time in the future for more."

"That wasn't part of our deal," Ryder protested, wiping the rain from his face with the back of his sleeve.

Delroy shoved the gun beneath Ryder's nose and bit out, "Our deal is whatever I say it is—got that?"

Ryder glanced toward Julia, standing patiently while the rain soaked her clothes, and nodded. "All right. But, then, you let her go."

Inside the mine, Delroy kept to the rear, one hand on Julia's arm, the other holding the gun between her shoulder blades as they followed in Ryder's footsteps.

In the cavern where Julia had been discovered by Ryder, he showed Delroy the vein of gold and how he'd kept it hidden by making a mixture of water, sand, and rock, and plastering it over his work area. Delroy was impressed by the man's cunning. He hadn't been able to find the vein when he'd snooped around looking for it before Julia and Ryder had returned that day.

"Okay, let's go." He motioned for them to precede him from the cavern.

Julia stumbled and would have fallen if Ryder hadn't caught her. "Can't you at least remove the gag?"

Delroy hesitated, then shrugged. Reaching for the knife strapped at his waist, he cut through the ropes around Julia's wrists. "Go on," he told Ryder, "take the gag off her."

Julia stood quietly, her eyes on Ryder's face while he loosened the gag. Rubbing at her wrists, she smiled at him, once the gag was removed. "Thank you."

"I love you," he answered.

Julia's eyes widened. He'd never said that before. She swayed toward him, filled with a love so powerful it almost defied Delroy to do his worst. And then Delroy intervened.

"This is a real touching scene, but we still got things to do. I want to know where you got rid of the tailings when you mined the gold," he said to Ryder. "I couldn't find nothin', that's why I was almost convinced I was wrong about the gold."

Ryder wasn't surprised to learn the man had been looking for the gold. "This way," he murmured. Putting his arm around Julia, he guided her along while speaking to her in low undertones.

"I didn't kill anybody. I want you to know that. A guard was killed when six of us broke out of prison, but I didn't kill him. Do you believe me?" he asked urgently.

"Yes," Julia answered. "But it doesn't matter, even if you had killed someone, I'd still love you."

"Don't you even want to know why I was in prison?"

"Only if you want to tell me," she answered softly, glancing back over her shoulder, meeting Delroy's speculative glare.

"I won Midnight in a poker game at the end of a round-up. The man who owned him was my boss, a big rancher in the Territory. I won him fair and square, but the boss didn't want to pay up. He took Midnight while I was asleep and lit out, heading for his ranch.

"He left me my own nag, not a bad horse, but a deal's a deal, and a man's only as good as his word. I went after him and stole Midnight back.

"He had me arrested for horse stealing, and I s'pose I should have swung at the end of a rope, but he had enough conscience to keep that from happening. He sent me to prison instead, and by the end of a month I was wishing he'd had me hanged. I was there for almost two years, till I couldn't take it anymore.

"Like I said before, a guard was killed, but I didn't have a hand in it." His grip tightened on her arm. "Do you believe me?"

"Yes," Julia whispered, "I believe you."

They'd reached the juncture of the two tunnels. Ryder stopped. "Down there is another tunnel," he told Delroy. "There's an underground river running through it. That's where I dumped the tailings."

"If you don't mind," Delroy mouthed sarcastically, "I'd like to see it for myself."

"Didn't you see it when you were here before?" Ryder was getting a real bad feeling.

"Maybe I want to see it again," Delroy answered with a slight motion from the gun.

Julia took hold of Ryder's arm and they continued down the path. At the edge of the cliff, Ryder stopped and drew back. "Here it is." He pointed toward the black rushing water below.

"That's fine." Delroy grinned in smug satisfaction. "Just what I was looking for—a way to get rid of trash without leavin' a trace."

Fear clutched at Ryder's insides. The man had lied to him! He'd never intended letting either of them go. He'd planned to kill them from the beginning. He was a fool for having believed the man's word.

Pulling Julia close, knowing they had only minutes to live, Ryder buried his face against her hair and breathed deeply of her perfume. "I'm sorry," he murmured brokenly, "I've brought you to this. If I could change things...I would. Forgive me."

"It doesn't matter," Julia said urgently, drawing back to place her hands against the sides of his face. "I love you. I don't mind dying—as long as I'm with you. Without you, life wouldn't be worth living."

"It isn't fair!" Ryder moaned, pressing kisses all over her forehead, cheeks and mouth. Lifting her hands to his face, he buried his lips against their callused palms. "I've just found you—I can't let you go—not now—"

"That's enough," Delroy barked. "Move away from her."

Ryder dropped her hands slowly and stepped back. He met the other man's cold eyes with a deep burning hate. "You said you'd let her go."

"I lied." Delroy laughed.

"Bastard—"

The gun thundered and Ryder's body jerked. Julia screamed and reached toward him as a large blossom of red appeared in the center of his chest. "No!" she cried in protest. "No—Ryder—no!"

This couldn't be happening! She'd traveled over a hundred years back in time to find the one man in all the world she could love. She *couldn't* lose him now! She reached toward him in desperation.

"I...love you...never forget that," Ryder whispered in an airless voice, his fingers reaching toward her. "I'll wait for you-o-o—"

Julia threw herself toward him, ripping her arm from the hand Delroy had locked on her arm the moment the gun had exploded at Ryder. She felt the touch of his fingertips—and the gun cracked again. The dark eyes locked with hers filled with silent protest... and pain. As though in slow motion, she saw his body jerk; watched as he took a faltering step back, and their fingers separated.

"J-u-l-i-a..." Her name echoed off the walls of the cavern as Ryder disappeared slowly from view. The last thing Julia saw were his fingers reaching toward her.

"Oh—God—no!" she cried, throwing herself toward the edge of the drop-off.

The gun spit again and Julia gasped as hot lead buried itself deep in her back. She waited for the pain, but felt nothing except thankfulness at the thought that now she wouldn't have to live in this world... alone... without Ryder.

As her body sailed toward the edge of the cliff—toward the churning black water below.

"R-y-d-e-r!" she cried, the sound of her own voice filling her head. "Don't leave me—wait for me—don't leave me... alone... again."

Her vision filled with blackness; it danced and undulated before her eyes, swirled inside her brain, filling her with emptiness. This is what she'd seen the first time she'd looked into the water's dark depths... death...

Somewhere above her the sound of a man's laughter rang out—then a loud war whoop, a man's scream followed and then silence.

Somewhere down below, the man she loved waited for her. Hand extended, heart filled to overflowing with love, she went to meet her destiny... Ryder... love... and eternity....

Chapter 15

Julia regained consciousness slowly. Her eyelids fluttered and opened. She was in darkness.

Where—where was she?

Testing an arm to see if she could move, she felt around the hard surface on which she lay. It was solid, hard and cold—she was laying on the ground. Shivering with the cold, she became aware of a dry, leathery taste in her mouth and a dull, throbbing ache in her head.

Was she dead?

No, the ground on which she lay was real and so was the pain in her head. But her thoughts were unclear, her mind filled with half-remembered images and impressions.

Again, she wondered where she could be. A moment later, she heard a slight sound, lifted her head and frowned in concentration as she spotted a tiny point of luminescence moving toward her. A shudder of dread coursed through her body. She'd heard all about the after death experiences people claimed to have had involving long black tunnels and bursts of bright yellow light.

Maybe she was dead.

Her eyes stayed with the point of brightness until a sluggish memory made her recognize it for what it was, a lantern, swinging at someone's side.

Once that had been established, a flood of memories tumbled through her head. The mine shaft, she must be in the mine shaft. Then it wasn't a dream....

The closer the light came the more it caused her head to throb with pain. Any kind of clear thinking was impossible. A sudden attack of nausea threatened her and she fought it back with closed eyes and slow, deep breaths.

An instant later, something cold and wet touched her forehead. Julia steeled herself to make no response. Her mind was groggy and her limbs leaden with cold, but one thing was becoming more clear with each passing second. *She was afraid!*

All at once, a picture of black churning water filled her mind. Her throat closed in protest as she gasped, trying to draw in air, the memory of water forcing its way up her nostrils and down her throat interfering with her breathing. She nearly cried aloud in protest at the memory of a sudden gunshot...and death.

Gunshot?

All at once she felt herself lifted in strong arms and moments later, a soft breeze stirred the short hair round her forehead and cheeks. It felt as though they were moving up hill. Opening one eye, she peered around the edge of the cloth covering her forehead.

There were stars overhead, but she could smell a lingering dampness in the air. It had stormed...yes, of course, she remembered that now, too.

It was storming when her car ran out of gas. She'd been lost and there hadn't been anyone around—the light! She'd seen a light...and a tunnel....

Oh, my God! She remembered now. Someone had shot her! She'd died in a tunnel, fallen in an underground river—

No, wait, that couldn't be real. She was here, alive, looking at the stars. It must have been a dream—the bump on her head! Yes, that was it, she'd knocked herself out on the low beam of the mine shaft....

Wait, how did she know that?

Closing both her eyes tightly against a mounting confusion, she took a deep breath and a scent tickled her memory. Tobacco, she could smell tobacco on the clothes of whoever carried her.

He had smoked, the man in her dream. A deep sadness, coming suddenly from nowhere, welled up inside her. He was gone!

Who was he? Where had he gone? Where had she met him? There had been no one on the road where she'd abandoned her car—wait, she remembered now. He'd found her in the mine shaft—yes, that was it. He'd put a damp cloth on her forehead and carried her....

Oh, my God! What was going on?

It was a dream—*it had to be!* But... There was one way to find out for certain. All she had to do was open her eyes and take a good look at the cabin...or the face of the man whose arms held her close to his broad chest....

No, she couldn't look! What if it was the other one? What was his name...Whitson, that was it...Delroy Whitson. The last expression she'd seen in his evil eyes floated before her mind's eye and no matter how hard she tried, she couldn't hold back a slight whimper.

The arms holding her tightened fractionally and Julia's breath became suspended. Did he know she was awake? Why hadn't he said anything? Was it because he knew she'd recognize his voice and struggle to get away?

But what if it wasn't him...wasn't Delroy Whitson? What if it was the other one...Ryder...

Along with the memory of his name came a tide of feeling so strong Julia felt tears start to her eyes. Oh...God...he was dead....

She'd seen him die...and she'd loved him.... No, love couldn't encompass what she had felt for the man. She would willingly have died for him—*she did die for him!*

Oh—she was so mixed up! Had it been real? No, of course it hadn't.

The wind stirred and Julia shivered. The mountain air was cool for summer, especially if you were dressed in wet clothing—

Wet clothing!

Was it true? Was she in the arms of the man she loved? But, how could it be? She'd seen him die—or else he hadn't existed in the first place...unless she'd really managed somehow to go back in time—no, that was ridiculous! It must have been a dream.

It didn't matter. Maybe she had experienced some mystical dream and seen the face of the man she would love before she met him.

And if it hadn't been a dream?

Then she wanted to go back! She wanted to go back, because suddenly she was completely cognizant of the events preceding her flight to Wyoming—her mother, her failed marriage, the loss of her child, her life in California—Mariette's death.

She hadn't had the opportunity to tell *him* about any of those things. She wanted to go back! Nothing in this life made it worth living. Life hadn't been worth living until she'd found *him*.

Her stomach cramped with nerves. The cabin, one look at the cabin, and she'd know the truth! Julia opened one eye and turned her head toward the building standing against the sky. No! Oh, no...

The rough cabin she had stumbled across in the dark was gone and in its place stood a modern two-story log cabin, with a wide veranda...and a light shining in the window behind lace curtains. Her eyes darted around in the moonlight, seeking something familiar and landed on a mound to the left of the cabin. The root cellar! She recognized the root cellar, this *had* to be the place of her dreams....

Julia closed her eyes and felt hot tears slide from beneath the closed lids. She wanted to cry out in protest, demand that he—this man, whoever he was—take her back, back to the mine, back to the black river where she'd last seen Ryder—*she wanted to return to that other time*...return to her love....

She felt her rescuer pause, climb three steps and cross what must be the veranda she'd seen. One arm moved and she heard a door open, a moment later they were inside.

The familiar sound of a crackling fire drifted to her ears. She prayed silently to open her eyes and find the inside of this cabin resembled the one in which she'd found shelter in the mountains of Wyoming Territory in the year 1876.

It was a futile prayer and she knew it.

She felt herself lowered gently onto something soft and the cloth on her forehead shifted to one side. Julia reached for it, blinking as soft yellow light dazzled her eyes.

For a long moment she lay and stared at the beamed ceiling overhead, filled with a profound regret. This was definitely not the cabin of her dreams. It seemed no amount of prayer would bring back what she'd lost.

It was time to face the music, time to make her rescuer's acquaintance, she realized listlessly. His identity no longer mattered . . . nothing mattered . . . now. . . .

Raising herself on one elbow, she glanced over the back of the couch and discovered she was alone. Would she have to go in search of him—as she'd had to go in search of *him?*

Julia dropped her feet to the floor and felt a wave of dizziness sweep over her. It might be more prudent to lie back down and let him come to her, but she was determined to meet this person on her own terms.

After a moment, she opened her eyes and caught sight of a man standing before the fireplace. His back was to her and while she watched, he bent to add another log to the low fire.

Julia's heart squeezed with pain. How many times had she watched Ryder place a log on the fire in just that manner?

She couldn't look at the face of the man moving toward her, too caught up in memories of another room . . . another fire . . . another night. . . .

Her host moved to within a foot of her and stopped. Julia's glance rested on the scarred brown boots sticking out from beneath a pair of well-worn jeans.

He held an object out to her silently and Julia accepted it curiously. Her eyes focused on it slowly, growing wide with disbelief.

No! It couldn't be! How was it possible? Before she could comment, a second item, similar to the first, was thrust into her other hand. Julia's vision swam with tears.

Tearing her eyes from the drawing of a woman with sleep-tousled hair, kiss swollen lips and passion-bright eyes, Julia looked up at the face of the man standing before her.

With leisurely calm, he lifted a hand and used two fingers to push back the wide, curled brim of a white Stetson, revealing a thick blonde mustache and deep brown eyes. Julia's heart skipped a beat and began to race.

The tears spilled down her cheeks as he lifted the hat and dropped it to the floor. Locking a pair of damp brown eyes with hers, he lowered himself to his knees beside her.

He removed the framed drawings from her trembling fingers and laid them on the cushion at her side. Taking her cold fingers in his warm grasp, he drew her slowly toward him. Julia swallowed tightly, smiled tremulously, and raised her lips for his kiss.

"What took you so long?" a deep, familiar voice whispered huskily against her quivering mouth. "I've been waiting for you, for a very long time."

* * * * *

**Silhouette Intimate Moments
is proud to present
Mary Anne Wilson's
SISTER, SISTER duet—
Two halves of a whole,
two parts of a soul**

In the mirror, Alicia and Alison Sullivan both had brilliant red hair and green eyes—but in personality and life-style, these identical twins were as different as night and day. Alison needed control, order and stability. Alicia, on the other hand, hated constraints, and the idea of settling down bored her.

Despite their differences, they had one thing in common—a need to be loved and cherished by a special man. And to fulfill their goals, these two sisters would do anything for each other—including switching places in a life-threatening situation.

Look for Alison and Jack's adventure in TWO FOR THE ROAD (IM #472, January 1993), and Alicia and Steven's story in TWO AGAINST THE WORLD (IM #489, April 1993)—and *enjoy!*

SISTERR

INTIMATE MOMENTS®
™ *Silhouette* ®

Silhouette
SPECIAL EDITION®

It takes a very
special man to win

That
SPECIAL
Woman!

She's friend, wife, mother—she's you! And beside each Special
Woman stands a wonderfully *special* man. It's a celebration of
our heroines—and the men who become part of their lives.

Look for these exciting titles from Silhouette Special Edition:

January   BUILDING DREAMS by Ginna Gray
Heroine: Tess Benson—a woman faced with single motherhood
who meets her better half.

February   HASTY WEDDING by Debbie Macomber
Heroine: Clare Gilroy—a woman whose one spontaneous act
gives her more than she'd ever bargained for.

March   THE AWAKENING by Patricia Coughlin
Heroine: Sara McAllister—a woman of reserved nature who
winds up in adventure with the man of her dreams.

April   FALLING FOR RACHEL by Nora Roberts
Heroine: Rachel Stanislaski—a woman dedicated to her career
who finds that romance adds spice to life.

Don't miss THAT SPECIAL WOMAN! each month—from some
of your special authors! Only from Silhouette Special Edition!

TSW

COME BACK TO

CONARD COUNTY

There's something about the American West, something about the men who live there. Accompany author Rachel Lee as she returns to Conard County, Wyoming, for CHEROKEE THUNDER (IM #463), the next title in her compelling series. American Hero Micah Parrish is the kind of man every woman dreams about—and that includes heroine Faith Williams. She doesn't only love Micah, she *needs* him, needs him to save her life—and that of her unborn child. Look for their story, coming in December, only from Silhouette Intimate Moments.

To order your copy of CHEROKEE THUNDER or the first Conard County title, EXILE'S END (IM #449), please send your name, address, zip or postal code, along with a check or money order (please do not send cash) for $3.39 for each book ordered, plus 75¢ postage and handling ($1.00 in Canada), payable to Silhouette Books, to:

In the U.S.	In Canada
Silhouette Books	Silhouette Books
3010 Walden Avenue	P.O. Box 609
P.O. Box 1396	Fort Erie, Ontario
Buffalo, NY 14269-1396	L2A 5X3

Please specify book title(s) with your order.
Canadian residents add applicable federal and provincial taxes.

CON2

INTIMATE MOMENTS®
Silhouette®

AMERICAN HERO

It seems readers can't get enough of these men—and we don't blame them! When Silhouette Intimate Moments' best authors go all-out to create irresistible men, it's no wonder women everywhere are falling in love. And look what—and who!—we have in store for you early in 1993.

January brings NO RETREAT (IM #469), by Marilyn Pappano. Here's a military man who brings a whole new meaning to macho!

In February, look for IN A STRANGER'S EYES (IM #475), by Doreen Roberts. Who is he—and why does she feel she knows him?

In March, it's FIREBRAND (IM #481), by Paula Detmer Riggs. The flames of passion have never burned this hot before!

And in April, look for COLD, COLD HEART (IM #487), by Ann Williams. It takes a mother in distress and a missing child to thaw this guy, but once he melts...!

AMERICAN HEROES. YOU WON'T WANT TO MISS A SINGLE ONE—ONLY FROM

IMHER03R

INTIMATE MOMENTS® ™ Silhouette®

NORA ROBERTS

Love has a language all its own, and for centuries
flowers have symbolized love's finest expression.
Discover the language of flowers—and love—in
this romantic collection of 48 favorite books by
bestselling author Nora Roberts.

Two titles are available each month at your
favorite retail outlet.

In December, look for:

Partners, **Volume #21**
Sullivan's Woman, **Volume #22**

In January, look for:

Summer Desserts, **Volume #23**
This Magic Moment, **Volume #24**

Collect all 48 titles
and become fluent in

THE
LANGUAGE
of **LOVE**

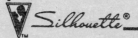

Silhouette®

If you missed any of volumes 1 through 20, order now by sending your name, address, zip
or postal code, along with a check or money order (please do not send cash) for $3.59 for
each volume, plus 75¢ postage and handling ($1.00 in Canada), payable to Silhouette Books,
to:

In the U.S.

3010 Walden Avenue
P.O. Box 1396
Buffalo, NY 14269-1396

In Canada

P.O. Box 609
Fort Erie, Ontario
L2A 5X3

Please specify book title(s) with order.
Canadian residents add applicable federal and provincial taxes.

LOL1292